Date: 4/16/18

LP FIC COBLE
Coble, Colleen,
The view from Rainshadow
Bay

THE VIEW FROM RAINSHADOW BAY

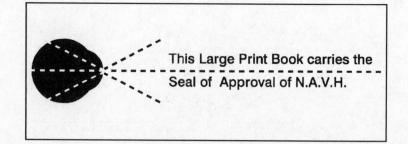

This Large Print Book carries the
Seal of Approval of N.A.V.H.

THE VIEW FROM RAINSHADOW BAY

COLLEEN COBLE

THORNDIKE PRESS
A part of Gale, a Cengage Company

Farmington Hills, Mich • San Francisco • New York • Waterville, Maine
Meriden, Conn • Mason, Ohio • Chicago

LIBRARY OF CONGRESS CIP DATA ON FILE.
CATALOGUING IN PUBLICATION FOR THIS BOOK
IS AVAILABLE FROM THE LIBRARY OF CONGRESS.

ISBN-13: 978-1-4328-4665-7 (hardcover)
ISBN-10: 1-4328-4665-5 (hardcover)

Published in 2018 by arrangement with Thomas Nelson, Inc., a division of HarperCollins Christian Publishing, Inc.

Printed in the United States of America
1 2 3 4 5 6 7 22 21 20 19 18

For my cousin, Tiffany Frank
Whose faith in adversity
shines Jesus to everyone

PROLOGUE

The wind blew her long black hair across her face and obscured her vision as she ran through the lavender fields, the sweet aroma mixing with her perspiration. Panic threatened to overtake her, but she had to push it back, push on. He would catch her if she wasn't smart and focused.

The shrubs of lavender caught at her feet, and she nearly tumbled to the dirt but managed to right herself in time to rush on. Her breath came hard, and her lungs burned.

The crash of Puget Sound waves pounding the rocks in the distance grounded her. If she headed for the water, she'd find people. He wouldn't dare kill her in front of witnesses.

All she'd wanted was justice, but she'd been stupid to think she could outsmart him. And what about her parents? Would they be his next target? She'd thought she could stop his evil plan that put so many people in jeopardy, but she was wrong, so wrong. She should have gone to the police at once, but she'd thought she needed more proof. Now she shuddered to think of how many people might die because of her obstinacy.

She had to get away, had to find help to make sure he was stopped before he hurt anyone else. It all depended on her.

She reversed her direction and ran toward the roar of a boat engine. A helicopter passed overhead, and she waved her hands at it, motioning for it to land, but the chopper continued on its path. The pilot hadn't seen her. She was on her own.

The air squeezed from her lungs. She'd never make it. Even now she could hear his feet pounding behind her, could almost feel his hot breath on her neck. A house loomed in the distance, and she ran that way, rushing as fast as she could. If someone was home, she could find an ally.

Night would be here soon. Already the sky threw out bright golds and oranges as the sun began to sink. The darkness might hide her or it could be her undoing if she stumbled and fell.

She managed an extra burst of speed, but it was too late. He shoved against her back, and she tumbled face-first into the lavender. Inhaling the sweet aroma, she turned her head and looked up into her attacker's face and the raised needle in his grip.

"Please don't." The whimper that escaped shamed her, and she struggled to roll onto her back. "You won't get away with this."

A hard hand held her in place on her shoulder. "Yes, I will."

The slight prick of a needle into her back was followed by a flood of warmth. She closed her eyes and let the darkness take her.

CHAPTER 1

One Year Later

She never got tired of this panoramic view. Shauna McDade dipped her helicopter, a six-passenger Airbus, low over the tops of the trees lining Puget Sound and saluted The Mountain that stood sentinel over Seattle, Mount Rainier. The glorious September color juxtaposed against the sky and sea made her reach for her camera. A ferry loaded with cars and passengers chugged through the waves toward Whidbey Island, and she snapped pictures of that too. With any luck, she could sell them as postcards.

She headed her chopper back toward Lavender Tides, the small town of four thousand residents that looked like it had been plucked from a Thomas Kinkade painting. Most of the Victorian buildings and storefronts had been constructed in the 1880s, and the town often drew in tourists searching for a short stopover on a trip from Port

Townsend to Sequim.

Many aging hippies had found its charm irresistible enough that they'd moved in and opened everything from coffee shops to pottery studios. In the golden glow of the late-afternoon sun, the town looked magical with its bustling pier stretching out into the blue water. The last of the Dungeness crab vendor trucks were closing and heading home for the night, leaving the pier to lovebirds and tourists.

She took a few more pictures, then flew her bird toward the municipal airport. After landing, Shauna stepped out onto the helipad and squared her shoulders. The piece of mail in the pocket of her denim jacket reminded her of the battle ahead. She swallowed the lump that formed in her throat. She'd deal with that once she got through the next half hour.

The small airport office was a simple metal Quonset hut that was beginning to rust. Through the window she saw Zach Bannister staring at his computer. The thought of asking him for help made her cringe, but she had no choice.

The wooden door boasted a new coat of blue paint, and the doorknob turned easily in her hand. Zach believed in keeping everything in tip-top shape. After he had gotten out of the Coast Guard, he took some Apple stock he'd inherited from his dad and built Hurricane Roost Airport. Though small, Hurricane Roost boasted a nice, flat runway and several helipads. It was a busy airport since Zach operated an emergency plane transport business out of here.

He stood when she entered, and surprise lit his deep-blue eyes. "Shauna, is something wrong?" He wore jeans and a flannel shirt that hugged his six-one, muscular frame. His hiking boots left flecks of mud on the concrete floor when he came around the desk toward her. A scabbed-over cut decorated his forehead, probably from his latest daredevil escapade. The last adventure she'd heard about had been BASE jumping off a bridge.

A flood of conflicting emotions swamped her just like always. Shauna and Zach had been friends once, but all she felt now was distrust and hatred. He'd ruined her life.

Her face burned, and she squirmed inside at what she had to say. For the past year she'd gone out of her way to make sure she didn't run into him. "I need to talk to you."

"Sure, have a seat." He indicated the chair across the desk as he retreated to the other side and regained his seat.

She forced herself to perch on the edge of the chair. "It's about Alex." Her five-year-old son was worth every bit of discomfort she felt in this moment.

Zach's eyes darkened, and he started to rise, then sank back. "Is he okay?"

She nodded, then shrugged. "Well, as okay as he can be without a dad." She should be ashamed at the sense of satisfaction she felt when he flinched, but she wasn't. He *should* flinch and feel some kind of pain. "There's a father-son hike at Freshwater Bay next Saturday. Alex cried himself to sleep last night because he can't go. I told him my dad could take him, but he just cried harder. So when he asked if you could take him, I promised him I'd check with you. It would mean the world to him."

Her son had gone through enough the past year, and he adored Zach, who had been like another father to him. Her dad was more of an embarrassment, and even if he agreed to take Alex, Dad was likely to show up drunk. She had been backed into a corner.

"I'd be happy to take him." His eyes narrowed as he stared back at her. "That hurt to ask me, didn't it?"

"More than you can imagine."

"Are you ever going to forgive me,

14

Shauna?"

"Can you sit there and tell me it wasn't your fault my husband is lying in his grave?"

He leaned back in his chair and shook his head. "It was an accident."

"You egged him on! If he hadn't been in such a rush to beat you, he never would have fallen."

"You think I don't know that?" He ran a hand through his dark, unruly hair. "Every time I close my eyes, I see his face as he fell." Zach's voice broke and he looked away. "I'd take his place if I could."

She squeezed her eyes shut against the horrific death scene playing out in her head. Even thinking about Jack's last moments brought immense pain.

After a long silence, she opened her eyes and exhaled. "The hike starts at nine, and the kids are supposed to meet at the Whale Trail sign. You can pick him up at eight thirty, and it should be enough time to get out there. Just don't let him out of your sight. He's all I've got left."

The Freshwater Bay hike was a safe trail, but little boys could scamper out of sight in a heartbeat, and the thought of leaving Alex in Zach's care made her heart want to pound out of her chest. She couldn't coddle Alex, though. It wasn't fair to deny him normal childhood fun because of her fears.

Zach stood and came around the desk toward her. "I won't take my eyes off him for a second." He looked deep into her eyes. "Thank you, Shauna. It took a lot of courage to ask me."

If he only knew how little sleep she'd gotten last night. It had been hard to keep her attention on flying today.

The crackle of the envelope in her pocket as she rose reminded her she had one more battle to fight after she left here. "Yes, well, Alex will be thrilled. I'll pack lunch for both of you." She hesitated. "If you don't mind, I'd appreciate an occasional text just to set my mind at ease."

"No problem." He stuck out his hand. "I hope this can be the beginning of putting the past behind us."

She didn't take his hand. "Don't get your hopes up about that." She spun on her heel and rushed for the door before she disgraced herself by crying.

Nothing he said or did could bring Jack back to her. She could only try to go forward.

Shauna parked outside the quaint two-story with cedar shakes weathering to a soft gray. The home stood on a hill and overlooked the waves of Rainshadow Bay as they rolled in to pound the rocks with foam before receding. In the old days Lucy would have met her at the door with warm cookies and hot coffee, but the death a year ago of the Glennons' daughter, Darla, had torn their marriage apart. Shauna prayed the current separation was only temporary.

She rang the doorbell and heard heavy footsteps heading her way. The door swung open, and Clarence greeted her. "Shauna, thanks for coming so quickly." At fifty-two, his blond hair was thinning on top, and his belly strained the black Harley-Davidson T-shirt he wore.

As he stepped back to allow her to enter, he kept putting his hands into the pockets of his jeans, then yanking them out. His normally florid face was pale, and his light-blue eyes held a trace of moisture. "It's terrible, terrible."

"Clarence, what's wrong?"

He didn't answer, so she followed him down the hall and spared a glance at the family pictures portraying a happier time before Darla's death. As she passed the doorway to his office and darkroom, she caught the faint stench of some kind of chemical and saw his mechanics overalls draped over a chair. He must have been working on his car, though it didn't exactly smell like gasoline or oil. There was a vague familiarity about the odor she couldn't place.

When they reached the living room, he sank onto the sofa. "I need a favor, Shauna."

She moved closer and looked him over. "Of course. What's wrong?" She'd never seen him in such a state. His hands trembled, and he kept glancing out the window.

Clarence had been her mentor and surrogate father ever since she got out of the navy eight years ago. He'd taught her everything she knew about mechanics and photography. He had been there when she got her chopper, and he'd held her when Jack died. Clarence and Lucy loved Alex like their own grandchild.

He reached toward the coffee table and picked up a box. "I need you to mail this box to Lucy. I'd do it myself, but I have to disappear for a while. I think he's on to me."

Her pulse sped up at the dread on his face. "Clarence, you're scaring me. What's this all about?" She took the box from him.

He shook his head so hard a lock of hair he'd combed over his bald spot fell down on his ear. "I can't tell you. I still can't believe it, but if I'm right, I don't want you in danger too. Once I know for sure, you'll

18

be the first to know."

"You can't leave it like that. I can keep a secret."

He shook his head again. "I have to figure this out before I go to the police."

His mention of the word *police* spiked her adrenaline, and she yanked out her phone. "Let's call Sheriff Burchell now. If you're in danger, let him figure out whatever this is."

His hand shook as he finger-combed his hair back into place. "I can't risk it. Not yet."

He rose and went toward the door, and she had no choice but to follow him. Clarence had always been his own man. Focused and intelligent, he generally knew what was right and tried to heed his conscience in everything. She'd never seen him scattered and scared like this.

He held the door open for her. "I'll be away for a few days, but try not to worry. Here, write down this phone number. I got a throwaway phone that can't be traced."

She copied the number into her phone and tagged it as Unknown. "I wish you'd tell me what this is all about."

"I will as soon as I can." He gave her a gentle push out the door. "Now get out of here before someone sees you."

"Who?" But the adamant expression on

his face told her he wouldn't budge in his determination to keep her in the dark.

Her knees felt shaky as she went to her truck and climbed inside. She started the engine and pulled away from the house and down the long driveway leading to the road. She heard a distant *thump,* and it almost felt as if an invisible hand pushed her truck forward.

She slammed on the brakes and looked in the rearview mirror — smoke poured from the open front door and flames shot through the roof. She gasped, then gunned the engine and wheeled the truck around. The truck tires slewed sideways, grabbed hold, and hurtled the vehicle back toward the house, where flames had engulfed the structure.

In front of the house she stopped the truck and threw the transmission into park before she leaped out. "Clarence!" She ran toward the house, but the intense heat drove her back. The place was a raging inferno. No one could get through. Maybe he'd gotten out the back way. She ran around to the back door, but the porch roof was already caving in.

Tears filled her eyes, and her hands shook as she pulled out her phone and dialed 911.

All she could do was pray he'd died instantly.

CHAPTER 2

Zach plotted the logistics for the flight from here to Alaska, then back to Seattle. It was a good way to keep his thoughts from drifting to Shauna's coldness.

Zach's greatest joy in life was flying his medical plane back and forth to Alaska, and it had become especially pivotal for his mental health since Jack died. The majority of his patients were kids, and helping take care of them made him happy. He'd always thought he'd have kids of his own by now, but life had kept him busy, and he'd never found the right woman. At thirty-three, he was beginning to think he'd always be alone, but helping hurt kids had filled that void nicely.

"Hey, buddy, want to grab some dinner?"

Zach looked up from his computer as Karl Prince's voice boomed from the front door. Zach stretched out his cramped back and shook his head. "Wish I could, Karl, but I just got a call that a little boy with a badly broken leg needs transport from Wrangell to Seattle. I need to figure out logistics for the crew."

Zach had always thought his friend's voice sounded like he was six four and built like a linebacker, but in reality, Karl barely reached five nine and had a thin frame he worked to keep by jogging. His wife, Nora, sold the best raw honey in the area. Karl's dark hair still showed no signs of thinning, and only a few threads of silver ran through the sides. CEO of Olympic Paper Mill, he was in his midsixties and had been a great encouragement to Zach after Jack died.

Karl shut the door behind him, blocking out the sound of fuel being pumped into Zach's plane. "What's got you upset? You've got those lines between your eyes like you're worried."

"Shauna visited me today. She asked me to take Alex to a father-son picnic next Saturday."

His friend's dark brows winged up, and he dropped into the chair on the other side of the desk. "Whoa, what's gotten into her? I thought she always crossed the street to avoid talking to you."

"It's the first civil word we've exchanged since Jack died. She let me know it wasn't her idea. I guess Alex cried and begged until she agreed." His heart hurt at the mental image of the little boy crying for his daddy. And it was all Zach's fault. He'd wanted to be there for Alex, but Shauna hadn't given an inch in her determination to make him pay for his crimes. He couldn't blame her.

Before Karl could offer up some wisdom, Zach's pager went off. "There's a fire. Gotta go." He grabbed his jacket and headed for his truck, with Karl behind him, then stopped as the address sank in. "Holy cow, that's Clarence's place!" He punched in a quick text to his friend, asking if he was okay.

Karl wheeled around and headed toward his SUV, a gleaming white Lexus. "I'll follow you there."

Karl and Clarence had been friends most of their lives, so Zach knew nothing would keep Karl from rushing there as well.

It was only a five-minute drive to the Glennon place, but it felt like an hour. He saw the smoke when he was still a couple of miles away. It looked bad, very bad. Clarence hadn't answered Zach's text, and by the time he turned into the dirt driveway, Zach's stomach was in knots.

Firemen were already hauling hoses from two trucks toward the fully engulfed structure. The smoke obscured most of the figures standing around watching. Zach parked his truck and grabbed his turnout gear before he jumped out. Where was Clarence? He scanned the crowd as he pulled on his jacket. He ran for the closest fire engine.

The fire chief, Stuart Ransom, motioned to him. "Haul that other hose around back."

Zach nodded and reached for the hose. "What about Clarence? Anyone seen him?"

Stuart, a muscular man in his forties, shook his head. "A witness saw him just moments before the explosion. We're afraid he didn't make it, but we won't know for sure until we get in there."

Zach felt light-headed at the chief's grave manner. Didn't make it? That couldn't be. He struggled to maintain his equilibrium as he moved into position. Water shot through the hose, and he aimed it at the back windows. The fire had too much of a head start, and he doubted they'd save more than some timbers. The water began to beat back some of the flames, but others sprang to life and devoured more of the roof like a giant dragon.

If Clarence was inside, all hope was lost.

The conflagration had died to smoking

embers. Spent from sobbing, Shauna sat on the wet grass and watched the firemen carry the body bag from the ruins. She should get up and do something, but she was numb.

Lucy. Shauna cringed at the thought of being the one to tell her. Even though the two were separated, Lucy would grieve terribly.

"Shauna, you okay?"

She looked up to see Zach's eyes peering down at her out of a smoke-covered face. His helmet dangled from his hand, and he still wore his firefighting uniform. "You tried to save him."

"The home was too far gone when we got here." His voice broke, and he rubbed his eyes. "Sorry, it's hard to take in. I loved Clarence."

They all did. "There was a bomb."

His blue eyes sharpened. "How do you know?"

"I'd just been here. It shook my car, and I saw everything erupt behind me." Her voice wavered. "Only a bomb could cause an explosion like that." Why was she even telling him all this? He was her enemy.

"Did you tell the sheriff? I don't think it's possible to know for sure what happened yet. Clarence had that darkroom where he worked with chemicals. It could have been an accident."

She rubbed her head. "Maybe you're right. I don't think Everett's here. If he is, I haven't seen him." She had to pull herself together. Jack's mother had already texted several times asking what time she was picking up Alex, but she hadn't been able to quit shaking long enough to call or text Marilyn. It was already an hour past the time Shauna usually got her son.

"I'll call him. I'm sure he'll want to hear about what you saw." Zach squatted beside her, and the stench of smoke wafted off him in waves. "Is there anything I can do? Get Alex, drive you somewhere?"

She shook her head. "I need to pick up Alex. And someone needs to tell Lucy."

He held out his hand and helped her up. "I can see Lucy."

She needed to guard herself from feeling like he was a friend. He wasn't. "I should probably do that. Nice of you to offer, though."

"How about if I go get Alex?"

"Marilyn would probably faint if you stepped foot on her property."

The hurt in his eyes returned and he nodded. "Probably. She ordered me to leave the funeral."

It had been a painful day, one Shauna

didn't like to remember. "I'll call her and tell her what's happening. She'll keep him overnight. He's got clothes there." She stepped a few feet away and placed the call to her mother-in-law.

Marilyn answered on the first ring. "Shauna, finally! I've been worried sick."

"I'm sorry I didn't call sooner. S-Something terrible's happened." Her throat closed, and she struggled to speak again. "There's been a fire at Clarence's house. He's dead. I've got to inform Lucy. Can you keep Alex overnight?"

"Oh, Shauna. Of course. Do they know how the fire started?"

"Not yet. I need to talk to the sheriff and tell him what I saw."

"You mean you were there?"

"Clarence was acting so funny. Like he was afraid someone was watching him."

"Don't worry about a thing with Alex. I've already fed him dinner, and we'll watch a Pixar movie or something before he goes to bed. Call me later."

"I will." Shauna ended the call.

Marilyn had been a rock for her since Jack died. A widow herself since the age of thirty-five, she understood all of Shauna's emotions. Though losing her only son had taken its toll as well.

28

Zach moved closer. "Let me at least go with you to Lucy's. You shouldn't have to do this alone."

Didn't he understand his presence was painful to her? Even talking to him about Alex had been like walking barefoot on hot lava. "I'll be fine. Thanks anyway." She turned her back on him and marched to her truck.

She reached for the door as Karl Prince headed toward her. He'd sent as much business her way as he could since Jack died, and he was one of those people she'd always felt she could turn to. He and Jack had been golfing buddies.

His gaze swept over her, then he enfolded her in a tight hug. "Sorry, Shauna. I know you loved Clarence like a dad."

Her face pressed against his Windbreaker, she nodded as she inhaled the scent of pipe tobacco. The pungent scent on his jacket was laced with something sweet. She took the comfort he offered, then reluctantly pulled away and reached for a tissue in her pocket. Her head began to throb.

She wiped her eyes and blew her nose. "I'm on my way to notify Lucy. I don't suppose you'd want to come?"

"Happy to. I already called Nora to let her know I was here and didn't know when

29

I'd be home. I'm sure she'd be glad to go along with us if you needed more moral support."

Shauna was already feeling like a five-year-old child afraid of the dark. She needed to buck up and do what had to be done. It would be a long evening. "You think I should call the sheriff first? Since it was murder, he might need to be the one to inform Lucy."

Unease flickered in Karl's light-brown eyes. "You think it was murder? I assumed it was an accident with the chemicals he was using."

Was she totally wrong about what she saw and smelled? Maybe she'd jumped to conclusions because of how strange Clarence had been acting.

"If there's any question about what happened, you should talk to Everett before you go see her."

She gasped and put her hand to her mouth. "He won't suspect Lucy, will he? You know, since they're separated?"

His jaw tightened. "I'm sure the sheriff will want to question her."

Shauna leaned against the truck door and wished she could go back to this morning. "I'll head to the sheriff's office now."

"I'll meet you there. I'll stop at Smokey's

30

and get you a rib sandwich and some coffee. I'm sure you haven't eaten."

She opened the door. "I'm not sure I can eat anything."

Karl zipped his jacket as the wind picked up. "I'll get something anyway. You may be at the sheriff's for hours."

She hoped not. The events had already played through her head a million times, and the thought of recounting it many more times was almost too much to take. But she owed this to Clarence. She'd make sure he received justice.

CHAPTER 3

The motion-detector light came on as Zach stepped out of the truck and approached Shauna's front porch. A full moon hung over the tops of the trees surrounding her five acres. Her house, a contemporary cedar home with soaring ceilings and prow-shaped windows, had been built in happier times in the first year of her marriage to Jack. His throat tightened at the memories here.

He settled into an Adirondack chair on the porch and waited. An owl swooped low over the treetops, and he could hear the distant sound of the surf. No neighbors were nearby, something he often worried about since Jack died. Not that Shauna would listen to his concerns.

The peaceful evening was in sharp contrast to the horror of a few hours earlier, and he wished he could erase the memories of that burned-out shell of a building. The lights switched off as he sat waiting. He pulled out his phone and opened his voice mail messages, then clicked on Jack's name.

His friend's laughing voice rang out. *"Hey, buddy, you're late."* Voices droned in the background. *"I already ordered the pizza so hurry up before it gets cold."*

The ache of missing his friend spread through his chest as Zach listened. The message ended, and his finger hovered over the next-to-last call from Jack, then he laid the phone on his knee and stared off into the darkness.

Zach had nearly died diving to explore that old wreck last week. Had he actually wanted to?

Bubbles rose around his mask as he kicked hard toward the bottom. There it was, just as he'd been told. The ghostly outline of the old *Diamond Knot* wreck. Getting here had been challenging since he faced a large swell that had combined with the choppy waves in the Strait of Juan de Fuca. The current changed on him at the last minute too, nearly pulling him off course.

But he'd persevered, and now the wreck, covered in white anemones, was right there in the emerald-green water. He stopped to admire some sponges growing on the hull,

33

but that capricious current took hold of him again and spun him around. He reached out and grabbed part of the hull, but it collapsed under his grip.

When he tried to withdraw his right hand, he couldn't move it. Several pieces of debris had trapped his wrist. A drop of blood floated in the water where something had pierced his skin. A large wolf eel peered at him from inside the hull and seemed to smirk at his predicament.

Not yet panicking, he looked around. He had stupidly come by himself, but surely there was another avid diver or two nearby. But the only things with fins close to him were schools of yellowtail rockfish. A movement drew his attention to his right, but it was just an octopus propelling by.

He tugged again on his hand, but it didn't budge. He reached for his knife with his left hand, but it was an awkward angle and he dropped it, then tried to grab it again. He couldn't reach it from here. He tried to pry back the part of the hull trapping his wrist, but it didn't even wiggle.

Zach glanced at his gauge. Only five minutes before he had to head for the surface. He had to slow his breathing. He was using up his oxygen too quickly. With renewed determination, Zach worked on the hull again, trying to pry it back with his fingers. No use.

He ceased his attempts and looked around at the beautiful scene. Jack would have loved this. And Zach didn't need to struggle. Maybe Jack would come to greet him as he died. His friend wouldn't blame him for the fall. Jack was happy now, dancing in heaven and seeing even more beautiful sights than the bright fish flitting by.

Why fight? Wasn't this what Zach wanted all along, to shed the guilt robbing him of every bit of joy in life? Maybe he'd even come down here alone hoping peace would find him. No one but his mother would mourn him, and he rarely saw her anyway. She had her own life since Dad died, and she wouldn't miss him. Shauna sure wouldn't either.

A light caught his attention to his left, and another diver swam down toward him. If Zach stayed motionless, maybe the guy would swim on and not even see him.

He blinked and shook his head, then waved his hand at the diver. As the diver took out his knife and freed Zach's hand, he pushed away those crazy thoughts.

Zach shook off the memory as headlights pierced the darkness and turned into the driveway. Shauna was home.

■ ■ ■ ■

Shauna's white Dodge pickup rolled to a stop, and she got out. The lights came back on, and Zach let himself stare at her. He'd always thought she was the most beautiful woman he'd ever seen. Her nearly black hair hung in a curtain down her back. Only about five two, she barely came to his chest. Because of her size it was always fun to see her behind the controls of her helicopter.

Since Jack's death, he'd rarely looked into her sea-green eyes, and he missed that. Now the accusation in them was always too painful.

Most of the time, he held the guilt at bay by keeping busy. Firefighting, skydiving, scuba diving, whatever it took. His dad had been an adrenaline junkie too, so it ran in the family, which hadn't ever seemed like a bad thing. No one had ever looked at his dad the way Shauna looked at him.

She stepped onto the edge of the porch and stopped. "Anyone there?"

He rose from the chair at the naked fear in her voice. "Shauna, it's just me." He emerged from the shadows. "Sorry I scared you."

"What are you doing here?"

He'd upset her. "Just making sure you're okay."

She stiffened. "Of course I'm okay. Thanks for your concern, but I'm exhausted. Good night." She turned back toward the door.

"Wait. I-I just wondered what the sheriff had to say."

The tension in her shoulders relaxed a bit as she turned back to face him. The warm glow of the porch light illuminated the pale skin that was such a contrast to her dark hair. "Just like everyone else, he thinks it was an accident. He could barely restrain himself from patting my shoulder and saying, 'There, there,' when I told him about the explosion I heard. He thinks he knows best. I had to remind him I'd been in the navy and had plenty of experience with explosions."

He suppressed a grin. She didn't suffer fools easily. "A fire inspector will determine what caused the blast so that will tell us a lot."

"I know." She hugged herself in the freshening wind. "I expect he'll be back to talk to me tomorrow." Her eyes widened, and she raised her hand to her mouth. "I just remembered the box!"

"What box?"

"Clarence gave it to me." She darted down the steps to her truck and opened the

37

passenger door. When she turned toward him, she carried a large Priority Mail box. "Clarence wanted me to mail this to Lucy. I should have told the sheriff."

Zach thought that very curious. "Why didn't he do it himself?"

"I'm freezing. Come in, and I'll make some coffee while I tell you about it."

He barely held back a gasp. Maybe she really was thawing toward him. Or maybe she just needed a sounding board tonight, and he was okay with that. He followed her inside where she led him to the kitchen in the middle of the open living space. It hadn't changed since he was here last, the morning Jack had died. The hardwood floors gleamed in the glow of the spotlights in the tongue-and-groove ceiling. The furniture was gray leather and comfortable enough that he'd fallen asleep on it a few times over the years. The sleek gray cabinets were a beautiful contrast to the marble counters and hickory floors. There were touches of red in the small appliances.

She put down the box on the farm-style table, then went to the coffee grinder and prepared the coffee.

He picked it up and shook it. "Did he give you any hint of the contents?"

"No, he didn't act like it was that important. He said he would have mailed it himself, but he had to disappear for a while because it was too dangerous."

His ears pricked at that. "He actually used the word *dangerous*?"

She tucked a dark strand of hair behind her ear. "He even bought a disposable phone and gave me the number."

Unease stirred in his gut as the aroma of coffee began to fill the kitchen. Could someone really have planted a bomb in Clarence's house?

"He's been teaching me aerial photography since I could use a second source of income. I'll have to figure out something else now." Color rushed to her pale cheeks, and she turned back toward the coffeepot and poured java into two mugs before joining him at the table.

Was she having financial trouble? She wouldn't tell him even if he asked. Jack had been an accountant and a good one. How could he have left her in a tough financial situation?

He placed the box on the counter, then wrapped his cold fingers around the hot surface of the mug she handed him. "Maybe you should take the box to the sheriff. It might be important."

She took a sip of her coffee, then shook her head. "Clarence seemed adamant that I deliver it to Lucy, and I want to honor his wishes. I doubt it has anything to do with his murder."

"If it was murder."

Her green eyes flashed his way, and her lips flattened. She glanced at her watch. "It's ten. She's probably still up. Maybe I should just take it to her."

"Shauna, listen to me. The sheriff needs to review the contents."

She jutted out her chin. "Lucy can give it to Everett. She needs to have it first. I promised Clarence."

He sighed. She'd always had that headstrong way about her. "You look like a stiff wind would blow you over. Get some rest tonight and deal with it tomorrow."

She took another sip of coffee and stared at him over the rim of her cup. "I wouldn't sleep anyway. I think I need to go over there and make sure she's okay."

He pulled out his cell phone. "Let me call her first." The phone rang in his ear, then went to voice mail. "Lucy's not picking up."

"Don't bother leaving a message. She probably doesn't want to talk. Let's just head over there." Shauna grabbed his mug and poured both of their drinks into thermal cups. "I'll let you drive."

She was actually letting him come?

■ ■ ■ ■

The condo complex where Lucy lived on the outskirts of Port Angeles had seen better days, and the bright lights lining the walkway clearly showed the structure's age. Built in the 1960s, the shingle siding had gone from a soft weathered gray to black and splitting apart. The door seemed a little crooked as well, and the scent of fish from someone's dinner lingered in the air.

Shauna paused outside the entry and listened. No sound arose from the other side of the door marked 311, though a dim light flickered through the condo window.

Zach was a comforting presence beside her, but she still couldn't believe she'd asked him to accompany her. She'd really needed someone to bolster her flagging courage, and her weakness confounded her. The last person's help she needed was his, so what had gotten into her?

He reached past her and pressed the doorbell. As it chimed inside, her stomach tightened and moisture flooded her eyes. She swallowed the thickness in her throat and squared her shoulders. She knew what it was like to be on the receiving end of a visit like this.

The door opened, and Lucy's reddened eyes locked with Shauna's. "You heard?" Lucy burst into fresh sobs and leaned against the door frame. "He can't be dead. I was going to go home this weekend." Her curly brown hair stood on end as if she'd raked her hands through it many times.

Shauna embraced her, and Lucy wept on her shoulder. Lucy's thin shoulders, clad in a baggy sweatshirt, shook with the storm of grief tearing through her. Shauna couldn't hold back her own tears.

Lucy finally released her and stepped out of the way. "Come in. I need a tissue, and so do you. Zach, thanks for stopping by."

The place was tiny. The living room was about ten feet square and ended with the countertop on a peninsula where the kitchen started. There was barely enough room for the worn brown tweed sofa in it. It was a dreary place to have heard the news. A partial bowl of soup sat congealing on the faded Formica counter.

Shauna accepted the tissue Lucy handed her and mopped her face before blowing her nose. "Want me to fix you some tea or coffee? Are you hungry?"

Lucy gestured to the sagging sofa. "I couldn't get anything down my throat, honey, but if you want something, help

42

yourself. You too, Zach."

"Nothing for me."

"Me neither," Zach said.

Shauna settled on the sofa and glanced at Zach as he sat on the other end. He had the box in his hands.

Lucy sank onto an ottoman and buried her face in her hands. "Who told you?"

"I called it in." Shauna told her what she'd seen. "I wanted to come tell you, but the sheriff wouldn't let me. He said he needed to be the one to break the news." She glanced at Zach. "Clarence gave me something for you. He'd told me to mail it, but under the circumstances, I wanted you to have it right away."

"H-he talked about me?" Lucy's eyes grew luminous with moisture again. "I always loved him. I just needed time to myself to accept what had happened to Darla. The good Lord forgive me, but I blamed Clarence for her death. I always thought he was too hard on her and that's why she turned to drugs. Alone in this dinky little place, I realized I was wrong. I tried to call him today but got his voice mail." Her voice grew choked, and she dabbed at her eyes again. "It wasn't his fault. It wasn't my fault. Darla chose her own path, as we all must."

Zach leaned forward. "He knew you'd

return to him, Lucy. I had lunch with him two days ago, and he told me you'd be back any day and that you would always love him."

Her hazel eyes searched his face. "You think he meant it? He really knew I still loved him?"

"I'm positive."

"How could the house just explode like that?" Lucy pushed her curls out of her eyes.

Shauna started to mention her suspicions about a bomb, but one look at Lucy's ravaged face changed her mind. She didn't need to hear that now.

Shauna reached over and took the box from Zach, then handed it to Lucy. "He didn't mention what was in this — just asked me to mail it to you."

Lucy exhaled and stared at the box. Her brown fingers began to pluck at the tab holding it closed. "Guess we'd better see what's in here."

The glue resisted her efforts, so Zach ripped the box open. Lucy pulled out the contents. Dozens of pictures, a key to something, a pink book closed with a clasp, and a map of the Olympic National Forest.

Lucy ran her fingertips over the book. "This is Darla's journal. I wondered where that had disappeared to."

Several of the pictures looked familiar to Shauna. "These are some of the aerial photographs I took a couple of months ago when he first started teaching me."

Lucy picked up the key. "Any idea what this unlocks? It's not a house or a car key."

Zach held out his hand. "May I?" She nodded and handed it to him. He rolled it around in his fingers and looked at the numbers on it. "I'm not familiar with a key like this."

"Safety deposit box maybe?" Shauna guessed. "Is that everything in the box?"

Lucy upended the box, and something fell to the worn beige carpet. A silver chain with some kind of black pendant glimmered in the lamplight. Lucy reached down to scoop it up, then held it under the light. "It's a necklace. How peculiar."

"Can I see it?"

Lucy dropped it into Shauna's palm.

"I think I've seen this before, but I'm not sure where." Shauna turned the pendant over to examine the front of the round black stone. An inlay of abalone flowers decorated either side of the imprint of a hummingbird. The pendant was large, about four inches across. A sick feeling coiled in her belly. It couldn't be the same one, could it?

"You look as though you're about to

faint," Lucy said. "Are you all right?"

"M-my mother had a necklace like this. It's a Haida hummingbird. Mom called it a symbol of health, and she never took it off. I asked my dad about it once, and he said it was missing when her body was found. It couldn't be the same one, could it?"

Seeing the jewelry again had brought back the pang of losing her mother all over again. That horrific time was something she usually pushed out of her mind, but it took extra effort to do that tonight and focus instead on her dim memories of the funeral. Had her mother been wearing the necklace in the casket?

No matter how hard she tried, Shauna couldn't remember. She'd only been eight, and her most vivid memory was how her father had fallen on top of the casket. He'd been drinking, though at the time she only knew his eyes were bloodshot and he didn't talk clearly.

"And if it is, why did Clarence have it?" Zach frowned.

"It's very strange," Lucy said. "Since Darla's journal is here, maybe all these things belonged to her, and he found them somewhere."

Shauna couldn't tear her gaze away from the necklace. "But how would Darla have obtained my mother's necklace?"

"If it is hers."

She nodded at Zach. "True. There might be thousands of necklaces like this out there. Maybe it means nothing." But it didn't feel like nothing. It felt hugely important, life-changing even.

Zach cleared his throat. "The sheriff will want to look at the contents."

"Especially if Clarence was murdered." As soon as the words were out of her mouth, Shauna wanted to call them back. She hadn't meant to upset Lucy even more.

Lucy's hazel eyes went wide. "Murder? I assumed it was an accident with his chemicals."

"The explosion felt bigger than something accidental to me," Shauna said.

Lucy rubbed her forehead. "Would you take these things then? I don't know what to do to keep it all safe."

"Let me take it," Zach said. "If you're willing, of course. I don't want to see either of you in danger. Especially not with Alex, Shauna. I'll take it to the sheriff in the morning."

At his concern for her son, her heart warmed just a bit. "That's probably a good idea. Okay with you, Lucy?"

Lucy dabbed her eyes as fresh tears fell. "Whatever you think."

CHAPTER 4

A campfire bloomed in the darkness down the street, and drunken laughter rippled on the wind. Good. No one was likely to notice him creeping up the steps, and if they did, it would make his mission more dangerous and exciting, which suited him just fine.

It was one in the morning, and he'd smashed the lone lightbulb in the stairwell once it got dark. There hadn't been anyone around then either, but he'd wanted to make sure no one caught a glimpse of his face. Any witness would most likely notice the deputy uniform he wore. One thing he'd noticed was that people paid attention to the badge and not the facial features.

He reached the woman's front door and paused to listen. There was only silence on the other side of the battered door. With such a flimsy barrier, all he had to do was slide a credit card down the jamb to unlock the latch. He slipped inside and quickly closed the door behind him. A cat gave a startled *meow,* then shot down the hallway. He'd have to move fast to make sure the animal didn't awaken her.

He pulled a ski mask over his face, then set his valise on the floor. With practiced care, he moved along the thin carpet to the first door on the right. Moonlight shone on the queen-size bed and illuminated her closed eyes and slightly open mouth. A light snore eased from her lips. He relaxed a bit as he stepped to the bed and clapped a gloved hand over her mouth.

Her eyes flew open, and she struggled to escape his grip. Her muffled cries couldn't get past his gloved hand.

"Easy. I just want to talk to you a minute. But if you scream, I have this." He held his sharp hunting knife up in the moonlight. Her eyes widened, and a tear slid from one eye. "Can I trust you enough to remove my hand?"

She gave a jerky nod, so he eased his hand away but kept the knife in sight. She licked dry lips. "What do you want?"

"Clarence gave the McDade woman a box to give to you. Where is it?" The device he'd put in the Glennons' house had yielded up that last nugget before the explosion.

Her eyes flickered to the closet, then back.

"I don't know what you're talking about."

Stupid woman. Why did she have to play games? He jerked her out of the bed and onto her feet, then marched her toward the closet. "Get it for me now."

"I don't have a box from Shauna. You have the wrong information."

"I had his house bugged. I know all about the box." He waggled the knife in front of her face. "Wonder how you'd look with a four-inch scar on your cheek? I might just cut you in a few places to see."

She shrank back. "Please don't hurt me."

"I want the box." He shoved her toward the closet door. "Get it!"

She opened the door and reached to the floor. A Priority Mail box was set back in the corner on top of a jumble of shoes. When she turned with it in her hands, he snatched it from her. "See, now wasn't that easy? Why did you have to make it so hard?"

She hugged herself in her flimsy night-gown. "Why are you doing this?"

He eyed the defiant tilt to her chin. "Come with me." The amnesia drug he planned to administer was in his satchel in the living room. One little stick, and she'd forget everything.

She shook her head and backed away. "I'm not going anywhere with you. You got what you wanted. Just go."

Reaching over, he laid the blade against her throat. "Do what I say."

Her lips trembled, and she moved toward the door. "I can't believe you'd do this to me. Clarence just died. I've had all I can take today."

He smirked at her. "You think I don't know that?"

Her eyes went wide and horrified. "You killed Clarence? Why?"

"I had no choice." Holding the blade to her throat again, he motioned her to move down the hall toward the front door.

She swallowed, then obeyed his silent command. They walked in lockstep toward the living room. The cat screeched and hurtled past their feet, and he jumped, nicking the woman's throat a bit with his blade.

She put her hand to her neck, then pulled her fingers back and looked at the blood on them. "You cut me." She jerked out of his grip, then ran for the kitchen. She grabbed a knife from the wooden block and turned to face him as he raced after her.

He stopped two feet from her and laughed. "You don't know how to use that. Put it down." He set the box on the counter and closed the gap.

She slashed at him with the butcher knife,

51

and he felt the wind of it on his arm. "Quit it."

He backhanded her, and her knife went flying and clattered on the kitchen floor. She reeled back, knocking over a glass of water on the counter. He moved toward her, but she threw a glass bowl at him, and as he ducked, she darted past him. Sprinting for the door, she stumbled over the cat and fell into the wall, smearing it with blood as she went down.

Rage darkened his vision as he pursued her. "You're making this harder than it has to be." His fingers closed around her arm, and he jerked her to her feet.

As he thrust the knife forward to threaten her, she jerked away again and lost her balance. Her shoulder hit the wall behind her and propelled her back toward him. When she crashed into him, the tip of the knife sliced into the base of her throat.

Great, just great. He'd have to finish this here, then get out before someone heard the ruckus. It wasn't supposed to be this hard.

When he was done, he wiped the bloody knife on her nightgown, then retrieved the box. It sure was light. He shook it but didn't hear anything. Frowning, he opened the end and peered inside. Empty. Where had the evidence gone?

Shauna used her key to unlock Marilyn's front door. She followed the sound of the TV and stepped into the living room. Sunshine slanted through the window and lit the red in Alex's auburn hair. "Good morning."

"Mommy!" Alex, watching cartoons, leaped up from the floor and pelted toward Shauna.

She caught him in a fierce embrace. After yesterday's horrible events, his hugs were especially precious. "Hey, Bug. You have a good time with Grammy?"

Marilyn had let him build a fort. Two blankets lay draped over the white leather sofa and chair. Remnants of pizza had hardened on paper plates as well. Alex's hair hadn't yet been combed, and a milk stain marred his Mickey Mouse pajamas. She didn't want to let go of his sturdy little body. When everything else was wrong with her world, being with her son made everything right. She forced herself to release him, then watched him go back to his cartoons.

Bright and perky, Marilyn stepped into the doorway between the living room and the kitchen. In her sixties, her hair was always colored to its original auburn shade and in a perfect chin-length bob. Shauna had never seen her in anything but designer slacks and blouses with perfectly appointed jewelry. She had one entire closet devoted to her shoes and accessories. In spite of being a slave to fashion, she'd been a bulwark for Shauna from the moment they met on that fifth date with Jack. Marilyn had taken one look at Shauna in her worn jeans and US Navy T-shirt and had decided she was perfect for her only child.

Shauna realized how fortunate that support was from the very first. She hugged Marilyn tightly. "Thanks for helping out. You're the best."

Marilyn released her. "Any more news?" She glanced at Alex. "Honey, you'd better go brush your teeth and get dressed. If Mommy is up for it, we'll go to Harvey's Pier for some seafood for lunch."

"Yay!" He abandoned the TV and rushed for the stairs.

With small ears out of the way, Shauna told her all she'd seen. "I'm sure the sheriff will be by today." She wanted to tell Marilyn about the necklace, but if it was an important clue to the investigation, she probably shouldn't reveal it. Clarence hadn't wanted anyone to know.

Her cell phone played, and Shauna pulled

54

it from her purse, then winced seeing the sheriff's name. Everett Burchell, about forty-five, had been sheriff for six years. His marriage six months ago to twenty-four-year-old model Felicia Tong had shocked the county.

Shauna answered the call. "Hi, Sheriff. I assume you want to talk to me again?"

"Why didn't you tell me about that package yesterday? You may have compromised the investigation! Lucy called me last night and told me about it. She said you were going to try to hide it from me. Is that true?"

She closed her eyes and sighed, then opened them and paced the floor in front of Marilyn's large living room windows. "Clarence asked me to keep it quiet. I wanted to honor his wishes. You'll see it all today."

The sheriff huffed. "I need you to go over every sentence Clarence said and every action he took when you were with him. Lucy says you identified the necklace as belonging to your mother."

"I'm not sure. I was very young when she died. I could be wrong. You could talk to my father about it."

"Can you come to my office right now?"

"Can it wait? I'm picking up my son. He spent the night with Marilyn. It would be better if he didn't hear any of this."

"No. You should have told me about the box last night. You're not far from my house, and I'm still there. Just come over here."

She sighed and rubbed her head, then glanced at her mother-in-law who nodded. "Okay, Marilyn can keep Alex a little longer. I'll be right there." She ended the call and went to tell her son that their outing was going to be delayed.

CHAPTER 5

Shauna's nerves still vibrated from the sheriff's reprimand. Had she messed up the investigation? She wanted the killer brought to justice with every fiber of her being.

She pulled up in front of a contemporary gray two-story overlooking the Strait of Juan de Fuca. The sheriff's house was the last one in the city limits of Lavender Tides. Rumor had it that his wife's money had paid for most of it since it had to be worth a million dollars. Shauna eyed the house as she parked her truck in the circle drive. Before she got out, she tried Lucy's number again. Still no answer. Maybe she was still asleep.

Shauna got out and went to the massive door. She didn't have a chance to press the doorbell before it swung open to reveal the Asian beauty she'd heard so much about.

The young woman's hair was in a ponytail, and she wore bright-pink yoga pants and a skimpy exercise top. Her olive skin glistened with perspiration, and her cheeks were pink. "Good morning. You must be Shauna."

Her voice had that smoky, husky tone men found so entrancing, but Shauna warmed immediately to the intelligence in her dark-brown sloe eyes.

"Guilty as charged." She held out her hand. "It's nice to meet you, Mrs. Burchell."

"Call me Felicia." Her handshake was firm and friendly. "Come on in. Everett is in the living room. I need to take a shower anyway, so the two of you can talk in private. But don't run off. I'd love a chance to chat. This area is a little standoffish, and I haven't gotten to know hardly anyone. Maybe you can give me the lay of the land."

Shauna followed her and took in the home's grandeur. The gleaming marble floors and huge living room with ceilings that soared at least twenty-feet high were impressive. A huge chandelier glittered down over a Persian rug warming the space. The place held the scent of Italian leather from the new red sofa. "Beautiful room."

"Thank you. It was fun to decorate, and Everett let me do whatever I wanted. I'll be back in a jiffy." Felicia sent a final smile her way as the sheriff rose from a leather chair by the massive marble fireplace.

He pointed to the sofa. "Have a seat. Want

something to drink?"

He capitalized on his dark good looks with an Elvis-style hairdo that glistened with product. Had he dyed it recently? She could have sworn he'd had some gray at the temples. He was handsome for a guy in his forties, though hardly in Felicia's attractiveness category.

"No, I'm fine." The leather still felt a little stiff to Shauna as she sank onto the couch. "Did you call my dad about the necklace?"

He nodded. "I didn't get him, though. Stubborn man doesn't have voice mail. I've already made some initial inquiries at some jewelry stores to determine where it was purchased. It's rare for sure, but it might not be one of a kind. I'm going to show it to your father as well once I get it. Zach is dropping off the box at my office first thing this morning."

Her father had become a drunk since her mother's death. Any mention of her was sure to send him on a binge. "Could I look at it again first? I don't want to bother Pop with it if it's unnecessary."

"Stop by the jail. I'll tell them to let you see it. But you were only eight or ten when your mom died, weren't you? I'm not so sure your memory of it is that clear."

"I was eight. Mom never took it off. I

59

played with it around her neck more times than I can count."

He shrugged. "Have a look then to set your mind at ease." A frown creased his forehead. "Have you spoken to Lucy this morning? I've called her three times but just got voice mail."

Her back prickled with gooseflesh. "I called her on the way here, but she didn't answer." Shauna raised her hand to her mouth. "Sheriff, what if the person who killed Clarence is after Lucy now? She might be in danger!"

"We don't know Clarence was killed. You're jumping to conclusions."

She failed to keep her voice steady. "I have a really bad feeling about this."

He rolled his eyes but got up. "I'll go check on her. Call her and tell her I'm on my way."

She fumbled her phone from her handbag and called Lucy, but she landed in voice mail after four rings. "Lucy, don't answer the door and keep it locked. The sheriff is on his way. We want to make sure you're safe."

Her hands shook as she ended the call and prayed for her friend's safety.

The scent of fish and chips hung in the

hallway. Morning traffic flowed past Lucy's apartment complex as Zach rang her doorbell and waited. When she didn't answer, he rang the bell again. Kids cried a few doors down, and he heard a woman's voice soothing them. After a furtive glance around, two teenagers below him in the stairwell exchanged something. Probably a drug buy. This neighborhood was notorious for drugs.

He glanced at the door and bit back a gasp when he saw it ajar by about an inch. His neck prickling, he nudged it open a few more inches. "Lucy? It's Zach."

No answer. His pulse sped up when her cat, Weasley, zipped past him from inside and disappeared around the corner of the outside hallway. He started to go after it, then looked back at the entry. Something was wrong. Lucy was always safety conscious. She wouldn't leave the door unlocked, let alone ajar.

He pushed it all the way open. "Lucy, I'm coming in." After stepping inside, he was struck by a thick coppery smell.

Then he saw the first smear of blood, a handprint on the beige wall. Acid rose in his throat as he walked toward the hallway.

And there she was. Lucy lay curled in a fetal position on the hall floor. He squatted beside her and pressed his fingers against her carotid artery. No pulse. She had multiple stab wounds in her chest, and defensive slashes scored her palms. She'd obviously fought hard against her attacker. A knife lay a foot or so from her outstretched hand.

He stood and pulled out his phone to call the sheriff's office when a strident voice called out, "Sheriff's department. I'm coming in!"

Zach stepped into the other man's view and held up his hand. "Over here, Sheriff."

Burchell barreled through the doorway and hurried toward him. "What are you doing here, Bannister?" His brows drew together, and his nostrils flared.

"I came to check on Lucy. She was understandably upset last night, and I wanted her to know we cared. Someone got here before me. She's dead, stabbed." He moved out of the way and motioned for the sheriff to go around him to the hallway.

The sheriff stopped and heaved a sigh. "Did you touch anything?"

"Her neck. I was checking for a pulse. And the door when I came in."

Burchell pulled out his phone and called in his forensic team. While he was talking, Zach wandered around the small apartment to look for clues, careful not to touch anything. A glass of spilled water pooled on the dingy counter, and a stool lay on its side. He suspected the sheriff would find the lock had been jimmied.

He stopped in the foyer and listened to the sheriff's end of the conversation. His ears perked up when he heard Burchell say, "C-4 isn't an easy explosive to get hold of. They're sure?"

The sheriff ended the call and motioned for Zach to join him in the living room. "What time did you get here?"

"About five minutes ago. I rang the bell a couple of times, then noticed the door was ajar. Her cat got out too, by the way. I should probably go find it."

Burchell's dark-blue eyes narrowed. "You have an alibi for this morning?"

"What, you think I killed her? She and Clarence were good friends. I cared about her, about both of them." When the sheriff continued to stare him down, Zach shrugged. "I was home alone from the time I dropped Shauna off at nine last night until I left the house this morning at seven. I stopped for gas, and you can probably find a video verifying it. I dropped the box off at your office at seven thirty, then had breakfast at the café before deciding to check on Lucy."

Though Zach should have expected the

suspicion, it still stung. His friendship with the Glennons was long-standing, but then, conventional wisdom said the murderer was usually someone close to the victim. The next thing the sheriff would say was that he was going to check out Shauna.

Zach's gut clenched. This would devastate her. First Clarence and now Lucy. "This has to be connected to Clarence's death. The C-4 proves it was no accident."

"You were eavesdropping? This is my investigation, not yours." The sheriff's mouth flattened and he looked away for a moment, head bowed, before he faced Zach again. "I don't know, but I'm going to keep an open mind about it. In this neighborhood, the perp could have been a punk looking to score. A knife is not usually an assassin's weapon of choice."

"You mind if I break the news to Shauna? This will be hard for her."

The sheriff stared at him. "I'm going to be here awhile, and I'd rather she didn't hear the news on TV, so yeah. And just in case, she shouldn't be staying alone. She is the only witness to the explosion and the last person to talk to Clarence. If we're dealing with the same killer, she could be the guy's next target."

Footsteps pounded up the stairwell, and

the forensic team arrived at the door. The sheriff grabbed Zach's shoulder and pushed him toward the exit. "Get out of here, and let us do our work."

Zach stepped out into the hallway, and Lucy's orange tabby peered at him from under the railing. He stooped and held out his hand. "Come here, Weasley. I'll scrounge up some food for you." The cat crawled out a few inches and licked his hand. He scooped it up. "Let's go see Shauna."

CHAPTER 6

"Where'd Everett go?" Felicia came down the stairs drying her long black hair. She wore slim-fitting jeans with boots and a figure-hugging red top that accentuated her dark eyes.

Shauna told her what had happened. "I should probably go get my son, but I was hoping your husband would call you with an update."

Felicia dropped onto the sofa and tucked her legs under her, then began to braid her hair. "Oh, Everett doesn't keep me informed of his comings and goings. I learned early on that he got mad when I questioned him."

Shauna didn't know what to make of Everett's new bride. She clearly said whatever she was thinking. "How do you like Lavender Tides? You're from New York?"

"Well, most recently from New York, but I grew up in Phoenix. My modeling career took me to the Big Apple five years ago."

"How'd you meet Everett?"

Felicia smiled. "I think you really want to know why I married him. That's what everyone wants to know. I see it in the sidelong glances as they look from him to me. All they see is a twenty-something model hooked up with an aging Elvis wannabe. The real truth is, I actually fell for the guy. Who can really explain how love hits? My uncle is in law enforcement, and he took me to a party in Seattle. Everett sat at our table. Within five minutes I knew I wanted to marry him."

"I'm glad it worked out." And when Shauna thought back to her own marriage, people had looked at her the same way. Jack had been six two to her five two. They didn't really go together, and she'd never felt worthy of him. He'd come from a good family, while her drunken father made her a constant source of pity and condemnation. Her heart warmed toward the young woman.

Love was a funny thing — experience in life sifted thoughts and feelings until you looked in someone's eyes and found a match you weren't expecting. She sometimes thought she'd been drawn to Jack because he'd grown up alone, just like she had. There was more to it than that, of course, but it was a bedrock common experience that let him understand her fears.

She'd been here longer than she planned. "I'd really better go. It's been great talking to you, Felicia."

The doorbell rang and Felicia rose. Shauna glanced through the big windows toward the driveway and recognized the truck. What was Zach doing here? She followed Felicia to the foyer.

Felicia opened the door. "Can I help you?"

"This is a-a friend, Zach Bannister," Shauna said.

Zach wore jeans and a Seahawks sweatshirt and cap. A frown crouched between his dark-blue eyes. His gaze went past Felicia to Shauna, but he didn't smile. Was that pity in his face? She shot to her feet and pressed her palm against her stomach. "What's wrong?"

He glanced back at Felicia then. "Do you mind if I come in? I need to talk to Shauna a minute."

Shauna gripped her hands together. "What is it? Is Alex — ?"

He held up his hand. "I'm sure Alex is fine. It's Lucy." He moved past Felicia to reach Shauna's side and put his hand on her shoulder. "I went by to check on her.

The door was standing open, and when she didn't answer, I went in. She's dead, Shauna. I'm sorry."

"Dead?" She shook his hand off her and stepped back. "That's not possible. D-did she kill herself?" The thought of such despair horrified her. She wanted to throw up, scream, or beat her head against a wall.

He cupped her shoulders. "No. She was stabbed."

Her head swam, and her vision darkened. *Don't faint.* "Stabbed. You mean murdered, just like Clarence."

"The sheriff isn't sure yet, but he says it's possible. You were right about the bomb. They found traces of C-4."

Her chest tightened. "Who would want to kill Clarence?"

"I'm worried about you. So is the sheriff. What if you're next on the killer's list? He might think Clarence told you something." Zach's fingers squeezed her shoulders. "You're moving into my place. I've got two spare rooms."

"That's out of the question." Every time she turned around she'd be faced with what he'd done. She couldn't handle it — not now, not ever.

Felicia shut the door. "You are a good man." She left them alone and went into the kitchen.

He gave Shauna a little shake. "You have to think of Alex. Who's going to protect him and you if that psycho comes back? Your dad? He's drunk all the time. Marilyn? He'd mow her down at the front door, and she lives out in the boonies with no neighbors just like you. You need a man between you and danger, someone the killer won't mess around with. And you need to be near neighbors who would hear glass breaking."

"I've done all right by myself for the past year. I can handle myself."

"It's not about you, Shauna. It's about Alex. He doesn't need to face any more trauma. He's had enough in his short life."

He was right.

She didn't even have a gun, though she'd grown up knowing how to shoot. She was rusty on her self-defense moves, but even if she'd kept up with that kind of thing, it wasn't much good against a gun or a knife. If she moved to Marilyn's, it would just put her mother-in-law in danger as well as Alex.

"You know I'm right." His somber and intent eyes willed her to listen to him. "I hope you're okay with cats. I took Weasley with me."

"Of course. There was nothing else you could do." She frowned. "Wait a minute —

aren't you allergic to cats? And what about your dogs?" His rottweilers, Apollo and Artemis, would terrorize the cat.

"The boys actually like cats, if you can believe it, and I couldn't leave the poor guy to run in that neighborhood. Some kid would probably set him on fire."

She thought through his offer. Her house sat in the woods where even a passing car wouldn't be able to see much. She could scream for help and no one would hear her. The big windows she loved made her vulnerable out there by herself. Someone could smash in one of them in the living room and step right inside. And she wasn't sure she could aim a rifle at a man and pull the trigger. She had to think of Alex.

She gave a jerky nod. "All right."

How was this going to work? Friends would think she'd lost her mind. Marilyn would have a fit, and even her dad would question the arrangements. She couldn't tell her son what was really going on because he'd be frightened.

She rubbed her forehead. "Any ideas on how to explain this to Alex?"

He lifted a brow. "He's five. I don't think he'll question anything."

"Let me grab my purse. I'll try to explain it to him. Let me know when you're heading for my house, and I'll meet you there, if you don't mind hanging out while we pack."

Zach's hands shook a little as he raked his hair out of his eyes and got out of his truck in front of Shauna's house. The moment Zach realized the killer might try to hurt her, he'd known what he had to do. He owed this to Jack, to their lifelong friendship. And it might help him come to grips with his guilt.

Her white truck sat next to the brick walkway to the porch, and he frowned as he climbed the steps. He'd asked her to wait until he arrived to go inside, just to be safe. She opened the front door before he could press the bell. The messy bun on top of her head emphasized the widow's peak on her forehead, and she looked cute with wisps of hair escaping to graze her high cheekbones.

Dark circles under her eyes emphasized her stress. "I'm still not sure about this. It's going to look bad to other people."

"We can both handle a little gossip. How did Marilyn react to the news you were moving in with me?" He stepped into the entry and shut the door behind him.

She hunched her shoulders. "I chickened out. She was already upset about Clarence and Lucy. I didn't have the heart to lay that on her too."

He thrust his hands in his jacket pockets. "It will be all over the county by tomorrow night. You know it will. How's she going to feel if she hears it from someone else?"

Shauna passed her hand over her forehead. "You're right. I know you're right. I'll go back over after dinner."

"Want me to take care of it?" He'd rather face an angry tiger than Jack's mother, but he'd do it if she needed him to.

She smiled then, a brief grimace that didn't reach her eyes. "She'd eat you alive."

"I think I can hold my own. Where's Alex? You told him?"

"I told him we were going to visit you for a while, that it would make it easy for you to take him on the outing. He didn't question it at all, just like you said. He's in his room. You know the way."

He nodded and headed down the hall, then heard a flurry of small feet skipping his way.

Alex launched himself at Zach's legs. "Zachster! Mommy said you were coming to get us. I thought she was teasing."

Zach's heart warmed at the nickname Jack had always used too. No one else ever called him that except Jack and Alex. He hoisted the boy to his chest. "Hey, little man, I've missed you."

Alex wound his small arms around Zach's neck. He smelled of jelly and little boy. "I'm not little anymore." The boy said it with all the seriousness of his four-foot stature.

Zach held him tight. Moisture blurred his vision. The boy's resemblance to Jack made his heart squeeze. Jack would be so proud of this kid. "You've grown four inches, I bet."

"I bet it's more like a whole foot." Alex squirmed to be let down.

Zach set him on his feet, then ruffled his auburn hair. "What do you think about going to my house? We have a cat to take care of too. Weasley is going to live with us."

"I love Weasley." Alex's turquoise eyes widened, and he danced around the hall. "We can have breakfast together. I haven't played Pac-Man since Daddy went to heaven. Mommy doesn't like it. You still have your game, right?"

Zach had paid a ridiculous price to buy two old Atari machines on eBay just to show Alex how to play the game Zach and Jack had played growing up. The boy liked it better than the modern games filling the cabinet in the living room. Every Saturday night they'd had a Pac-Man marathon. Zach had

74

thought Alex would have forgotten it by now.

"I sure do, and I think I'm up for the challenge tonight. I'll make my famous Mickey Mouse pancakes for breakfast."

"Yay! I'm going to go tell Mommy!" Alex ran down the hall.

Zach followed at a slower pace. It had been a year since he'd been here. An interminable number of days filled with self-loathing and guilt. He had a chance to make it up to Alex and Shauna. Alex would be easier than his mother. The accusation in Shauna's eyes wouldn't fade overnight. He didn't deserve for it to leave easily either. Maybe never.

He found Shauna and Alex at the kitchen island. Alex was already stuffing his mouth full of an almond butter and jelly sandwich. He was allergic to peanuts, so peanut butter wasn't allowed in the house.

Zach hadn't eaten since breakfast, and his stomach rumbled. "Mind if I have one of those?"

Shauna glanced at him. "Help yourself. You know where the stuff is. I just put it away."

His throat was tight as he went to the corner cabinet and pulled down the almond butter and the bread, then got the jelly out of the fridge. It was about three, still a couple of hours to dinner. Should he offer to cook tonight or ask her if she wanted to? He would need to tread a very cautious line.

"Anything special in mind for dinner?" He forced a lighthearted tone. "I could buy pizza for our Pac-Man challenge."

"Pac-Man," Shauna said in a choked voice.

He shot her a glance and saw tears filling her eyes. This was going to be harder for her than he'd realized.

CHAPTER 7

Shauna was only too happy to escape from the sound of Pac-Man. It brought back way too many memories, and even bearding the lioness named Marilyn was preferable to watching Alex playing with Zach.

The salty scent of the sea blew in her open window as she drove to her mother-in-law's. The quiet drive along the water with the lights of houses glimmering in the dark settled her jitters. She could do this, even though it would be unpleasant. She ran up the windows before she reached the lavender fields. The plants were still in bloom, and the aroma would make her head pound.

The lights were on in the barn and the chicken coop when she pulled into the drive. An incoming text message dinged, and she glanced at it. A friend, Ellie Blackmore, wanted to have lunch, but she turned off the screen. She hadn't had an outing with a friend since Jack died, and she still wasn't ready.

She eyed the barn, then got out and headed that way. Marilyn must have gotten to her chores late. Shauna found her mother-in-law in the barn tossing hay to her milk cow, Ellen. She wore a tailored pink shirt over slim gray slacks. She refused to wear jeans, even though Shauna had bought her several for her birthday one year.

Even doing chores, she wore her nice clothes. Though Shauna had never asked Marilyn why she dressed that way, Jack had told Shauna it was part of his mother's need to control circumstances. Marilyn's dad had been a high-profile judge who never wore anything but a suit. She'd married Walter, a man just like him, and he'd insisted she present the proper facade to the community. One day she'd dressed in capris in defiance of his decree and had gone for a walk along the beach with Jack. That afternoon Jack's father choked on a piece of food at a restaurant over lunch and died. Her picture in the capris arriving at the hospital had been on the front page of the paper. According to Jack, she never dressed casually again.

The familiar blend of farmyard smells made Shauna nostalgic. In the early years of her marriage, before Alex came along, she'd spent a lot of time helping Marilyn in the barn. She'd learned a lot about gardening and farm animals. Though, since Jack died, she'd let weeds take over her own small plot of tomatoes and jalapeños.

Marilyn turned to hang the pitchfork on the wall and spotted Shauna by the door. She put her hand to her chest. "Goodness, you about gave me a heart attack. Has something else happened?" She came toward Shauna.

Shauna reached over and plucked a chicken feather from Marilyn's hair. "Nothing else has happened, but it might. I didn't want to talk about it in front of Alex, so I came back alone."

Marilyn lifted a brow and frowned. "Where's Alex now?"

Here it comes. Shauna wetted her lips. "Well, that's part of all this. The sheriff thinks it's possible that whoever killed Lucy and Clarence might hunt for me next. For protection, Zach Bannister has invited us to move into his spare rooms, just until we know Alex and I aren't in danger."

Marilyn's perfectly shaped brows drew together, and her mouth grew pinched. "That's ridiculous, Shauna. Kick him to the curb and stay here with me. You don't want to owe *that man* anything."

"We'd be no safer with you. You're in the country as well with no close neighbors. We'd have no protection, and I'd just be putting you in jeopardy as well."

Marilyn's scowl deepened. "How can you stand to be around the man who murdered my boy? And to let him be around Alex is worse yet!" She brushed past her and exited the barn.

Shauna followed and pulled the door shut behind her. She hurried to catch up with Marilyn, who was marching toward the house. "I knew you'd be upset, but it seemed to make sense. My dad is never sober enough to be any help. And Zach offered."

Marilyn swung around with her eyes ablaze. "Of course he did. He's trying to dump his guilt, but that's an impossible goal. Nothing he says or does could make up for what he did. Murder. Pure and simple murder."

Shauna reached toward her, but when Marilyn flinched, she dropped her hand back to her side. "That's a little harsh. What he did was stupid and foolhardy, but it wasn't murder. I can see he's suffered too. He loved Jack. You know he did. They were like brothers."

"As a kid he was at this house more than

he was at his own, and he repaid my kindness by killing my only child." Marilyn's voice grew thick with unshed tears. "I can't even wrap my head around this." She turned and rushed for the door.

"Don't tell anyone the real reason we're there," Shauna called after her. "I don't want Alex to be frightened. We can stand a little gossip to protect him." She hurried toward the porch.

Marilyn slipped inside, and Shauna heard the *click* of the lock. She shook the doorknob. "Open up, Marilyn. Let's talk about this."

There was no reply, but she heard the quick retreat of Marilyn's feet. Then the living room light went out, and a few moments later, the upstairs bedroom light came on.

Shauna rubbed her forehead. That had played out even worse than she'd imagined. She and Marilyn had never had so much as a spat in all these years. Should she use her key and go in anyway? She shook her head and went to her truck. Maybe if Shauna gave her some time to cool down, Marilyn would be more reasonable tomorrow.

Did she even want to go back to Zach's yet? She'd rather wait until the TV had fallen silent. She sighed and started the truck. This was going to be her life for a little while. All she could do was pray the sheriff found the people who did this right away so she could expel Zach from her life.

The sound of the video game left Zach feeling a little bereft. He'd misjudged how hard it would be to face the constant reminder that his best friend was dead. Alex was practically asleep sitting up when Zach put him to bed, and the clock by the fireplace had just chimed nine times when headlights swept past the big front windows.

He wiped suddenly damp hands on his jeans as the dogs ran to the front door, stubby tails wagging. Was Shauna going to pack up and leave? It was one reason he hadn't gone to bed. Marilyn just might have succeeded in derailing this idea, and he had no alternate plan to keep Shauna safe.

The bigger question was, why was it *his* job to keep her safe when she clearly didn't want him around? The look on her face across the table over dinner had curdled the pizza in his stomach. Pursed lips, hooded eyes that didn't meet his gaze, and curt answers to any questions. It was going to be a long, hard few days here. Or however long it took. What if they didn't find the killer right away? This could drag on in a very painful way.

The lock clicked, and he dropped into a chair by the fireplace and tried to appear nonchalant. She stepped inside and loved on the dogs, who were going crazy with excitement, though they didn't bark. They only barked when they didn't recognize someone. They'd taken the arrival of the cat better than Weasley had taken their interest. The cat hadn't come out from under the couch all night until it was bedtime. He now slept curled on the foot of Alex's bed.

The light from the chandelier gleamed on her dark hair. She had always been gorgeous, but grief had pulled her strong features into sharp planes and angles that translated into dramatic beauty. She wouldn't appreciate him saying something like that, though.

He'd always thought Jack was a lucky guy. Not that he'd ever told his friend that. Jack had met Shauna in a coffee shop after she got out of the navy. She was twenty-seven, and Jack was twenty-eight. They married, and a year later Alex was born, and their life seemed set for perfection.

Until Zach's rashness had ruined it all.

Her expression enigmatic, Shauna glanced his way as she shed her denim jacket. "Alex is in bed?" The dogs followed her to the sofa.

83

"Yeah, he was about to drop where he sat so I read him *The Blessings Jar* and tucked him in. He was out before I turned off the light." He rose and scooped the bowl of popcorn kernels off the coffee table. "Sorry, I should have cleaned up." He dumped the kernels in the trash, then put the bowl in the dishwasher before he turned back toward her. "How'd it go with Marilyn?"

"Worse than you can imagine. She locked me out of the house." Her eyes filled with tears, and she twisted around to adjust the afghan that had fallen off the back of the sofa. She'd made it for him for Christmas in a happier time. "She's always been a mom to me, so it was hard to take." She sat on the sofa, and Apollo settled at her feet.

"I'm sorry. I could try to talk to her, but I know how well that would go over."

She shuddered and gave a forced laugh. "I wouldn't even want to be within firing distance." Her green eyes looked enormous in her pale face. "She wanted us to move in with her, exactly as I predicted. When I pointed out she couldn't keep us safe, she stalked off."

"So you're not moving back to your house?"

She grabbed a pencil, then wound her hair up on top of her head and stuck it in the

84

wad of locks to hold it. "I don't have much choice, do I? I can't say I'm happy about it. It's harder to be around you than I anticipated." She pointed to a picture of him at age sixteen BASE jumping with his dad. "Jack took that picture. It's a reminder of how you always egged him on to bigger dangers."

She was right. His fingers curled into his palms. "You're not the only one suffering. I hear Jack's laugh over your shoulder and look up. I can almost catch a glimpse of him tossing a pillow at me. I miss him too." He cleared his suddenly husky throat. "I loved him too, Shauna. You can't really doubt that."

Artemis, the smaller of his two rottweilers, came to nose at his hand, and Zach petted him. "I'm okay, boy."

Shauna's chest heaved as she exhaled, and she went to poke at the fire, dying to embers. The scent of smoke intensified in the room, and it made him think of all the camping trips he'd taken with Jack. The entire day had been almost more than he could take. "Maybe I should go to my room and leave you alone. I know this isn't easy." He started for the hall.

"Wait. I'm sorry I'm such a bear. I know you loved him."

He thrust his hands in the pockets of his jeans. "All I want to do is keep you and Alex safe. This will be over soon."

Those green eyes were like sea glass, clear and pure, as she stared back at him. A sudden urge to cup her face in his hands startled him, and he took an involuntary step back. "Um, you hungry? There's a little pizza left. I think I'll warm up a piece."

"No, thanks. I don't think I could eat." She followed him into the kitchen and settled on one of the bar stools at the island.

He threw a piece of pizza on a paper plate and tossed it in the microwave. He wasn't sure what to talk about. Was Jack off-limits? It was probably dangerous ground, though the desire to talk about him, to remember, rose in a flood.

The microwave dinged, and he pulled out the steaming pizza and bit into it so he didn't have to say anything. The house never used to be silent when the three of them were together.

As the silence continued, he swallowed, then joined her at the island. "How's your dad? You mentioned he's still drinking. You see him much?"

"I make an obligatory visit every two weeks. He's gotten worse since Jack died. I'll have to talk to him about that necklace, but I'm afraid it's going to send him into a weeklong binge." Her mouth twisted. "The sheriff said I could take another look at it, but I haven't had a chance to stop at the jail."

He grinned and felt the tension roll off. "I made copies of all the photos and took pictures of everything else in the box before I delivered it to the sheriff. I even made an impression of the key."

Her mouth gaped. "You're serious?"

"Yep. I thought we might need to go over things to figure this out. Your lives are depending on it."

"I'm shocked! Can I see?"

He nodded and grabbed a box on the breakfast bar. "Here are the pictures, and here's the one of the necklace. That's what you want to see, isn't it?"

She nodded and reached for the photo. "I have to know if this is Mom's." She went through the pictures one by one. "I really think this might be hers, Zach."

"How did she die? You've never really said. You were eight, right?"

At first she said nothing and stepped across the kitchen to get water from the refrigerator dispenser. When she turned back around, her fair skin was as pale as the marble counter. "It's not something I ever talk about. Jack knew, of course, but it was an incredibly painful time in my life."

"Forget I asked then. Sorry."

A lock of hair fell from the knot on her head, and she pushed it out of her face. "Maybe I should talk about it. It might not hurt so much when I have to talk to Pop." She took a sip and eyed him over the rim of her glass. "It's not a pretty story, Zach."

"Losing a parent rarely is. It's probably why Alex is so well adjusted, even after losing Jack. You know what it's like, and you were able to help him through it."

A bit of color came to her cheeks. "You really think he's doing okay? I'm never sure if I'm doing enough."

He held her gaze. "You're an amazing mother, Shauna. The finest I've ever seen. Alex is a lucky little boy."

The column of her neck rippled with the convulsive swallow she made. "Thank you." Carrying her water, she headed back to the living room. "I think I have to sit down for this."

CHAPTER 8

When was the last time she'd allowed
herself to remember that horrible day?
Shauna couldn't recall. She sat on the sofa,
and Apollo settled at her feet. She sipped
the water and stared into the fire, then
began to recount the events to Zach.

"Mommy, I want to go play." Shauna tugged
her hand out of her mother's grip and took
hold of Connor's hand. "I'll look out for Connor." At eight, it was her responsibility to take
care of her baby brother, who was six years
younger.

The market had tables, blocks, and other
toys in the back corner of the building, right
next to the candy department, though Mommy
didn't often buy it for them. She said it would
rot their teeth, but Shauna didn't see how that
could be true. The kids at school sometimes
had candy bars in their lunch pails, and their
teeth all looked fine. She'd even asked to look

in her best friend's mouth once after she had a Snickers bar.

Her mother was the most beautiful person in the world, even with her belly sticking out. Her hair was the color of the night, and she was always smiling. Shauna sometimes put her ear on Mommy's tummy to see if the new baby would talk to her, but she never heard anything other than her mommy's tummy gurgling. Little Peanut was supposed to be here anytime, and Shauna was hoping for a baby sister, just because she didn't have one.

Mommy touched her head. "Okay, stay in the play enclosure. I'll come fetch you when I'm ready to check out. I have to get a lot of groceries so it might be a little while."

That was just fine with Shauna. She led Connor through the aisles of canned goods and bags of chips. She stopped by the purple flowers lining the windowsills. Mommy loved lavender, and Shauna had brought her allowance. She touched the lavender, then buried her face in it. She'd buy her some after they played.

She and her brother hopped onto the small plastic teeter-totter. He shrieked with laughter as Shauna bounced down and lifted his small rear end into the air.

But in the next moment, she catapulted off the end. She bounced to her feet. "You pushed too hard."

But Connor was on the floor too. And the carpet was *moving.* There was some kind of low rumble that made Shauna want to hide under the small table covered with puzzles. Was it a T rex about to come eat them? She wasn't supposed to watch scary movies, but she'd seen a little bit of *Jurassic Park* last week at a friend's house. The shaking intensified and kept her and Connor on the ground.

She hugged her brother as Connor began to cry. All around the store things crashed to the ground, and people were screaming and calling out to each other. "Mommy!" Her scream sounded like a whisper with the awful noise going on all around.

Then her mother was there. She covered them both with her body. "It's going to be okay, little ones. Stay still."

The ceiling started to cave in, and big chunks of wood fell. Shauna peeked past her mother's arm and saw blue sky above. What was happening? She was too frightened to even cry. Pieces of the ceiling hung over them like some kind of tent, and there were only small tunnels here and there.

Her mother gave a strange *oomph* sound, then didn't move. Shauna shook her, but she didn't respond. Connor was still crying, and Shauna tried to move to hug him, but she was trapped under her mother's heavy arm.

"Mommy!" She tried again to get her mother to open her eyes, and finally Mommy stirred a little and looked at her. "Mommy, you scared me."

A little bit of red dribbled from Mommy's mouth, and she licked it away. "My good girl. Lie still. It's an earthquake. Someone will come to help us soon."

An earthquake? Didn't those only happen in California? But Mommy didn't seem too scared, so Shauna tried not to cry. The rumbling that seemed to last forever finally stopped. "Can I get up, Mommy?"

Her mother winced as she moved her arm far enough for Shauna to crawl out. She turned and helped her brother up too. The place was a mess, and she heard water running from somewhere. "Let me pull you up, Mommy."

Her mother's eyes closed again. "I can't move, honey. There is something on top of me. We have to wait for someone to come help us."

"I'll get help!" Shauna climbed through the tunnels formed by the concrete and fallen beams, sometimes coming to a dead end until she retraced her path and found another way. A man with a green shirt lay motionless on the floor with blood on his head. She was afraid to move closer, and her chest started to feel tight. She had to find help.

She crawled through the tunnels until she found a woman seated in the crumbled concrete with her head cradled in her arms. Shauna touched her wrist. "My mommy is trapped. Can you help her?"

The woman had blonde hair and looked friendly, and she put her hand on Shauna's arm. "Where is she, honey? I'm a paramedic."

Shauna pointed. "Back in the play area with my little brother. It's not easy to get there, though. I can show you."

The woman peered through the tunnel Shauna had exited. "I think the worst of it is over, but there might be aftershocks. We're trapped here until someone comes."

Shauna led the way back and only went down the wrong tunnel once before emerging into the small, cramped space where her mother lay with Connor.

Shauna pointed out her mother, who wasn't moving. "There she is."

The paramedic lady made her way to Mommy and touched her shoulder. "Let me see if I can move this beam off your legs."

She grabbed another broken piece of wood and propped it under the big beam on a piece of concrete. Grunting, she pushed on the thing until the big beam rolled off Mommy.

Mommy cried out a little and put her hand to her tummy. "I think the baby's coming."

Shauna backed away and reached for Connor's hand. He didn't move his fingers. Maybe he was sleeping. It was dark by the time she heard a baby cry. The paramedic lady soothed the baby, then everything fell silent.

Her cheeks wet and her vision blurry, Shauna looked across at Zach's stricken face. "We were stuck there for hours. I think my mom died as soon as Brenna was born. I named her and held her, but my mother never spoke. The paramedic found some formula and bottles in the debris and managed to feed Brenna. I heard her cry a couple of times. Some aftershocks struck and another beam fell on Connor. I thought he would die before help arrived. He was in terrible pain. My dad found me at the triage center, but he never found Connor and Brenna. I told him they died, but I didn't know that for sure. I just felt it."

The grief in her chest was a mountain too big to ever move off her. She wiped at her cheeks. "I can understand why Pop fell headlong into the bottle. I couldn't do that, though."

Zach leaned forward. "You lost your entire family that night."

She grabbed a tissue and blew her nose. "So that necklace being found now makes no sense."

"Was she wearing it when she died?"

"I don't remember. She hardly ever took it off, so probably." She moved the cat off her lap and leaped to her feet. "I have to go to bed now. This is too hard."

He wouldn't sleep for hours, not with the horrific details of that night still lingering in his brain. Zach went to his room and pulled his laptop from his backpack. Maybe there was an article about the tragedy online. He settled on the side of the bed and scanned through news reports of devastation from the quake with pictures of damaged buildings. The death toll had been thirteen, and he finally found a list, but the only Duval he saw listed was Theresa, Shauna's mother. The children's names were missing.

Frowning, he read through the article more closely.

Pandemonium still rages through the small town of Lavender Tides, Washington, after a 7.8 magnitude earthquake ripped through the community on Tuesday. Numerous buildings were destroyed, including a school and the town grocery store.

The children left wandering the streets were of particular concern to authorities who called in Child Protective Services for help. Two days later some parents are still trying to locate their children.

There was more, but he stopped reading and frowned. Lost children? Did they actually find the bodies of Brenna and Connor? It was a delicate question to ask, so maybe he should talk to Shauna's father. He'd always gotten along well with the older man, at least when he found him sober.

This probably wasn't something Shauna would appreciate him poking into, but the story was so horrendous he couldn't let it go. Had anyone tried to locate the paramedic who delivered Brenna and took care of them all? She might be able to shed more light on what happened when the authorities showed up. Connor was injured, so perhaps he really did succumb to injuries, but what about the baby? She had been fed and cared for, so what happened to her?

Maybe Zach was reading too much into it, but the nagging feeling that something was off wouldn't leave him. He glanced at the time on his phone. It was eleven, and most normal people might be heading for bed, but Lewis Duval, Shauna's father, was probably sitting in his living room only halfway through his beer stash for the night. Zach found his name in his contacts and placed the call.

" 'Lo." Lewis's voice was only a little slurred, which was a good sign.

"Hey, Lewis, it's Zach Bannister. How you doing?"

"Zach." The older man's voice grew more alert. "Haven't heard from you in a while, boy. Doing just fine."

Lewis lived in a cabin in the Olympic Forest. The place had been falling down around his ears for years, but he did what he had to do, and no one could budge him from the place his grandfather had built. At one time it had been a vacation retreat for the family, and from what Zach remembered of the story Jack had told him, Lewis moved in permanently when Shauna was a kid. The guy seemed to get crazier by the year, probably from the alcohol.

"That's good to hear. Listen, I have a question and it's personal, but I'm going to ask it anyway if that's okay."

"Got no secrets, boy." He slurped on a liquid, then cleared his throat. "Ask away."

"It's about your other children. Were you able to retrieve their bodies after the earthquake and bury them?"

"Bury them, you say? Who you been talking to? Shauna? She don't remember that time even half right."

"What do you mean?"

"My poor babies were dead when they were hauled out of the ruins. It just took a few days, maybe a week, to get confirmation."

"But did you identify their bodies?"

"I didn't have no money for burials, so the state took care of it."

"But did you *see* the bodies?"

A long pause followed. "You implying I'm lying, boy?"

"Of course not. But I was reading about the disaster, and CPS had trouble finding the families of some of the children. I just wondered if it was possible there was a mix-up is all." He held his breath and waited.

Something in Lewis's vehement denials left a bad taste in his mouth. Zach had expected Lewis to grow maudlin about the family he'd lost, but he'd been, well, defensive. That was the only word to describe his tone.

Lewis let loose a long round of cursing. The next moment the phone went silent.

"Hello? Lewis, you there?" Zach pulled the phone away and looked at it. No connection. Lewis had hung up on him.

Lewis's reaction struck Zach as odd. He was determined to get to the bottom of it.

CHAPTER 9

The night was dark with clouds covering the moon. He parked his truck on the road and crept through the pine and birch trees to the clearing that opened up at her house. No lights shone in the windows, but he assumed she'd be asleep at three in the morning. He felt sharp and alert with anticipation.

She had to have it. The Glennon woman wouldn't have given it to anyone else, and it was the only explanation for the way she'd tried to trick him. She'd recognized its importance and had to have given it to Shauna McDade.

The grass was slippery with dew as he hurried to the porch and peered in the large prow-shaped windows. Darkness cloaked the interior, and he saw only the dim glow of the clock on the microwave at the back of the great room. He'd checked the architectural drawings for the house and knew the master bedroom was to the left of the great room and two guest rooms were to the right.

He'd grab the kid first. The woman would do whatever he wanted to save her son. Not that it would make any difference to the outcome. He hated having to hurt a kid, though. At times like this he wondered if he should just let the chips fall and vamoose for a country that wouldn't extradite to the United States. Crazy talk. He wasn't about to allow that to happen, even if the tasks before him turned unpleasant. Too much money was riding on this. And his future happiness.

He'd come too far to lose it all now.

He could jimmy the door, but it would probably scare her more if she heard the glass breaking and came out to find him already with the kid. Raising his tire iron, he brought it down on the glass, then reached inside and unlocked the door. In moments, he was outside the boy's room. He flipped on the light and moved to the bed. Empty.

He stood perplexed. Maybe the kid was sleeping with her. That was unfortunate. He turned and ran for the master bedroom. He pulled out his knife, ready for the attack, but when he entered the bedroom, he found it empty as well.

Where could she be at this hour? He went back to the great room to the kitchen area and opened the door to the garage. Empty.

Rage nearly choked him, and he spun on his heels and slammed the tire iron down on the table. The resulting crack felt satisfying, and he gritted his teeth. He'd show Shauna what would happen to her and the kid if she didn't give him back his property. He whipped around the kitchen smashing everything he could find. When he was finished, he stopped and wiped perspiration from his forehead.

Maybe the box was still here. She might have just gone out for the night to Marilyn's or a friend's. If that were the case, she might not have taken it. He made a systematic search of the entire house, upending drawers and ripping open the bellies of stuffed animals. Nothing!

Rage surged again, and he grabbed his tire iron. Let's see how she liked having her possessions taken from her.

An hour later his chest heaved from exertion, but it was done. Needing to hear his sweetheart's voice, he pulled out his phone. His pulse calmed when she answered. "Did I wake you up?"

"No, I was lying here thinking about you."

He smiled. "She wasn't here, but I left her an explicit message. Now tell me what we're going to do as soon as we hit the beach."

Shauna's phone woke her from sleep. No light came through the blinds so she glanced at the time. Who on earth was calling at 5:00 a.m.? She peered at the screen, then rubbed the sleep out of her eyes. "Sheriff, what's wrong?"

"Someone broke into your house, Shauna. The front door is standing open. I had a deputy drive by every few hours, and he called in the report fifteen minutes ago. I'm sorry to say the place is trashed."

"Trashed?" Holding the phone to her ear with her shoulder, she pulled on her jeans. "I'll be right there."

"We'll want to know if anything was taken."

"You think the person who killed Lucy and Clarence did this?"

"If they're related. Lucy lived in a rough area, so I need to investigate every angle. I also had a deputy go by Marilyn's. Her place appears undisturbed."

Praise God.

"I'm sure it's all related. Talk to you in a few minutes." She ended the call and pulled a sweatshirt over her head. Her hair was braided so she left it alone, and she jammed her feet into slip-ons and opened her door.

She nearly collided with Zach in the doorway. "Whoa, sorry."

He put his hand on her shoulder. "What's wrong?" His eyes widened as she recounted what the sheriff said. "Good thing you and Alex weren't there."

She hadn't stopped to count her blessings in that department. "You're right. He might have hurt Alex." She shook off his hand. It felt way too intimate to be standing close with him in basketball shorts with no shirt.

"I need to get over there. Will you watch Alex?" She started past him.

He blocked her way. "Sure, unless you want me to grab him and come with you."

"I'd rather he didn't see it. This might deflect gossip too. I'll be able to say we needed a place to stay until things can be repaired."

"People will talk no matter what we say. If you need me, text or call and I'll take Alex to play with Jermaine's kids." A smile flickered on his face in the dim light starting to break through the blinds. "I'll even endure Marilyn's wrath and take him there."

"Brave man." She eased past him, catching a sensation of heat from his bare skin.

He followed her to the front door, where

she grabbed her denim jacket from the hall closet. "Let me know what it looks like."

She nodded and stepped out into a dew-scented yard. A few lights were on up and down the street as people prepared to go to work. The cold seat made her shiver as she started the engine. The thought of what she might find filled her with dread. It was too much to hope that it had been a random break-in. All these crimes had to be connected.

Squad car lights flashed from several deputy cars parked in Shauna's drive. The rising sun shot shades of magenta and orange across the sky just over the treetops. The front door stood open, but even as she got out of the vehicle, she saw the window in the door was smashed. Whoever broke in wasn't worried about being heard. Did that mean he knew she wasn't staying there or he didn't care if he warned her before he entered?

The sheriff turned as glass crunched under her shoes. "Sorry to call you out so early, Shauna."

"It's not your fault." Her stomach did a nosedive as she looked around at the devastation.

Someone had picked up chairs and thrown

them randomly. The legs on most of the small tables were broken. Nearly every vase or piece of glass was shattered. It seemed as if he had taken a baseball bat to the clock and pictures that had been on the wall.

"It's worse in your bedroom."

How was that possible? She followed Everett to her room, where she found everything out of the drawers and all the clothes off hangers, heaped on the floor of the closet. "I thought maybe he was searching for something, but this looks like rage."

In a trancelike state, she followed the sheriff all through the house. No room had been spared, not even Alex's. The intruder had even cut up all his stuffed animals. She'd make sure he never saw this destruction.

She curled her fingers into fists until her nails bit into her palms. "There was no reason to do this." Pain pulsed in her head, and she rubbed her temple.

"I think the thug was sending a message that he could do whatever he wants."

She trailed Everett to the kitchen and looked around at the broken pottery and glasses. "I'll need to replace everything." Was the insurance even up-to-date? She'd cut expenses everywhere she could, so the thought that she might not have insurance terrified her.

But no. The bank paid that yearly as part of her escrow payment. Even though she was a little behind on the mortgage, the insurance had been paid four months ago.

She reached down to pick up a broken plate, part of her wedding china. "What does the psycho want?"

"It could have been kids or something random."

She put her hands on her hips and glared at the sheriff. "You can't still be saying that kind of thing. Clarence and Lucy are *dead* and now this. All these crimes are related — they have to be."

He pursed his lips. "You might be right, but I don't want to jump to conclusions."

"I think Lucy didn't tell her killer what was in the box or where it was. The guy is still looking for it."

"Maybe. I'm still going over everything in the box. The key might be important, but I don't know what it unlocks yet. I'm working on it."

She exhaled. The box's contents had not been anything earth-shattering. "It makes no sense. Have you found out anything about the necklace?"

His black hair, shiny with product, glistened under the glare of the overhead light as Everett shook his head. He glanced at his watch. "The owner of one of the jewelry stores on my list told me it looked like the work of a Haida artisan who used to display her things in her shop. She gave me the artist's name, but I haven't been able to track her down yet."

"A woman?"

He nodded. "Dorothy Edenshaw."

Where had she heard that name before? Maybe her father would know. She would have to go see him and show him the picture of the necklace, though it seemed highly unlikely it was her mother's. She had to know the truth for her own sanity.

CHAPTER 10

Alex chattered to Zach all through their breakfast of pancakes cooked in the shape of Mickey Mouse, and he didn't seem upset by his mother's absence. Zach relaxed in his chair and listened to the boy prattle on. He'd missed the little guy so much. His two dogs didn't move from their watchful gaze at Alex's feet, and the boy dropped bits of pancake for them. Weasley was hiding again, this time in Alex's room. Zach blew his nose, then took some allergy medicine.

Alex swallowed the last of his milk, then wiped his mouth with the back of his hand. "Can we go to your church this morning? I haven't gone with you in a long time."

"I don't think your mom would mind. I'll text her and let her know." Zach ruffled the boy's hair. "You need to get dressed, though. I don't think your camo pajamas are church attire. But we'll need to hurry. Sunday school starts in forty-five minutes, and it will take us fifteen to get there. So you've got thirty minutes."

"I can do that!" Alex jumped to his feet and headed for the bathroom.

"Don't forget to brush your teeth," Zach called after him. He picked up the plates, sticky with maple syrup, and rinsed them under the faucet before placing them in the dishwasher.

Had Shauna even noticed he'd redone the kitchen? The last time she was here, the cabinets were still the old pine ones. He'd made the sleek black shaker cabinets himself, and a buddy had installed the quartz countertops that mimicked marble. Zach had put up a marble subway backsplash and laid travertine floor tiles. It looked pretty good, but she hadn't said a word about it.

But why would she after the day she'd had? A kitchen remodel didn't even deserve a remark after losing Clarence and Lucy.

He clicked the latch on the dishwasher and started it, then went to pick up the living room after last night's Pac-Man marathon. Near the spot where Shauna had sat, he pulled a crumpled piece of paper from the crack where the cushion met the arm of the sofa. He didn't remember looking at mail there, but he opened up the single sheet and smoothed it out to read it.

The heading was from the local bank, Lavender Tides Savings and Loan. He scanned half of it, then realized it was addressed to Shauna. She was behind on her loan for the helicopter. By three months. They were going to start legal action to claim her chopper if she didn't get caught up in fifteen days.

He clenched his fists and sighed. Poor Shauna had a heavier load than most could bear. What could he do to help? Paying the debt would be easy for him, but how did he help and still keep her pride intact? She wouldn't take assistance from him if she had a choice. *Especially* not from him. And why hadn't Jack taken better care of her? He was an accountant, for Pete's sake! He should have left adequate insurance.

The lock snicked on the front door, and he quickly pushed the paper back into the crevice where he'd found it before Shauna entered the house. He picked up the empty glasses and turned toward the door as the pine-scented wind practically shoved her inside.

"Whew, it's blowing like a hurricane out there." The wind had tugged strands of dark hair out of her braid, and the cool air had chapped her cheeks. Worry marred her face in a frown and the press of her lips.

"Was it bad?"

She shrugged out of her jacket. "You can't even imagine. The entire place is destroyed. It's like whoever broke in wanted me to know how upset he was. Every dish and glass was shattered in the kitchen." Her eyes filled with moisture. "I don't even know how to tell Alex that all his toys were ruined. I wouldn't want him to see the way the intruder took a knife to his stuffed animals. It was bizarre and horrifying." She swiped at the tears on her cheeks. "Even the box of wedding mementos was ripped open and scattered. He tore several pictures in two."

"I'm sorry." He wanted to comfort her, but any encouraging words died on his tongue. "I'd like to replace some of Alex's things. And if you're hungry, there's a pancake left. It just needs to be warmed in the microwave."

"I might do that." She went past him to the kitchen on the other side of the great room. "I don't even know where to start at the house."

His thoughts shot to the bank letter. "What about insurance? Is the damage covered?"

Relief lit her eyes, and she nodded. "It's paid in my escrow. Fully up-to-date." She bit her lip as though she realized she might have given away too much information about her financial circumstances. "I mean, that's the way it usually works. I'm sure they paid it on time so there's no worry. I have a call in to my agent to start the process. I think the insurance is pretty good — replacement, I think. Jack wanted the best when we got the house, and I never changed it. So I hope I won't be out anything."

He watched her heat up the pancake and drizzle maple syrup on it. "I'll get you some coffee."

She carried her plate to the farm-style table in the dining area and settled in the seat he usually used. "It's a good thing we weren't there."

He set the coffee in front of her, then carried his own to the other side of the table where he could see her face. "I had a feeling the guy would be back." Should he tell her he'd called her dad last night? "Listen, I hope you're not upset, but I was really curious about the history you told me last night. I did a little looking around, and as far as I can tell, there's no mention in the newspapers of the deaths of your brother and sister."

Her eyes widened, and she put down her fork. "That can't be right."

"I called your dad. He was a little defensive."

"Defensive? What do you mean?"

"I asked him if the saw the bodies, and he asked if I was implying he was a liar."

"He'd probably been drinking." She took a bite of pancake, then washed it down with coffee. "That's ancient history anyway, Zach. I'm not sure what you were trying to find out."

"Your mom's necklace is ancient history too. The past has a way of rising up and stepping into view when we least expect it."

Her green eyes were pensive as she studied him over the rim of her coffee cup. "I need to talk to him about that necklace anyway. I thought I'd go out today."

"How about we go to church first? Alex wants to go to mine." They all used to attend the same church, but she'd stopped after Jack's death. He wasn't sure she'd ever found another.

She winced. "That will set the tongues to wagging."

"We can talk about how your house is totally destroyed. That should calm any speculation."

She put down her coffee. "If you say so. I'd better change and do something with this rat's nest hair."

Shauna dabbed her eyes and willed the frantic pounding of her heart to settle. For the past year she'd struggled to even think about going to church. She'd been afraid she would sit and cry, but so what? Everyone had been wonderful since she'd stepped inside the door this morning. There'd been tears, yes, but good ones. People here loved her, and she should have known better. Her natural inclination had been to huddle in her house to lick her wounds like some animal. It had been the wrong decision.

Her heart soaked up the music and the sermon, and she leaned over to Zach as the service ended. "I'm glad we came. I needed to be here."

His smile washed over her. "Me too." He looked past her shoulder and waved. "Jermaine, Michelle, hold on."

She turned to see Jermaine Diskin, the paramedic who flew on Zach's mercy flights, wave. He steered his wife their way. About five eight, he was slightly built with green eyes that stood out in his mocha-colored skin. Michelle was part Asian and had a lavender farm on the outskirts of town. She was nearly as tall as her husband and always wore colorful flowing skirts. Her raven hair fell nearly to her waist. They were in their late twenties and clearly doted on one another.

Michelle started to hug her, then took a step back. "Sorry, I put lavender oil on this morning. I don't want to give you a headache."

Nice of her to remember. "It's good to see you. How's the farm doing?" Luckily all she could smell was the hint of Jermaine's pipe tobacco.

"I had a great harvest this month, but I've been dealing with EPA headaches. I'll survive it, though. You look good, girl. I've missed you. Jermaine has kept me posted on you, but it's not the same as seeing your sweet face." She ruffled Alex's hair. "And how's my boy?"

He grinned and sidled closer to Shauna. "We're staying at the Zachster's, and we had a Pac-Man marathon last night."

Michelle's face was a study of contrasts: disbelief, joy, and curiosity. She glanced at Zach. "Is that so? Sounds like a good time to me."

Zach touched Alex's head and shot Michelle a quelling glance. "I'll tell Jermaine about it tomorrow. It's complicated."

"I'll bet." Michelle smiled and took Jermaine's arm. "We'd better go rescue the Junior Church workers from our two hoodlums. Let's get together for dinner soon."

"Sounds great." All Shauna's warm feelings evaporated. The tongues would go to wagging all over town now.

Zach's voice spoke softly in her ear. "She's not going to gossip about it. Michelle is one of the good ones."

He was right, and she knew it. "I'm just being a little touchy."

Karl's voice boomed behind her, and she turned just in time to be enfolded in a hug. "I thought that was you. How are you doing, Shauna? I heard about Lucy. Terrible thing." He shook his head. "Nora and I had gone to the Gulf of Thailand for our anniversary, and we stopped to see her on our way back from the airport. Nora barely got through our trip without her best friend. I had to call the doctor to give her a sedative when we heard the news."

She pulled away. "It's hard to even believe it." Her head began to throb, probably from catching a whiff of Michelle's lavender oil.

His lionlike mane of salt-and-pepper hair fell over his forehead. "Anything I can do?" He glanced sideways at Zach, as if trying to figure out why they were there together when the whole town knew she hadn't given him the time of day for a year. She would have to explain to him too.

Zach spoke in a hushed voice. "Shauna's house was broken into last night. The killer must think she saw or knows something. I insisted she and Alex stay with me so I can protect them. It was a good thing I did, or they would have been home when he came calling."

Karl raised his brows. "You're a good man." He looked over Zach's shoulder and waved. "I'd better go. Nora is waiting at the door, and she'll have my hide if we miss our lunch reservations, especially today. She's heading for her sister's soon and will be gone for two weeks, leaving me with the bees to take care of." He touched Shauna's arm. "Let me know if you need anything."

She took Alex's hand. "Let's get out of here before we have to explain it to anyone else."

Zach pressed his lips together and led her to a side door out into the sunshine. He stopped on the stoop. "People care, Shauna. Everyone loved Jack, and they love you and Alex. Quit putting up such a fence around yourself. Let people in."

She bit her lip. "I don't know how to do that. Growing up, I was constantly dealing with snickers and whispers from other girls because of my dad. I thought I'd outgrown fearing things like that, but since Jack's death, I've regressed. I'll try to quit hiding, but it's not going to be easy."

He nodded, then scooped Alex up in his arms and headed for his truck, where he buckled her boy into his booster seat in the back. "Let's go see your dad and try to forget about all this for just a little while."

She climbed into the passenger seat and fastened her seat belt. Easier said than done.

CHAPTER 11

Trees pressed close to the vehicle on both sides of the road. Shauna had huddled with her thoughts on the drive out to Pop's cabin. Her earlier euphoria about being back in church had ebbed. The message at church had given her pause as the pastor talked about trusting God in the hard circumstances. Ever since Jack died, she'd found trust hard. If God would take Jack and leave her and Alex in such dire circumstances, then his promises seemed fickle to her.

She didn't know how to reconcile her faith with the reality facing her. If she had another bad month, she'd lose her helicopter, and her home would be next. How could she support Alex? She pressed her hot forehead against the cool glass of the door. And now their very lives were in danger.

"You doing okay?"

Zach's voice broke into her chaotic thoughts. She lifted her head and checked the backseat to make sure Alex was still asleep. "I'm just dreading talking to my dad about the necklace. He doesn't like to discuss the old days."

"I could tell when I questioned him." Zach turned into the long track that led back to her dad's cabin on the lake.

She pulled up the picture of the necklace on her phone and stared at it. Maybe Pop would keep it civil for Alex's sake.

"If he turns belligerent, you could take Alex out to the lake while I continue to question him," Zach suggested.

She looked at Zach again. After the way she'd treated him since Jack's death, she didn't deserve the kindness and concern he'd been showing. "Thanks. I hope it doesn't come to that."

The cabin came into view through the fall foliage, and she curled her fingers into her palms. Maybe she should have called first. For all she knew her dad was already drunk. Some days he started off with beer for breakfast.

The gravel crunched under the tires as the crew-cab truck rolled to a stop. She inhaled and squared her shoulders. Putting a smile on her face, she turned to look into the backseat. "Hey, buddy, we're at Grandpa's."

Alex's eyes flew open, and he smiled. "You think Gramps will take me fishing? It's a good day for it, isn't it?"

Zach got out and opened the back door for her son. "If he is feeling under the weather, one of us will take you."

He was really good with Alex. Shauna had forgotten the bond between the two of them. Or maybe she hadn't wanted to remember. There were times when Jack was alive that she'd felt like the odd one out. The three were tight, always on the same wavelength.

She pushed open her door and stepped down into the tall grass surrounding the cabin. The three-bedroom home had been built in the fifties, but it looked like it had been there since pioneer days. The logs had weathered more since last winter, and the chinking needed to be replaced all over the structure. Moss grew in patches on the roof, and she suspected the ceiling leaked during hard rains. Her dad had the money to fix it, but he lacked the motivation. Ever since she'd gone off to the navy and then married Jack, he'd spiraled deeper and deeper into the bottle, until his thirst was all he cared about.

She had tried to help him many times, but he brushed off her concern.

Alex ran for the front door and pushed it open. "Gramps, we're here to see you!"

She slanted a glance at Zach, then trailed after her son. At least she wasn't the one surprising her dad. Despite never being sober when they came, he always seemed to welcome Alex.

When she reached the door, she caught the familiar odor of beer and cigar smoke. This time it was mingled with the sour stench of vomit. "Dad?" Her pulse kicked up, and she rushed inside. She stepped over a pool of nastiness just inside the door. "You okay, Pop?"

"Fine, I'm fine." He sat huddled under a Seahawks throw on the threadbare green sofa. He tossed off the blanket, then struggled to an upright position.

His rheumy eyes lit on Alex, and he brightened. "Sit here beside me, boy. You've grown since I last saw you." He glanced at Shauna. "You should have called first. The place is a little bit of a mess."

What an understatement. Shauna bit back more questions. "I'm sorry. It was spur of the moment."

From the corner of her eye, she saw Zach go to the kitchen, then emerge with a pan of water and a rag. He went to the door and stooped to clean up the mess. She folded up the throw and tossed it over the back of the sofa so Alex could sit by his grandpa.

If she got some food down him to counteract the alcohol, he'd be more apt to talk sense. "Have you eaten today? I brought some vegetable soup in a thermos in the truck. Want some?"

He rubbed his nicotine-stained hands together. "Sounds good. You make it just like your mom did."

Had he changed his dirty jeans and red plaid flannel shirt in the past month? Both items looked like they could stand up without help.

She glanced at Zach, who was already heading out the door. "Zach will get the soup. Listen, I'm glad you mentioned Mom. I want to show you something." She turned on the phone screen and showed him the necklace. "Mom had one like this, didn't she? Zach's got a bigger picture of it if you need to see it."

Her dad ran his fingers over his grizzly chin as he stared at the picture. "I bought that for her on our first anniversary. She never took it off."

"Do you remember where you bought it?"

"Little shop in Vancouver. We got to know

the designer a bit."

"Are you sure it's hers?"

"Sure, I'm sure. This designer only made one-of-a-kind pieces."

"Do you remember the jeweler's name?" She watched him fidget. What was up with his discomfort? It was a simple question.

He rose as Zach came in. "Sure could use some of that soup."

"I'll get it for you." She followed Zach into the kitchen and washed a bowl from the overflowing pile in the sink, then took the thermos from Zach and poured some soup into it. *Thanks,* she mouthed to him.

He nodded and motioned to Alex. "Hey, buddy, let's go check out the lake and see if the fish are jumping."

"Yay!" Alex followed Zach out the rickety back door and onto a porch that leaned precariously out over the water.

"Be careful," she called after them. "That deck isn't very safe."

"We'll go down to the water." Zach shut the door behind them.

She set the soup in front of her dad at the table. "Here you go. Now, about that designer. Surely you remember the name."

He slurped a spoonful of the soup. "Can't say as I do. It was a long time ago."

She recognized the stubborn tilt to his

chin and sighed. "Was it Dorothy Eden-shaw?"

His eyes widened, and he choked on the soup sliding down his throat. She looked around for a napkin or something, but there was nothing around but a dirty kitchen towel. It was better than nothing so she handed it to him.

He coughed into it, then sat back and gasped. "Shew."

"You okay?"

"I'm fine." He went back to the soup, and that chin jutted in an even more determined manner.

"That's the name, isn't it, Pop?"

"Why do you care? That was a long time ago." He set his spoon down on the dirty table. "I'm not answering another question until you tell me what this is all about."

"When did you last see the necklace?"

"I thought it was buried with your mom." He didn't look at her.

"Did you see it on her?"

He rose and started for the door. "This conversation is done."

"This necklace showed up at Clarence's, Pop. It was in a box of stuff he wanted me to give to Lucy for safekeeping. Where did it come from, and how did he come to possess it?"

Her dad hitched up his baggy jeans and made a slow turn back around. "You'd better ask Clarence then."

"He's dead, and so is Lucy. Someone wanted that box very badly. He broke into my house last night too, evidently looking for the box. Could this necklace be what the killer wants?"

Her dad's muddy green eyes shifted away from her gaze. "I don't know anything about this, Shauna."

She had no answers now, only more questions. And Pop knew something.

Zach had tried his best to keep up a steady patter of conversation with his guests since the visit with Lewis, but Alex had whined all afternoon about not catching any fish, and Shauna stared blankly into space and answered in monosyllables. By the time Alex grumpily went to bed, Zach was out of words and out of patience. None of this had been easy for him either, but he was a big believer in making the best of circumstances.

Shauna stood and stretched, lifting her thick, nearly black hair off her neck as she did. "I think I'll unpack a few things. I still have a couple of boxes of Alex's toys in my truck."

"I'll get them." When he stepped outside, he heard a car engine roar off. His senses went on high alert, but it was too dark to make out more than the shape of a full-size car. Hopefully, it was nothing.

He used her key to unlock her crew-cab truck. Two boxes were in the backseat, and he carried them to her room and set them down on the floor by the closet.

She looked up from her task of putting clothes on hangers. "Thanks."

While he was outside, she'd pulled on a Seahawks sweatshirt, and her hair was up in a messy ponytail. He averted his gaze from the enticing sweep of her bare neck. "You know, we haven't examined the pictures in Clarence's box at all. Seeing that necklace threw us a curveball, but maybe there's evidence pointing to the killer's identity in a picture. Maybe there's one that implicates him. Want to go through them?"

She looked adorable with her hair half falling out of the ponytail. Her slight frame swam in the baggy sweats she wore.

He stopped his thoughts before they could head in an even crazier direction. "Let's take a look."

She rubbed the back of her neck and nodded. "Let's make it fast. I want to go to bed. It's been a rough week, and I have to work tomorrow."

After seeing the fatigue and discouragement in her eyes, he almost told her to forget it, but that car outside had made him uneasy. He still believed she and Alex were in danger, and he didn't think the sheriff was going to move fast enough to figure this out on his own. "Let's go to the kitchen. The box is on the table."

She followed him into the kitchen, and he retrieved the box of duplicate pictures he'd made. She settled onto a stool and watched as he pulled a sheaf of photos out and put them on the counter.

He made a cursory glance through them. "Looks like aerial photos." He picked up the closest one and studied it. "Looks like it's a shot of the paper mill." He set it aside and moved on to the next one and then the next. "These are all of the paper mill. Did Karl commission him to take some photos?"

"He commissioned me. It was my photography job. I didn't take all these pictures, though. Some Clarence must have taken. Lots of the businesses around like to have shots from the air to assess maintenance issues." She picked up another picture and perused it. "This doesn't seem to be a photograph of anything except dirt with cracks in it." She shuddered and put it down. "It makes me think of earthquakes." She studied another picture. "This one is just a building in the forest." She squinted. "I don't recognize the area."

He was only listening with half an ear. She'd been paranoid about earthquakes ever since he'd known her. Though now he understood why.

"This one is of Rainshadow Bay. What's that blob in the water? It almost seems like oil. I didn't notice it when I took the picture."

At the interest in her voice, he took the photo from her and held it under one of the pendant lights over the island. "I'm not sure. I can scan it and enlarge it if you think it's important."

"Maybe it's some kind of pollution." Her voice rose, and pink rushed to her cheeks. "You might be right, and some of these pictures are incriminating to someone."

"The blob could be algae. It's probably nothing, but just in case, we should check it out. Who are you taking up tomorrow?"

Her gaze remained on the photo. "Some biologists with the EPA hired me to fly in and out of river areas and throughout the bay. They want to assess if placing boulders and logs in some of the waterways will help fish spawning grounds, and they're looking for toxic runoff."

"So you'll be in a perfect spot to check out the bay. You have a camera?"

She nodded. "Clarence bought me a good one."

"I'm picking up a patient in Alaska first thing in the morning and flying him to the hospital, so I'll take a gander myself." He picked up several photos. "I'll scan these, and we can assess what you see tomorrow night. It's nearly ten. Get some rest."

The smile that lifted her lips made the past year fade from memory. He was beginning to remember how much he'd always liked being with her.

CHAPTER 12

With her headset on to block out the roar of the rotors, Shauna guided the chopper over the treetops. Up here at the controls, she found that the joy of flying always caused her troubles to slip away. She spotted several eagles on high branches. From this altitude she caught glimpses of several waterfalls and saw fishermen hauling up Dungeness crab pots out in the Strait of Juan de Fuca. She itched to pull out her camera.

One passenger sat in the front with her, and two more were in the back. They all wore microphones and sound-canceling headphones to communicate. Guy Rosenthal, head biologist with the EPA, had hired Shauna several times before today. A slim man in his early thirties, he always reminded her of a sleek puma with his light-brown hair and almost golden eyes. He'd asked her out every time they went up, but she refused. She wasn't ready for romance again. Maybe she never would be.

She hovered the chopper over a clearing. "What are we looking for?" A sparkling river ran through the area, rushing past wildflowers and gurgling around rocks. It was a pretty place.

Guy adjusted his mic. "The river below is too shallow in places. Spawning fish can't reach the head. We're trying to figure out the best locations to drop boulders or logs. Can you drop us a little lower right there?" He pointed out the area.

"Want me to land? There's a flat spot in the clearing."

"That would be great."

She brought the helicopter down and settled back to check whatever e-mail messages had come in before she lost a signal. They could explore the river to their heart's content. A couple of e-mails were from possible clients asking for price estimates. She answered those and prayed they decided to book.

What was she going to do about the bank? Her eyes burned, and she leaned back against the seat. They wanted the loan caught up, and she had no way of doing that unless some miracle happened. The last letter demanded payment immediately.

She straightened. Wait. Didn't the house insurance pay for rental of a place to stay? Maybe she could talk to Zach about it, and he'd let her borrow that rent money until she could pay him back. At least it was a sliver of hope to cling to. The thought of asking him for anything made her cringe, but what choice did she have? If she lost her helicopter, she wouldn't have a way to support Alex. She'd lose the house and everything else.

She rubbed her eyes and sighed. If only Jack hadn't died.

The men returned, and Guy climbed back into his seat. "I think we have our site picked out. Now we'd like to take a gander at the bay."

"You bet." She started the chopper and got it airborne.

Minutes later they were swooping over Rainshadow Bay. The view from up here always staggered her senses. Waves foamed from the sea and threw themselves against the base of the soaring cliffs. She'd seen this scene on many postcards over the years, but she never tired of viewing it with her own eyes. From the beach you'd never know about the waterfalls or the sea cliffs on the other side.

She swooped the chopper over the landscape, and Guy snapped pictures through the window at the water below. He asked her to take them to the west, and she changed direction. She saw him stiffen, then realized what had caused his reaction. A large blob of something marred the pristine blue of the water. Exactly like the pictures she'd taken. If anything, it was darker. It had also moved a bit.

"What do you think that is?" She took the chopper lower, barely skimming the tops of the waves.

Guy was furiously taking pictures and didn't answer at first. He straightened and put his camera down. "Not sure. It could be an oil spill or even runoff from a construction project, though none have been approved in this area. I don't like it. I'll examine these pictures back at the office. And we'll need to send a boat out to collect samples. You can take us back now."

They weren't far from the airport, so Shauna nodded and flew the helicopter back to its pad. There was still time to go to the bank. But first she had to talk to the insurance company and Zach so she had a decent plan in place.

The biologists scurried away to their vehicles, even Guy. He must have finally taken the hint that she wasn't interested in dating.

Before she got out of the chopper, she called the insurance agent. He confirmed she'd be given a lump sum of money to start replacing items that had been destroyed as well as money for lodging. The amount of money made her gasp, then smile. And he was meeting her this afternoon to deliver it. Now all she had to do was see if Zach would agree to her plan.

She slid out of the cockpit and proceeded to the office. Zach was talking to Jermaine, and she waited until the paramedic finished and went to his office.

She tapped on the window and entered the Quonset hut. "Hey, you got a minute?"

"Sure. I didn't expect to see you back so soon. Did you see that blob?"

Had he always been so tall and good looking? His muscles bulged under his T-shirt, and even from here, she could catch a faint whiff of his cologne. Those dark-blue eyes seemed to look right into her soul.

She shifted from foot to foot. "We did. The biologists are concerned and are going to check it out." She shut the door behind her and went to join him at his desk. "They suspect it is some banned chemical making its way into the water."

"So those pictures might have something to do with this."

"I think it's too soon to say." She stood awkwardly on the other side of the desk. How should she even start this conversation?

He eyed her. "Have a seat and tell me what's bugging you."

"What makes you think anything is bugging me?" She perched on the edge of the chair and clasped her hands in front of her.

"You keep twirling your hair around your finger and you're biting your lip hard enough to leave imprints. What's up?"

She made herself stop biting her lip. "Um, I've got a situation. I'm a little behind on the payments for my helicopter. My mortgage too, for that matter. I got to thinking about the insurance payment. My agent confirmed I am getting funds to pay for temporary housing and to replace the property that was destroyed. The money for the housing will come to you, of course, but I was wondering if I could borrow it from you and pay it back in installments. I could take that money and get caught up."

He stared at her. "I wasn't sure how to bring this up myself."

Her heart sank at his words. Was he kicking her out? The thought of being on her own terrified her for Alex's sake. "You want us to leave?"

He reared back, and his eyes went wide. "What? No, of course not. I meant I found the letter from the bank. I was going to offer to pay it for you, but I thought you'd be offended so I hadn't mentioned it. And if you don't mind me saying this, I'm surprised Jack didn't plan better for the future."

She stared at her clasped hands. "I've wondered the same thing. He let his life-insurance policy lapse. It was so unlike him, but he'd been a little distracted the last few months before he died." She looked up and met his concerned gaze. "But this isn't your problem. I just want to borrow the insurance money. I don't want a gift."

"I don't want you to pay me the insurance money. It's yours." He opened a desk drawer. "In fact, let me write you a check for what you need now, and you can give it back to me when you see your agent."

"He's bringing me a check this afternoon so there's no need." She stood, her face burning as she remembered how harshly she'd treated him. "You've been far kinder to me than I deserve, Zach."

He rose and slid his hands in his pockets. "I hope we can be friends again, Shauna."

"I'd like that." To her surprise, she found

she meant those words.

Zach listened to Jermaine soothing the ten-year-old with the broken leg. They'd left for Ketchikan at five this morning, and the poor kid had been white with pain. The leg was a compound fracture and broken in multiple places. It would require surgery, but it hadn't taken long for Jermaine's funny stories to get the child's mind off his predicament. His parents were with him in the back of the Learjet and had visibly relaxed once they were airborne.

Zach's copilot, Valerie Baer, studied the flight plan. "We should be to Seattle in half an hour. No problems." In her late thirties, Valerie was a beautiful blonde who was all business. She was married with twelve-year-old twin girls, and she was one of the finest pilots Zach had ever met.

"Surgical team is waiting?"

Valerie nodded. "Just received an update a few minutes ago."

Zach took the plane below the clouds. A ferry chugged past Sequim just below. Just past the lavender fields he saw the smokestacks of Olympic Paper. It would only take a slight deviation to fly over the area where the mysterious blob showed on the pictures and wouldn't take any extra time.

"I'm taking a bit of a detour." He guided the Lear a bit to the east. "You've got the controls, Val." He grabbed his camera, then snapped off half-a-dozen pictures.

"What was that all about?" Valerie wore a disapproving frown.

"I've been helping Shauna look into the murders of Clarence and Lucy. We saw some kind of blob in the water on some pictures Clarence gave her." He stabbed a finger in the direction of Rainshadow Bay. "That blob."

"Huh." She peered through the window at the water for a long moment. "Probably algae. The EPA will figure it out." She blew her bangs out of her eyes with an exasperated puff. "They sure won't leave us alone. Always wanting to inspect the apple orchard and poke into what pesticides we're using. Richard can never seem to catch a break. Even in years where we have a great crop, he gets slammed with new regulations for the next year that eat up any profit he makes. I've told him we should sell the orchard. I've about had it."

"You've got a beautiful place." Their apple orchard produced some of the best fruit he'd ever tasted, and the trees were healthy and vibrant.

She slid him a sidelong glance full of

speculation. "So, what's up with Shauna and Alex moving in with you? I thought she hated your guts." The crew was like a big family, poking into one another's business and offering advice even when it hadn't been requested.

"She does. If she'd had any other choice she would have taken it." He told her about their suspicions and about the way Shauna's house had been trashed.

"I bet that makes for uncomfortable evenings. How's Alex act with you?"

"He's great. And she's warming up. At least she's not staring daggers at me anymore."

Valerie shot him another glance from her too-perceptive blue eyes. "Is it doing anything for that big weight you carry around all day?"

There was no way he was looking at her. "I'm fine."

"You haven't been fine since Jack died. Your daredevil spirit has gotten downright dangerous. BASE jumping, cave diving. You even went bull riding."

"I've always liked extreme sports."

"You think since you challenged Jack to that climb that it's your duty to do things even more dangerous until it kills you too."

Heat crept up his neck to his cheeks.

"What can I say — I'm an adrenaline junkie."

"You and Jack always liked to be active, but this is more than that. And you need to stop it. It won't bring Jack back."

"I'm not trying to do that."

"Maybe not consciously, but you think you deserve to be punished. Zach, look at me."

He couldn't ignore the command in her voice. Her eyes were filled with tears, not the anger he'd expected. "Hey, don't cry."

She sniffled. "I'll cry a lot more if I receive a call that you killed yourself. Jack's death was an *accident.* Do you think he would want you to flay yourself with guilt like this?"

His buddy had been a man who caught every moment of happiness and treasured it. He always had a smile and a kind word for everyone. In school, he was the one who noticed the kid sitting alone at lunch and made a point to be friendly. In college, he refused to join a fraternity because he didn't want to haze anyone.

Zach tried to be more and more like him, and since Jack's death, he'd undergone a massive change. "Probably not. He always tried to make people feel better about themselves."

"He would be horrified if he saw the way you risk your life. I want you to cancel that volcano-surfing trip you have planned to Nicaragua next month. I haven't been able to sleep since you told me about it."

He flashed her a reassuring grin. "It's not that dangerous. I'm great at skiing. Piece of cake."

A tear ran down her cheek, and she swiped it away. "I've had a terrible foreboding about it, Zach. Please, just call it off."

"I'll think about it." What else could he say when someone he respected as much as he did Valerie said that to him? But thinking about it was as far as he was willing to promise. By the time his trip rolled around, he might need the distraction to clear his mind of Shauna's face.

Her smile was watery but genuine. "You've always liked Shauna. Surely she won't be able to resist your charm."

He scowled. "What do you mean by that? I never tried to steal her away from Jack. He saw her first."

Her mouth dropped open, and she snapped it shut. "A little defensive, aren't we?" Her gaze sharpened, and a frown crouched between her eyes. "You're attracted to her, aren't you?"

"Oh, come on. That's going too far,

Valerie. She's been a friend from the moment Jack introduced us. I care about her like a sister."

"Liar, liar, pants on fire," she chanted. "You can't hide anything from me. I can't think of anything better for you than falling in love with her. Alex already adores you, and he needs a new daddy."

"He has Jack! I wouldn't want anyone to take his place."

"You'd rather Alex was lonely and pining for a father figure?"

Zach focused on flying the plane. "The airport is just ahead."

"That's the real problem, isn't it? You'll fight any attraction to Shauna with every bit of fortitude you have because you think it would be wrong for her to love again too. Just like you think Alex shouldn't have another dad. Life goes on, Zach. That's the way it's supposed to be. Jack would want them to be happy."

"Look, just drop it, okay? I'm not taking Jack's place." He clammed up and concentrated on landing the plane. Valerie couldn't be right, could she?

CHAPTER 13

This street had neighborhood watch, and even parking in front of Bannister's house had brought several biddies to their windows this morning when he first cased the place. He parked down the street in the dark and walked toward the house. The street was quiet at this hour, and none of the houses had lights on.

But there were way too many streetlights here, and their glow cast light into the yards. How was he going to enter the house to look around? He couldn't jimmy the door and slip in with the porch light on either.

She had to have brought it with her. And he had to get it back.

He cut through Bannister's yard, brushing past a big pine that released its aroma. A motion sensor triggered a light on the corner of the house, and he darted for the darkness under the branches of a maple tree. His heart pounded at the sudden light.

Now what? Even if he could get inside, Bannister was home. So was Shauna, because both trucks were in the drive.

There'd been no response from inside so maybe everyone was asleep. He eyed the front door again. Not a good option, but maybe the back would offer more seclusion.

He skirted the side of the house, but his movements triggered more lights. It was bright enough to read out here. The guy must have had professional security installed.

What if Bannister was a light sleeper? The illumination out here might bring him to investigate. He cursed under his breath and scurried for the backyard, but more lights came on. The backyard was surrounded by a six-foot fence. He could scale it, but it wouldn't gain him much. He wasn't breaking in here undiscovered. If he chose to do it when Bannister was home, he had to be prepared to take the big man down instantly.

He patted his back pocket and its reassuring bulge. Bannister shouldn't be a problem, not with the gun and silencer. Better to move now than when Bannister was on his guard.

He stood poised outside the fence, then jumped and grabbed the top with his gloved hands and hoisted his foot up. He balanced precariously, then slung himself down inside the backyard. The space was large, probably half an acre, with steps leading down to the bay. He could have saved himself some trouble by walking to the back.

Jeez-Louise, the place was lit up like Fort Knox. The bright lights illuminated a barbecue and outdoor kitchen with a fire pit in the middle of the yard. Flowers and shrubs were everywhere. It was like a little garden paradise back here.

He moved to the partial darkness cast by a big tree and considered his options. A light came on inside, and he grinned as adrenaline surged. He shrank farther into the shadows. Maybe he should hightail it down the slope to the water. Before he could decide what to do, the back deck light came on, and the door opened.

Bannister flipped off the light and stepped into deeper shadows. "Who's there?" Dogs barked and snarled as they sprang forward, eager to get outside.

He squinted. Was that a gun in Bannister's hand? He turned and bolted toward the back fence. The dogs were on his heels by the time he climbed over. Bannister shouted after him, and he thought he heard feet thunder down the deck steps.

A smile stretched across his face as he ran

down the slope toward the water. Bannister was making the night interesting. He ran until his chest burned and his head pounded. He fell a couple of times on the shale but sprang back up and continued to rush away.

When he reached the rocky shore, he paused and slanted a glance back up the hillside. Bannister was hot on his trail, but he'd left the dogs behind. Maybe he should just kill the man now and be done with it. Clear out here, the surf would muffle any sound from the silencer. Then he could go back to the house and force McDade to turn over the box. He curled his hands into fists and grinned. This kind of adventure made life exciting.

He ran down the beach a short way and crouched behind a rock. Bannister would follow the footprints right to the ambush. He brought the gun up to wait.

Zach's chest still pounded from his mad run out the door and down to the water. His feet were bare, and he wore only a pair of basketball shorts. At least he had his Glock, but he didn't like leaving Shauna and Alex back at the house alone, though he'd put the dogs on alert. They'd tear into any intruder.

But what if more than one man was out here? He'd only seen one in the backyard, but that was no guarantee he was facing a lone adversary.

His feet sank into the cold, wet sand as he stood in the moonlight and tried to decide what to do. The salty ocean air mingled with the scent of fresh-cut grass from the neighbor's yard. Continuing to search in the dark might be foolhardy, but everything in him wanted to keep tracking that guy. What if he was the one who had trashed Shauna's house?

But more important, what if he'd been out here to lure Zach away from the house?

Zach whirled around and ran back up the hillside toward the backyard. His bare feet slipped on the rocks, and he went down on one knee, then sprang up and sprinted for the back gate. Something whizzed past his cheek, and he flinched at a sharp sting. He didn't stop to assess but continued to run for the house. The gate squeaked as he yanked it open, and he raced for the house.

He eased inside the kitchen door and threw the dead bolt behind him, then stopped. Shauna stood there with a butcher knife held in front of her. Ears forward and alert, the dogs stood guard at her feet.

She lowered the knife. "Someone's out

there, isn't he?"

"Yes." He touched his cheek, then looked at his finger.

"You're bleeding." She grabbed a paper towel and doused it under the sink, then wiped his face. "It's like a crease on your skin. How'd it happen?"

"A bullet." When she winced, he wished he'd kept his mouth shut. "I'll look around when it's daylight."

"Did you see him?"

He shook his head. "Just the shape of a man. I chased him down the steps to the water. Did you hear anything else outside?" He didn't wait for an answer but rushed to the front door and checked it. The alarm was engaged and the dead bolt in place. He closed the blinds, then went back to the kitchen. "We'd better call the dispatcher and let the sheriff know what happened."

She huffed out an exhale. "No going back to bed for us then. Deputies will be crawling all over the yard."

"We wouldn't sleep anyway. We'd be watching for the lights to go on or for someone to break in."

"True."

"I'll grab my phone." He strode down the hall and across the living room to his bedroom and retrieved it from the bedside table. He relayed what had happened to the dispatcher, but then declined to stay on the line. Still carrying his phone, he returned to the great room, but Shauna wasn't there. He heard noises in her bedroom, so he went down the hall and found her packing.

He felt like he couldn't breathe when he was near her. What was up with him that she set his heart to racing? It had to stop. She had no interest in him romantically. She hardly even considered him a friend. And that wasn't what he was feeling either, was it? It would be very inconvenient if he developed feelings for a woman who couldn't stand him.

"What are you doing?"

"I can't drag you into danger too, Zach." Her voice was choked. "I was only thinking of myself and Alex when I agreed to come here. I don't want to be the cause of your death."

He took the suitcase out of her hand. "You're not going anywhere. Where else would you be safe, Shauna? At least here we have the dogs, good security, and my gun. This place gives us the best chance of staying safe until they catch that guy. You have to think of Alex. I'm fine, and I'll stay fine. Just trust me."

A tear tracked down her cheek, and she

swiped it away, then sank onto the edge of the bed. "I hate this."

"I do too, but we'll be okay. Think of what might've happened if you'd been somewhere with no security lights and no dogs."

She nodded and looked up at him. "You're still bleeding. At least let me put a bandage on it."

"Okay." With law enforcement on its way, he followed her to the hall bathroom. He inhaled the clean scent of her while she tended to his cheek. Her hair was a bit damp from a shower, and he liked looking at the gold flecks in her eyes.

Her gaze flickered to his bare chest, and he took a step back. "I should probably start wearing more at night. I get hot."

"Jack always did too." Her smile came, and she sounded a little breathless. "He even had those same shorts."

Best not to go there. "Let's wait in the living room."

She followed him down the hall, and the dogs greeted her with excitement as she went to the sofa. With Apollo's head in her lap and Artemis lying across her feet, she looked completely at home. And cute. Very cute.

He dropped into the armchair across from the sofa. "What did you hear?"

She absently rubbed Apollo's ears. "I didn't hear anything except you running across the wood floor. I wasn't sleeping, and I saw the lights go on outside. I told myself it was a raccoon or a deer that had triggered the motion sensors, but I was still worried. Then I heard you."

He jumped up. "Let me check on Alex."

"I did before I came to the kitchen."

"I want to make sure." He hurried to the boy's room and peeked inside. Alex lay snuggled up to his favorite stuffed animal, a blue bear named Blueberry that Jack had gotten him the last Christmas he was with them. He backed out into the hall, pulled the door partly shut, and bumped into Shauna. "He's asleep."

She moved out of the way. "Sorry. So what do we do now?"

"How about some coffee?"

"We might as well have some help keeping our eyes open. I'm hungry too. I think I'll have an omelet and a piece of toast."

Lord help him, he couldn't stay away from her and found himself moving to join her. Anything to be near her and catch a whiff of her lemon-scented hair. "Sounds good."

She opened a loaf of bread and popped two pieces into the toaster. "Are deputies on their way?"

"Yep, but it's going to be fifteen minutes or so." The aroma of coffee began to fill the air. "Dispatch wanted me to stay on the line, but I wanted to watch things here. So far the lights have stayed off so I think the guy is gone."

She chopped peppers and vegetables with practiced precision, then poured the omelet into a hot skillet. What had it been like for her with Jack gone? He wished he'd been allowed to be there for her and Alex. With every fiber of his being he hoped things stayed good between them once the danger was gone.

CHAPTER 14

How had she known Zach so long and never noticed his character? Shauna sipped her coffee in the living room by the crackling fire. He had charged outside after the intruder without a thought to his own safety. When it was over, he'd been quick to check on Alex, and yesterday he'd cleaned up her dad's vomit. What kind of guy did that? Not even Jack, as perfect as he was, would have done that. He had a weak stomach, and if he'd tried, there would have been even more of a mess to clean.

The front door shut, and the dead bolt locked into place. She glanced around to see Zach turn off the entry light. "The deputies finally gone?"

He brought the scent of early-morning dew into the house with him. "Yeah, but they'll be back after daylight. The sheriff found tracks in the tree line leading to the fence and then an indentation where the guy jumped down into the backyard. And he found a bullet casing."

She set her coffee down and shuddered. "It's the same guy, isn't it?"

"No way of knowing for sure, but I think so." His eyelids drooped sleepily, and he dropped into a chair across from her. "That coffee didn't do much for me. Maybe I need more."

She eyed the bandage on his cheek. "You need some sleep."

"It's already four. I'd have to get up in two hours anyway."

"Two hours is an eternity after what we've been through. More coffee then?"

"Yeah, sure. At least Alex slept through it all."

She felt strangely wide-awake and ready for the day as she went to fetch him another cup of coffee. "That kid could sleep through a parade."

He accepted the mug and took a sip. "You hear anything from Marilyn?"

Her heart squeezed with a pang. "Alex got off the bus at her house yesterday like usual, but when I went to get him, he was waiting on the porch and told me his grandma said not to bother coming in because she was going to take a nap."

He winced. "Did Alex act like he knew

she was mad?"

"Not that I could tell. I'll have to go talk to her when he's not around."

"Want me to give it a try?"

Another checkmark in his favor. Marilyn could make anyone's knees tremble, but he would do it if she asked. "I doubt it would help."

His eyes drooped more, and he took another sip of coffee. "You never know. She used to like me. I mean, I practically grew up at her place. She thought of me as another son, at least that's what she'd always said. And maybe that's why she's so mad. She feels I betrayed her friendship."

"You had a strong bond with her."

His gaze stayed down. "My dad died when I was seventeen. He taught me to fly, and I wanted to be just like him. I loved watching him do stunt flying. Marilyn and Jack were with me when his plane crashed into the trees. Marilyn was wonderful, and I always thought she really loved me." His voice thickened. "It's been hard knowing I hurt her so much."

"Your dad was a daredevil too. Is that why you're such an adrenaline junkie?"

He shrugged. "Maybe. I feel close to his memory when I'm doing one of the things we used to do together. Like skydiving."

She remembered many fun times around the table at Marilyn's after Shauna married Jack. It was like another era, one that might never return. And did she want it to? She'd been flummoxed at the easy camaraderie that had rekindled between Zach and her. A week ago, she would have said nothing would induce her to speak to him again. Now here she was in his living room noticing what an attractive man he was.

What was wrong with her? Maybe it was time to start dating again, but if she did, Zach would be the last man she'd choose to spend time with. Especially if she didn't want to start an all-out war with Marilyn.

"We didn't get a chance to talk about our day other than we both saw the blob in the bay. Any idea what it is?"

He shook his head. "No clue. It looked like it had moved a little ways from the location in Clarence's picture."

"Guy is going to try to collect a sample. I'll check to see what he finds out."

He raised a brow. "I heard he's asked you out a few times."

How on earth? Was nothing secret in Lavender Tides? "He's a nice man. Maybe I'll say yes sometime."

When dismay flashed across his face, she twisted her hands in her lap. Why did she say that? She didn't want to make him jealous, did she? And why would he be jealous? There was nothing special between them now — just two people who loved Jack and were trying to make the best of a difficult situation.

But as much as she tried to tell herself that wasn't what she'd intended, the more she savored his brief expression. Unless she was reading more into it than had been there. Maybe he'd been taken aback at the idea that she might move on someday. She hadn't thought she'd ever be ready, and Marilyn for sure didn't want anything to change.

But Shauna had already started to change in subtle ways these past few days. And it wasn't okay. She'd promised to love Jack, and she wasn't about to go back on that promise — not for anyone.

She rose to her feet so fast she nearly tripped over the red throw dangling from her lap. "I think I'll go take a shower and get ready for work. I'm not really sleepy."

He yawned again. "Maybe I'll try to rest my eyes a few minutes."

She wanted to see if he watched her leave, but she didn't turn around until she was safely ensconced in the bathroom. The sooner she got out of Zach's house, the better. Then things could go back to the way they were.

Zach sat in his truck outside Marilyn's house trying to get up the nerve to open his door. The bus wouldn't drop Alex off for another forty-five minutes, so if he could make his frozen muscles move, Zach intended to march in there and throw himself on Marilyn's good heart. He had faith that it still existed somewhere down in that rigid exterior.

This might be the dumbest idea he'd ever come up with — and he'd come up with plenty — but Shauna's expression after the police had left tugged at his heart. He'd already caused her a lot of grief, and he needed to do whatever he could to make things easier for her.

Get moving.

As he approached Marilyn's front door, he heard her talking to the chickens in the barn. Maybe their discussion would be better out here anyway. He dragged his feet as he went to the open barn door. The structure's red paint was wearing in spots. If she'd let him, he'd paint it for her. He had a professional sprayer he seldom got to use.

He stopped and watched her. Just a year had brought quite a few changes. More lines around her mouth and a weary droop to her eyes. She carried a basket and reached into the straw to gather eggs. A few chickens squawked in outrage. She wore slim gray slacks and a blue cashmere sweater, one he'd bought her for Christmas a few years ago.

"Oh, hush," she told the chickens as she swung back toward the door.

He knew the moment she saw him because she stilled, and her mouth started into the smile he'd always loved. Then she squelched it and pressed her lips together. The glare she gave him would have sent him and Jack scurrying when they were ten.

He wasn't ten now.

"Hello, Marilyn. You look wonderful."

Something in her eyes flickered. "What are you doing here? I told you I never wanted to lay eyes on you again."

He took a step into a line of dust motes dancing in a swath of sunlight. "I still love you, you know. You've always been like a mother to me, and I find it impossible to dislike you now that you hate me."

She shifted her basket of eggs to the other arm. "I don't hate you. I simply don't want you to ever hurt me again."

He blocked her path of escape. She'd have to deal with him to get to the house. "You plan to punish Shauna in your vendetta against me?"

She sighed. "Oh, for heaven's sake, such melodrama. I have no vendetta. You killed my son, Zach." Her mouth worked, and tears filled her eyes. "No one would want to see your face after that. And you still haven't changed. I've heard about your escapades this past year. If not for your foolhardiness, Jack would still be busting through the front door asking for cookies."

They'd done exactly that countless times, and she'd always been there with those cookies. "You think I don't agonize over that every single day? You think I don't hear his voice in my head?" He dragged his phone from his pocket. "I can't bring myself to delete him from my phone, and I listen to all the voice mail messages he's ever left me. He was my brother in every way but blood."

His voice broke and he swallowed. "I punish myself quite enough without your help. But you're hurting Shauna. Did you want her to stay in that house with Alex and wait for the murderer to come for them?"

"I doubt he would have."

"He already did. If you'd talked to her, you'd know that she's lost everything in the house. The guy broke in and destroyed

162

everything, even Alex's stuffed animals. If they had been there, they'd be dead."

Marilyn flinched. "You're lying. Alex never said a word about it."

"He doesn't know. She didn't want to scare him, but ask her and see. And the man tried to get to them last night at my house too. I have excellent security, so the motion-sensor lights alerted me." He touched his cheek. "The dude shot at me. He was heading for the back door when I went to check on things."

Her hazel eyes studied him as if she still was uncertain he was telling the truth. "They could have stayed here."

"You have any security? Any lights that activate with movement? Dogs? How would you protect her? You don't even own a gun."

She started toward him. "Oh, for heaven's sakes, you're making a mountain out of a molehill. It was probably kids."

He gripped her arm and stopped her from brushing past him. "Look at the groove in my cheek. You think that was kids with a gun? Call the sheriff and ask him what went down."

"Let go of me," she said through gritted teeth.

He instantly released her. "Let's call a truce, Marilyn. Shauna will go home as soon as it's safe, and you can all go back to hating me. But in the meantime, can we work together to keep her and Alex alive? For Jack's sake?"

She exhaled. "I'll have to think about it. And pray about it."

"Not much to pray about. The Lord tells us to forgive."

"But he doesn't tell us to go right back into the same situation!"

"Turn the other cheek. Forgive your brother seventy times seven."

She blinked and shook her head. "Trying to turn Bible verses around for your benefit."

"I wouldn't be here if it weren't for Shauna. She adores you, and this is hurting her. She doesn't deserve that."

Marilyn squared her shoulders. "And why should you care? You've already hurt her as much as anyone could."

The jab hit home, and he took a step back. "She's a friend. She's been part of my life since Jack brought her home. I'm Alex's godfather. You think all the love I have for them just evaporated when Jack died? I just want to keep them safe." He stuck out his hand. "Truce?"

She brushed past him. "I said I'd have to think about it. You could always talk Jack into anything, but I'm not that gullible. Just leave me be, Zach Bannister." Her voice cracked, and she ran for the house.

The slamming of the door echoed on the wind, and he heard her throw the dead bolt. That hadn't gone well. He'd better leave before Alex arrived.

CHAPTER 15

The sidewalks of Lavender Tides had only a few window-shoppers strolling along Main Street. Small Victorian storefronts painted in happy colors lined both sides of the street and marched down the hill toward the seashore. The line at the Crabby Pot food truck parked by the pier stretched out twelve feet. The scent of their Dungeness crab cakes made her mouth water.

Shauna waited to cross the street after three cars bearing kayaks on their roofs passed, then waved at a client as she ducked into the sheriff's office, located in a building built in 1895. The receptionist directed her back to his office, a musty-smelling room with greenish-gray paint that would have fit right in with its original color. The old wooden bookshelves were battered as well and held a picture of the sheriff and his deputies receiving some awards.

Sheriff Burchell rose from behind his

desk. He was out of uniform and wore jeans under a long-sleeved red shirt that highlighted his dark good looks. "Thanks for coming down."

She caught a glimpse of a picture of his wife. "Not a problem. I'd just quit work for the day." She sat down on the chair opposite him. "Something new about the attack last night?"

"No, but I have some information about the necklace." He settled some readers on his nose and picked up a paper on his desk. "It seems to be one of a kind and was made by —"

"Dorothy Edenshaw. You already told me, and Pop confirmed it. He didn't seem to know if she's still alive. Did you find her?"

Everett nodded and leaned back in his chair. "She's very much alive and still designing jewelry. She works exclusively out of a shop in Vancouver."

"According to Pop, she only created one-of-a-kind necklaces, so the one you have has to belong to Mom."

"I tried to call Ms. Edenshaw, but she didn't pick up and hasn't returned my message. I'm trying to find the funds for a trip to Vancouver to speak with her personally."

She leaned forward. "I'm flying a client to Vancouver tomorrow. There's room for you or a deputy if you want to tag along."

He lifted a thick brow. "For free? What's the catch?"

She caught and held his gaze. "I get to go with you."

A smile tugged at his lips. "You'll need to keep quiet and let me do the talking."

"Okay." Unless he didn't ask the questions she had. She'd plumbed her memories and thought she might remember Dorothy a bit. She had been tall and willowy with a booming voice. At least in Shauna's memory. She'd find out tomorrow.

He picked up a pencil and flipped it through his fingers but remained silent for a long minute. She could see from his knitted brows he had something more to say. "What is it?"

"It's kind of personal, so maybe it's not the time to mention it."

"You can tell me. I don't plan on keeping any secrets from you. I want to find the killer."

A blush washed up his neck. "It's not that. It's Felicia. She was elated that you stayed to visit with her. The reception in town has been less than kind. People look at her and then at me and wonder why she married me."

"I'm sure that's not true." A feeble response, but Shauna hated to see his hurt expression. She'd heard enough of the scuttlebutt around town to know that was exactly what people wondered. "I really liked her."

"She liked you, and she could use some friends and a little championing. Would you consider asking her to meet you for lunch sometime? You're well respected in town, and if others could see you'd accepted her, maybe it would smooth the way for her."

"I'd be glad to. I could use a friend right now."

His lips curved and he straightened. "Thanks, Shauna. I appreciate it."

"My pleasure. But about last night — did you find any other evidence on Zach's property today?"

"Footprints." Everett frowned. "It appeared the intruder was lying in wait behind some rocks on the beach. There were knee prints, and then his footprints went back to the steps. He appeared to be running after Zach when he fired at him."

She gripped the arms of the chairs at the horrific mental image. "He was planning an ambush? So if Zach had continued following him, he likely would have been killed."

"Maybe."

There was something in his voice she

couldn't quite follow. Was he hiding something from her? "Who is doing this? I don't understand what he wants."

"I don't have a clue, not yet anyway."

Not what she wanted to hear. "And Clarence's death? Lucy's? Surely there is some news."

A lock of black hair fell over his forehead when he shook his head. "I do want to talk to you about Lucy's death. Bannister discovered her, and he has no good alibi."

"You can't seriously suspect him. Someone tried to kill him last night!"

"It appears that way, but appearances can be manipulated. I don't want to leave any stone unturned in my investigation. How well did he know Lucy?"

She didn't like the suspicion in his eyes. "Very well. We all did. She and Clarence, along with Zach, were often at our home when Jack was alive. We've been friends for years."

"The killer is usually someone known to the victim. And he was one of the first firemen at Clarence's house too."

She leaped to her feet with clenched fists. "Sheriff, you're completely wrong! Zach would never hurt either of them. He wouldn't hurt anyone."

One of his brows arched. "You blame him

for your husband's death."

She barely managed not to roll her eyes. It wasn't the same thing, not by a long shot. "Well, yes, but only for urging Jack to climb fast. He didn't *deliberately* kill him. It was an accident."

"That's not what you've been saying for a year."

Maybe she had been overzealous about her hatred, but being around Zach again had started to show her that maybe, just maybe, she'd been wrong. "If you waste time looking at him as a suspect, you won't find the real killer."

"We'll see. I don't plan to turn a blind eye in any direction. And you're staying at his house. Be very careful, Shauna. And keep your ears open. You might pick up on something he says."

"I'm not going to spy on him! He didn't have anything to do with this."

"I've had two murders in two days, and those are the first ones in my town in over a year. We haven't had one since Darla died."

She'd started for the door, but she swung around at his comment. "Wait a minute. She died of a drug overdose, didn't she?"

He made a face. "My bad. I didn't mean for that to slip out. The injection that killed her wasn't self-inflicted. The injection site was on her back in a place she couldn't have reached."

"Clarence never told me. Are you sure? Did he know?"

His lip curled. "I'm not incompetent, Shauna. Of course he knew. He and Lucy both knew."

Her knees felt so shaky she grabbed the back of the chair for support. "Why would he keep something like that from me? And there was never a word in the papers."

"We managed to keep it quiet. I wanted to investigate in peace."

"So who killed Darla?"

"I assume her drug pusher. Maybe she owed him money. There was very little evidence, and I never found out for sure."

"She'd been clean for two years." This was all more than she could wrap her head around. Maybe Zach would offer some perspective.

Shauna was quiet after she brought Alex home, but the boy made up for it with constant questions to Zach about clocks. At school he'd started to learn about time, and he was full of queries about how it all worked. Zach kept shooting glances at Shauna over dinner. Had Marilyn mentioned his visit? If so, he was probably going to hear an earful once Alex was in bed.

"Mommy, can I watch *Sesame Street*?"

"For a little while. It's bath night, and we need to wash your hair."

Alex made a face, then raced for the TV remote. Zach had recorded dozens of children's shows for him on the DVR, and Alex was making his way through them.

Shauna loaded the dirty dishes in the dishwasher. "Thanks for dinner, Zach. I had no idea you were such a good cook. The extent of your culinary skills used to be springing for pizza."

He carried his soiled tableware to the sink and rinsed them. "After Jack died, I didn't want to go out much. That meant I had to learn to cook, and I found I enjoyed it."

Tonight he'd fixed Cajun chicken Alfredo, and his mouth still tingled from the hot spices.

Her green eyes sparkled like emeralds when she smiled. "And Cajun seasoning. I was impressed. Just the right amount too. I might have to revise my opinion about your tenderfoot mouth. You usually don't even use pepper."

"I know how much you love spicy food, so I found the recipe today online."

She ladled the leftovers into a glass dish and put it in the fridge. "Well, I think I need that recipe."

"Sure." He eyed the side of her face and admired the curve of her cheeks and her determined little chin. Being around her was starting to really get to him. "Did Marilyn speak to you today?"

She swung toward him with bright eyes. "She did! She even offered me cookies and tea, which is why I was a little late."

"She apologized?"

"She didn't unbend *that* far, but she acted like nothing had ever happened between us. At least she wasn't still shouting for me to get away from you. That's progress." She turned toward the stove. "I think I want hot chocolate. Join me?"

"Sure." What would she think if he told her he'd talked to Marilyn? It was hard to tell if his attempt was the reason for Marilyn's sudden warm-up, but he hoped he'd done some good.

She put the teakettle on to warm. "Listen, there's something I wanted to talk to you about while Alex is occupied. I saw the sheriff today. He still considers you a suspect in Lucy's death. He also pointed out you were early on the scene of the explosion at Clarence's too."

He straightened from putting his utensils in the dishwasher. "You've got to be kidding me! After getting shot last night, he still thinks I had something to do with all this?"

"I know. I know. I said the same thing. He said he wasn't eliminating any avenue of investigation. It's crazy, but I wanted you to know."

He went to the corner cabinet and got down the chocolate mix and marshmallows. "Not much I can do about it."

The teakettle shrieked, and she brought it to where he stood scooping chocolate mix into mugs. "I think we might have to figure this out ourselves. It felt like the sheriff smelled fresh blood and was going to pin this on you."

Steam curled from the cups as he stirred and tried not to let it bother him. "I don't believe he's serious. He'll get evidence back from the murder scenes and figure it out."

Her hand brushed his as they both went to grab marshmallows. The shock of touching her made him pull his hand back quickly. "Sorry, you first."

She dug out a handful of mini marshmallows and dropped them into her mug. "How did Darla die?"

"Whoa, where did that come from?"

"What have you heard? Did you talk to Clarence about it at all?"

Where was she going with this? "A heroin overdose. I'd really hoped she'd kicked it, so her death by drugs hit him hard. Lucy too, of course."

Her piercing green eyes locked on him, and she had an intent expression. "That's what Clarence said too?"

"Clarence didn't talk about it much. I always thought it was too painful. Why are you asking about that now?"

"Sheriff Burchell told me she was murdered. The coroner found an injection site on her back she couldn't have reached on her own. He's investigating it as a homicide. The entire family, just wiped out. It can't be a coincidence that they're all dead. The same person has to have killed them for a specific reason."

And now that person was on Shauna's tail. Zach wanted to shudder, but instead stirred his hot chocolate and tried not to let her see his panic. Would he be able to protect her and Alex?

She blew on her chocolate. "I'd thought Clarence was paranoid for no reason when he talked about how someone was after him. It seemed too outrageous to be true. I should have believed him. Maybe he was looking into Darla's murder on his own."

"It's possible. Clarence was not one to let

176

anyone else do what he thought was his duty. Maybe we need to go through more of the pictures in the box."

"That odd blob in the bay doesn't seem likely to be related, does it?"

"I don't know what's related and what isn't, Shauna, but I think you're right and we need to poke around. Maybe speak to some of Darla's friends. They might talk to us when they wouldn't talk to the sheriff."

Her eyes brightened. "I'm glad you're with me on it."

He stopped himself from telling her he was with her no matter where she wanted to go. "Um, I bought some stuff for Alex. I wasn't sure when you wanted to tell him about the destruction of his toys, so I stashed them in my bedroom closet. I got some stuffed animals and all of his favorite Legos, plus a bunch of *Star Wars* stuff. I hope that's okay."

Her eyes went soft. "Thank you, Zach. You can show them to him now if you like, and we'll tell him what happened."

CHAPTER 16

Rings and Things was in a three-story brick building on Granville Street that looked like it had been built in the late 1800s. Shauna swiped her damp palms on her jeans and tried to shore up her shaky knees as they approached the store. She paused to look in the windows at the exquisite jewelry. All the pieces were very different — some with sea glass, some with diamonds, and others with the same black stone called argillite that had been used in her mother's necklace. There was nothing exactly like the necklace the sheriff carried, but the style looked similar enough she was sure they were in the right place.

The sheriff held the door open for her, and she stepped onto old brick floors. The ceilings soared overhead with exposed ductwork. The place smelled expensive — a combination of luxury furnishings and high-end perfumes carried into the space by wealthy patrons.

A perky, dark-haired woman smiled their way from behind glass display shelves. More items glittered on shelves beyond her, probably of lesser value but still beautiful. "Good morning. Can I help you?" Maybe a little younger than Shauna, she had the high cheekbones and bone structure of someone with Native American heritage.

The sheriff stepped forward. "I'm looking for Dorothy Edenshaw. Is she here this morning?"

The woman eyed them. "She's in the design room in the back. Who may I tell her is asking for her?"

"Sheriff Everett Burchell. From Lavender Tides, Washington."

"You've been pestering her." The friendliness in her face vanished. "I don't think she wants to speak to you."

"It's just a friendly inquiry about a piece of jewelry she might have designed. I'd like to see if she recognizes it. I can go to the Vancouver police instead and ask them to bring her in."

The sheriff had already told Shauna it was unlikely they'd receive local support, but the threat worked because the woman shrugged. "Let me ask if she'll see you." The black swinging door gave an indignant *whoosh* as she exited into a back room.

Shauna let out the breath she'd been holding. "I was sure she was going to kick us out."

"Most people don't want to be hauled down to the police station. It's much more discreet here." He bent over the shelves. "Felicia would love this." He pointed out a beaver etched into a teardrop pendant of argillite. It's only five hundred dollars. I think I'll get it for her."

She wouldn't have guessed the sheriff made enough money to drop that much on a bauble, but she shrugged and turned away to browse another display case.

The door opened, and the woman appeared with an older woman on her heels. The two were clearly related. The shape of their dark eyes was identical, and they both had the same long necks and full lips. Mother and daughter? Shauna met the younger woman's defiant gaze. Yep, the protectiveness was a sure giveaway.

Shauna looked over the woman's shoulder and felt a strange sense of déjà vu as she stared into Dorothy's eyes. She'd seen her before, but when? The older woman wore her salt-and-pepper hair in a long braid that hung over her right shoulder. Her skin glowed with a warm tan, and her dark-brown eyes tilted up at the corners. She wore a loose-fitting dress that came nearly to the tops of her fur-lined boots. The design on the dress looked Native American, though Shauna stumbled at recalling the name of the pattern.

A frown appeared on Dorothy's face, and she stared back. "Theresa?" She shook her head. "Forgive me, but you look like someone I knew a long time ago. You can't possibly be her. She's been dead for many years."

"My mother, Theresa Duval?"

"Brenna?"

Shauna caught her breath. "I'm Shauna. How do you know about Brenna?" Very few people even knew the baby's name. "Did my dad mention her?"

Dorothy waved a hand glittering with two rings. "Shauna. Of course, how silly of me. Forget everything I just said. I'm befuddled."

Shauna could hardly form a sentence with her mouth so dry. Was the name only a slip of the tongue? And something about Dorothy's manner put her off.

Dorothy's gaze swiveled to the sheriff. "You have a piece of jewelry you wish me to identify?" She glanced around. "There are no customers right now, so I think we can take care of this quickly enough here."

In other words, if anyone comes in, please get out. The unspoken command rankled Shauna, but she stepped back and said nothing as the sheriff pulled out the necklace.

He unwrapped it from its leather pouch. "Did you make this?" He rolled out the necklace, and it sparkled in the overhead lights.

Dorothy inhaled. "Oh yes, one of my finest pieces. I thought it was buried with . . ." She glanced at Shauna.

"With my mother."

The older woman's nod was curt. "Obviously Lewis saved it for you. Which is wonderful." The sour tilt to her lips gave lie to the words.

"He says he doesn't remember what happened to it."

The sheriff shot Shauna a stern glance. "Let me handle this." He turned back to Dorothy. "She bought it from you?"

"No, her husband bought it from me for their anniversary. It's worth more money now, I suspect. Many of the pieces I designed back then are collectibles today. I think it might fetch twenty-five hundred dollars at this point."

The sheriff never took his attention from

her. "Have you ever heard of a couple named Clarence and Lucy Glennon?"

Dorothy frowned and shook her head. "No, I don't believe so. They are customers?"

"We don't know. This necklace was found in their possession. They also happen to now be dead."

Dorothy gasped and put her hand to her throat. "I'm so sorry. I can't help you, though. I haven't seen this necklace in many years."

The door behind them opened and a laughing couple staggered in, arm in arm.

The sheriff wrapped the necklace and put it back in his coat pocket. "Thanks so much, Ms. Edenshaw."

Back outside in the stink of car exhaust, Shauna wanted to stomp her feet. "She's lying. I know she is."

The sheriff shrugged. "Why would she? This necklace doesn't really seem to be related." He studied her face. "In fact, I'm going to give you the necklace. It was your mom's, and I think you'd like to have it."

"I would." Shauna's eyes burned. Even if the necklace had nothing to do with the murders, she wanted to pursue this and find out what Dorothy knew about her family. What about Brenna? Shauna resolved to ask

183

her dad about Dorothy. His manner had been evasive when he'd first heard her name.

The fire crackled in the fireplace, and the faint scent of wood smoke hung in Zach's living room. The dogs curled at Shauna's feet, and the cat had finally come out, as evidenced by Zach's burning eyes. He sat beside Shauna on the sofa and went through the links that had popped up in his search.

"Look here." He stabbed a finger at his computer screen to show Shauna. "Dorothy's daughter's name is Penelope."

Shauna sat snuggled up in a fleece throw beside him. Wisps of hair had escaped her topknot and drifted around her face.

"Yeah. It doesn't list a father in the birth announcement." He stopped to listen. "Was that Alex?"

"I think it was the cat."

He glanced around for the source of his runny nose and found that Weasley had curled up on the afghan in the armchair. He made a mental note to wash it. "You said Penelope seemed angry. Why do you think she seemed antagonistic?"

"She had this challenging look in her eyes, and though it's a little too strong of a term, she almost had her lip curled in contempt.

I've never met her so I don't know what her problem was."

"It might be something she heard from her mother about your family." Would either of the women talk to him about the family? He didn't think Dorothy had anything to add to the murder investigation, but maybe she knew something about what happened when Shauna's mother and siblings died.

He'd like to give Shauna some closure on that, especially with that necklace popping up again. It was all such a mystery.

The house felt more homey with her and Alex in it. When it had been just him rattling around alone, Zach often looked for excuses to go out and do something. Now he was more than content to sit on the sofa with her and lean in to watch the way her eyes caught the light. Playing Go Fish with Alex was something he looked forward to. What was he going to do when they left?

The thought made him wince.

She must have seen it. "You okay?"

"Sure, just thinking about everything that's happened."

She pulled the throw around her neck and turned to stare into the fire. "I'm having a joint funeral for Clarence and Lucy on Sunday. Three o'clock."

"You're planning it?"

Shauna nodded. "There's no one else. With Darla gone, I'm the closest thing they had to family around here. I called Clarence's brother, but they've been estranged for years, and he wasn't interested in attending."

"That's pretty cold."

"I thought so too, but I didn't argue with him."

"Lucy doesn't have any family?"

She shook her head. "Her mother died in childbirth, and her dad passed away when she was ten. She went into foster care then. I've never heard either of them mention any family except Clarence's brother."

"Do you know what caused their estrangement?" Could this brother have had anything to do with Clarence's death? Zach was grasping at straws, but there seemed to be no good leads to the murderer.

"The brother was engaged to Lucy, and she broke their engagement to marry Clarence."

"Whoa, that's a hard one. But still, they're family. You'd think he would have gotten over it years ago."

She took a sip of the hot spiced cider beside her on the side table. "And if they'd lived near each other, maybe they would have, but he lives in New York. He's a bank executive, always busy, and he never married. So they drifted apart and stayed that way."

"Still, to hold a grudge even at their deaths seems pretty extreme. Did you tell the sheriff? He might want to look into the guy's whereabouts when Clarence and Lucy were killed."

She set her mug back on the table. "I can tell him, but I think that's a dead end."

"You aren't paying for burial expenses, are you?"

"No, that will come out of their estate."

Their estate. "Who's their beneficiary?" Greed was a common motive for murder.

Clarence had told Zach the mortgage was paid off, and his place overlooked the water. The land itself would fetch half a million or more. Maybe closer to a million with its panoramic view out over Rainshadow Bay. And then there would be the insurance money for whatever the house had been worth.

"I don't know. I'm not even sure the sheriff knows if they had a will or not. They might have left it to the church. Clarence never talked about that kind of thing."

Zach watched the cute way she pursed her lips as she considered it. The fleeting thought of kissing those lips passed through his mind, and he pulled away a few inches. What was wrong with him? He needed to get over this attraction to her and fast. The thought of stepping into Jack's place was unacceptable.

"You need some help planning the service?"

"The pastor is handling it. I wanted to provide a space for friends to come and gather, to remember what they meant to us. They already had plots together in the cemetery, so I didn't have to worry about picking anything out. They'd even done all the prearrangements for their funerals."

She yawned and kicked off the throw, then stood and folded it. "I think I'll go read for a while. Hopefully, we'll be out of your hair soon."

He watched her slim form walk away from him, and a sense of hopelessness swept over him. Once the killer was caught, she'd be walking out the door forever. That day wouldn't be a happy one for him.

CHAPTER 17

Customers crowded the aisles at Wagner's General Store for their annual sale on fall flowers. It was a crazy day to shop for new jeans for Alex, but Shauna hadn't had a choice. His old ones were beginning to look like high-water pants. She navigated the shopping carts and people back to the children's section and grabbed three pairs of jeans, then headed for the checkout.

She bumped her cart into another on the way out the door. "So sorry."

It wasn't until the woman turned that she recognized Kristy Gillings. An attorney, Kristy didn't dress the part in her generally wrinkled khakis and oversized sweaters. Her gray hair was usually messy, but she had the reputation of being one of the best lawyers in the area. She'd drawn up Jack's will and had been helpful after his death, but seeing the woman always brought a hard knot to Shauna's stomach. She didn't like to relive those days.

Kristy stopped and smiled. "I tried to call you a little while ago and got your voice mail."

"I didn't hear my phone, but it's loud in here. Is everything all right?"

Kristy's blue eyes twinkled. "I think you're going to say things are more than all right. Do you have time to come to my office right now?"

The office was just across the street, so Shauna nodded. She parked her shopping cart at the front door, then walked with Kristy. The Victorian building had been redone in Painted Lady colors, and the interior boasted fresh gray paint since Shauna had been here last.

Kristy led her past the receptionist to the spacious back office that had huge windows overlooking a park by the bay. She shrugged off her ratty blue cardigan. "Have a seat." She dropped into her black leather desk chair.

Shauna perched on the edge of the seat across from the gleaming black desk. "What's this all about?" She thought she'd paid all the taxes due after Jack's death, but what if there was a bill outstanding? Or what if the mortgage was about to be foreclosed? She'd gotten it caught up, but it was possible the bank had already started proceedings.

Kristy opened a folder and pulled out a sheaf of papers. "I have Clarence and Lucy's wills here. You are their only beneficiary."

The words didn't make sense to Shauna. She sat blinking at Kristy until the words coalesced in her head. "You can't be serious."

"You were an equal beneficiary with Darla until their daughter's death, and then they changed their will. Everything goes to you." She slid a paper across the desk. "Here is a list of the assets."

Shauna couldn't bring herself to take the paper. She didn't want to benefit from losing such dear friends. "Why would they do that?"

Kristy shrugged. "Seems simple enough to me — they loved you."

"I-I loved them." Her throat was so tight Shauna could barely whisper.

Kristy nudged the paper closer to her. "It'll take some time to settle part of the estate. The house was insured for six hundred thousand, but the land is worth over at least twice that. They had some stocks as well as cash in the bank. All told, you stand to inherit about two million dollars."

Two million dollars.

The breath escaped from Shauna's lungs, and she shrank against the seat back. "That can't be possible."

"Barring anyone contesting the will, of course, but I don't foresee that. They had no close relatives."

Shauna gathered her wits. "Clarence's brother. I contacted him about the funeral, but he's not coming. They've been estranged for a long time."

"Well, he could possibly choose to contest it, but he wouldn't have any grounds. They were both of sound mind and in good health. Their wishes will stand any kind of court judgment."

Shauna still couldn't take it in. She could pay off her mortgage and her helicopter, but it felt wrong to be happy about that when her friends were dead. "Thank you for telling me."

"Probate will take a few months. I have some documents for you to sign so I can open probate and settle it all." Kristy lifted more papers from the folder. "We can take care of that now if you have time."

Even as she numbly went through the motions of reading and signing the paperwork, she forced back tears. What would people think when they heard this news? Would they think she had finagled her way into their hearts for money?

It was going to take some time for Shauna to wrap her head around the news. She parked in Clarence's driveway and got out under a spectacular sunset that painted the sky in glorious bands of red and gold. Her eyes burned, and the lump in her throat refused to go down no matter how much she swallowed.

How could they have done this for her? They'd never even hinted at it. She stood against the yellow crime-scene tape and stared at the burned ruins of the house. The charred beams and timbers still reeked of soot, and she flinched as the memory of that night filled her head. Hot tears rolled down her cheeks, and she swiped at them with the back of her hand.

Who had done this to Clarence and Lucy? What could be worth their lives?

Tires crunched on the drive behind her, and she turned to see the sheriff's car roll to a stop. Everett got out and studied her face before taking several steps toward her.

"Any news, Sheriff?"

"What are you doing here?"

"Just missing them, remembering the good times." Her voice quivered, and she pressed her lips together.

He propped a booted foot on a blackened truss. "They were good people. I wish I could tell you I know who did this, but I've got so little to go on that I'm not sure I'll ever solve it."

She had hoped for answers. "Are you coming to the funeral on Sunday?"

"Yep. The killer often shows up, and I want to check out attendees. Maybe some of their family will show up. I still haven't tracked down their heir yet."

"His brother is the only living relative, and he's not coming. They've been estranged for years."

He lifted his black brows. "Hmm, maybe he's their heir. Do you have his name? I want to check him out."

The need to talk moved up her throat. "They left me everything."

The sheriff pulled his foot off the beam and straightened. "They left you their estate?"

She nodded and stuffed her hands in her pockets. "I had no idea until today. Kristy Gillings tracked me down and told me about it. It seems unreal." Shauna glanced up at him. "Why are you looking at me like that?" His expression had gone somber and calculated.

"You were the last one to see both of them

194

alive. And you stood to gain from their deaths." He sighed. "Look, I don't think you had anything to do with the murders, but my lead detective is not going to be so sure. And the state boys are helping us on this, so I'm guessing you just moved to the top of the suspect list."

"But I didn't know anything about it until an hour ago."

He put his hand on her shoulder. "Go home, Shauna. Don't talk about this to anyone. I don't want their suspicions to misdirect the investigation."

She crossed her arms over her chest. "When do you think I can go home? I've been at Zach's for five days already. If you don't think you'll ever find the killer, I need to decide what to do. I can't stay at his house forever."

"We are still sifting through evidence at your house. There's a lot of destruction, which makes for a lot of debris to search. We should be done in a couple more days." He frowned and zipped up his jacket against the wind stiffening off the ocean. "I don't want you to go home just yet. Give us a few weeks to see if we come up with a suspect."

She nodded and didn't argue with him. "I've got to pick up Alex."

No matter what the sheriff said, she had

to get on with her life sooner or later. It seemed clear neither the sheriff nor the state police would be able to do much to help her. They had no clues and no real direction, so what was she supposed to do?

She got in her truck and pulled away. It wasn't until she turned onto the road to Marilyn's when a thought struck. Once the will was executed, she'd be able to hire all the security she needed.

CHAPTER 18

Shauna had been quiet all evening, but Zach hadn't wanted to push her on what was wrong.

She stepped back into the living room after she put Alex to bed. "I think I'll go to bed too."

He patted the sofa beside him. "Tell me what's on your mind. You haven't said two words since you got home."

She bit her lip and looked away. For a long moment, he didn't think she was going to explain her mood, but she finally shrugged and came to sit on the sofa beside him.

Apollo immediately leaped onto the sofa and put his head on her lap. She stroked his ears, and he practically melted into a black puddle. "I still can't believe it." She paused and looked up at Zach. "I'm Clarence and Lucy's only heir. Kristy says the estate will be worth about two million dollars."

The shock of her words took a moment.

He blinked, and a warm rush of joy rolled up his chest. "Shauna, that's great! I always knew they loved you, and no one deserves a streak of good to come out of this any more than you do." He leaned over and brushed her cheek with his lips. She always smelled so good — a mixture of lemon and some kind of herbal scent in her shampoo or lotion. Her skin was incredibly soft under his lips, and he quickly pulled away before she noticed he'd like to linger.

"It feels wrong to benefit from their deaths."

"They wanted to take care of you. I'm not surprised they did this. You won't have to worry about money any longer."

"The sheriff says I went to the top of the suspect list. I was the last one to see both of them alive."

"I went with you to see Lucy," he reminded her. "Try not to worry. They'll take a look at you and realize you had nothing to do with their deaths. They'll check out your alibis for both time frames."

"I suppose, but it feels weird to know anyone might think I'd hurt them." She yawned. "I've got to get to bed. I have an early-morning flight." She nudged Apollo's head off her lap and rose. "Thanks for caring."

The living room felt lonely as soon as she left. Zach should be heading to bed himself, but he grabbed his laptop and scrolled through more links of information about Dorothy Edenshaw. He read half a dozen interviews with her about jewelry design, then read another on her views about women in the art field. When nothing there gave him any new information, he stopped and yawned.

The fire was out, and it was time to go to bed, but he couldn't make himself close the computer. He could search for information on Darla. Shauna's revelation about her death being a murder had rocked him. Nothing online indicated that she'd been murdered, just a dry rendering of the discovery of her body in a field of lavender. A small news article a week later mentioned a drug overdose, and that was it.

This was getting them nowhere. He closed the lid of his laptop and stood. The cat meowed in complaint. "I didn't bother you," he told Weasley. Sniffling, he carried his empty mug to the kitchen and took an allergy pill.

The backyard lay shrouded in darkness. No motion-activated lights flipping on tonight. After hardly any sleep last night, he should be exhausted, but in spite of yawning, he wasn't sure he'd be able to drift off yet.

The floor creaked, and he whipped around to see Alex staring. "Hey, buddy, you should be asleep."

Alex didn't respond, so Zach touched his head. The boy was sleepwalking. He'd done it since he was a little guy.

He picked up the boy, who snuggled into the crook of his shoulder as if it were made for him. He wore *Star Wars* pajamas much like the ones Zach had worn once upon a time. Jack too. They'd had every *Star Wars* figurine on the market and often traded them back and forth.

Would it be so terrible to get to be a dad to this little guy? He had no one but Shauna, and while she was an excellent mother — the best — every boy needed a dad. It was Zach's fault Alex didn't have a dad. Shouldn't he be the one to make sure someone filled that role?

Everything in him yearned to be a dad to Alex, but it wouldn't be right, not really. He didn't deserve it. But maybe he should try to find someone for Shauna, someone who would love Alex too. Zach began to run through the single men he knew, and none of them was up to the high standard he had in mind for Shauna and Alex.

Alex stirred and lifted his head. His eyes were clear now, wide-awake. "Would you lie down with me for a little while, Zachster?"

"Sure thing, little man." Zach shut off the lights and carried the boy back to his bedroom.

As they passed Shauna's room, he noticed her light was out. She was probably sound asleep, which was why Alex was able to slip out of his room without her on his tail.

Alex's room held a queen-size bed with the gray duvet hanging nearly to the floor on one side. Zach straightened it and tucked the boy beneath the covers, then went around to the other side and slid in next to him.

Alex rolled over and threw his arm around Zach's neck. "Snuggle me!"

Zach obliged and breathed in the scent of little boy. He could get used to this.

Alex yawned and buried his face in Zach's chest. "Zachster, where do you think Daddy is? Mommy says he's in heaven, but where is that and what is it like?"

Zach's eyes burned, and he felt a sharp pain in his chest. He'd often asked himself that very question. He'd believed in God since age eight when Jack took him to church, but since his friend's death, Zach had found himself asking God how he could do something like this. Jack's family needed him. Zach needed him.

He swallowed hard. "Your daddy's in heaven for sure, but we don't really understand where that is. It's where God is. That's really all we know. It's beautiful and filled with plants, animals, and fruit. The rivers are crystal clear, and your dad has a beautiful mansion somewhere. He's laughing there and happy. He feels no pain."

"But doesn't he miss me and Mommy?" Alex's voice held a tragic note.

"He probably misses you terribly, but time isn't like it is here. Your daddy's been gone a year, but in heaven, he might feel like he just got there. I'm sure he's watching out for you."

Alex's fingers twisted a lock of Zach's hair. "Do you think he can see me now? Does he know I got an A in reading this week? Does he hear me say my prayers at night?"

Gosh, the kid was asking hard questions. "The Bible says we're surrounded by a great cloud of witnesses, so I think he can see us when God lets him." Zach pulled him closer and rested his chin on Alex's thick thatch of auburn hair. "You'll see him again someday, but for now, you get to help your mommy and your grammy. You get to grow into a man and become the kind of good guy your daddy was."

He paused, and Alex began to breathe more deeply. A slight snore came from his mouth. Thank the good Lord he was asleep and wasn't asking more hard questions. He pressed a kiss to the little guy's damp forehead, then eased out of his tight embrace.

When he tiptoed to the door, he nearly ran into Shauna. He grabbed her by the shoulders. "Sorry, I about knocked you over."

"I-I heard what you told him." Her voice was thick with tears. "I'm so sorry for the way I've treated you. I was wrong. You're a good man, Zach. Can you forgive me?"

"I never held it against you. You didn't say anything I wasn't already thinking."

In an instant her arms were around his neck, and he felt the warm touch of her breath before her lips brushed across his cheek.

"Thank you," she whispered.

She was gone from his arms before he could react, and he sagged against the doorjamb. How could he stop her from creeping into his heart when she did things like that?

Alex hadn't stopped talking from the moment Zach buckled him in the booster seat and headed for the father/son hike at Freshwater Bay Park, commonly known as the Whale Trail. The rocky cove along the Strait of Juan de Fuca was a popular spot with kids.

He parked in the lot. "We're here."

"Yay!" Alex unbuckled his seat belt and grabbed his backpack. "I've got cookies Grammy made for a snack."

Zach grinned at the boy's excitement. "Your mommy packed us some sandwiches too, and I brought water. And gummy bears." He grabbed his backpack from the passenger seat and got out of the truck.

Stuart Ransom waved to him from the sign denoting the start of the Whale Trail. "Hey, Zach, I didn't know you were coming." Stuart had been the chief for the volunteer fire department for about ten years and also owned a local gym where he was a fitness trainer and looked the part.

Zach shook his hand. "Who are you with?" Stuart wasn't married and didn't have any kids. He'd dated Darla for a while, but that hadn't worked out.

"My nephew. My brother-in-law was called up to active duty and is out of the country. Sis didn't want Brandon to be left out."

"Brandon!" Alex rushed past Zach to join another little boy who was blond like his uncle. The two kids knelt to study the pebbles along the beach.

Stuart lifted a brow. "Heard he and his mom were staying with you. What's she think about your upcoming volcano-surfing trip?"

"I haven't told her." And he was wishing he hadn't told Stuart. "It's not until next month anyway."

"She never did like the way you talked Jack into crazy adventures." Stuart grinned and shook his head. "I thought she was going to pass out when Jack told her he was going skydiving. I thought maybe after he died, you'd lay off the dangerous sports."

"I like adventure." And he'd really like to change the subject.

Stuart smirked and nudged Zach. "Good thing you were there at the right time. I've asked her out at least three times, but she wasn't having it. Good luck."

Zach went cold then hot. He curled his hands into fists. "There's nothing going on, Stu. She's been my friend ever since she started dating Jack. My only plan is to keep her and Alex safe. Jack would expect that of me."

Stuart's smirk widened. "Whatever you

say, buddy."

Zach started to shoot out a sharp reply, but the teacher called them all to gather together for the start of the hike. Zach took Alex's hand and gave Stuart a wide berth. He didn't need to hear any more insinuations. Was that what the whole town thought? No wonder Shauna had been reluctant. He'd believed people would understand.

He took the list of plants and trees the teacher handed out, then led Alex along the shoreline. A barge and a ferry rolled past on the waves, and several sailboats, mainsails gleaming in the sunshine, added to the scenic view. Alex kept up a steady chatter, and Zach led him up a hillside toward several pockets of plants.

"Hey, Alex, wait up. Brandon wants a buddy to look for the plants with."

Zach turned at Stuart's voice, though he wanted to keep on walking. Brandon ran up to join Alex, and the two of them scampered off with the list of plants clutched in Alex's hand. "Stay in sight," Zach called to the boys.

"Look, I realize I was out of line," Stuart said. "I struck out with her, so I admit I was a little jealous. I hope you won't hold it against me."

"No problem." Zach wanted to hold on to his anger, but it ebbed at Stu's contrite tone. He stopped and frowned. "I've never seen that crack before." He pointed out a big fissure in the soil near the top of the hill they were climbing.

Stuart stopped and examined it. "We've had a ton of small earthquakes lately. Everyone is expecting the big one any day. I don't scare easily, but I have to admit I'm a little freaked out by all the reporters acting like Armageddon is about to erupt here. The town board even authorized a rooftop shelter on the school in case of a tsunami. They started construction on it last Monday."

"I hadn't heard that." Zach had read the news reports, but it sounded like fearmongering to him.

He took a long, hard look at the fissure again. Maybe he'd better report it.

CHAPTER 19

With Alex on the hike with Zach, Shauna cleaned the house, then took her laptop out to the back deck with the dogs. She should be spending her time looking for the killer, but she couldn't squelch her curiosity about Dorothy Edenshaw. Her comment about Brenna was never far from Shauna's thoughts.

The links that popped up in her search held no surprises. Mostly news articles touting her designs or jewelry blogs mentioning her talent.

Apollo lurched to his feet and growled low in his throat. Artemis did the same, and both dogs leaped off the deck and ran to the west side of the fence. Artemis snarled and leaped up on the fence.

The hair prickled on the back of her neck, and Shauna rose. "Is anyone there?"

When no one answered, she grabbed her laptop and ran for the house, her heart pounding by the time she shut the back door. The dogs could scare off whoever was out there. It might be that same guy who'd lured Zach out on Monday night. She snatched up her phone from the counter and called the sheriff. When he didn't answer, she left a message asking him to send someone by to check on things.

She paced the floor for several minutes. What should she do? She could get in her truck and leave, but she hated to feel like a coward. She could call Zach, but she didn't want to interrupt Alex's fun. They should be home within the hour anyway.

She found her purse and reached inside to feel around for her can of bear spray. As soon as her fingers closed around the metal, she gained a bit of courage. Shauna carried it with her and made the rounds through the house. There was no evidence of anyone trying to sneak in a window or the front door.

She went back to the kitchen and peeked through the window into the backyard. The dogs were sleeping on the deck again, so whoever was out there was gone now. She exhaled and sank onto a bar stool. Her relief was short-lived, the sound of the garage door opening had her on alert again. She rose and faced the door into the garage with her finger on the nozzle of the bear spray.

Alex's giggle in the garage was the sweetest sound she'd heard all day. She quickly dropped the bear spray back into her purse and pasted on a welcoming smile. The dogs began to paw at the back door so she went to let them in. Nails clicking on the wood floor, they raced to greet Alex and Zach as they entered from the garage.

Alex threw his arms around Apollo's neck. "Mommy, we had the best time! Me and Zachster found the most plants and trees, and I won a book about the forest."

"That's great, honey. I'm so proud of you!" As soon as he let go of the dog, she hugged him. "Ooh, you smell like a fish, and you're a little muddy. Let me run you a bath."

"I want to take a shower like Zachster. I'm too big to be a baby and take a bath." He puffed out his chest. "When I grow up, I'm going to go on adventures like him too. He's going volcano surfing next month!" He pulled away and headed for the hall. "Can I have a cookie when I'm done showering?"

Volcano surfing. Adventures. Her gaze collided with Zach's. Her chest compressed until she couldn't breathe. "Sure."

Zach held up a hand. "Look, I didn't tell

him anything about it. He must have heard Stuart grilling me about it."

"Volcano surfing. Really? You get Jack killed, and now you want to take out his son as well?" Aware that she was nearly shouting, she tried to temper her tone, but holding in her rage made the pressure in her chest build. "Doing this kind of thing is crazy, Zach!"

Patches of mud had spattered his jeans and sneakers, and his eyes were tired. "It's just sliding down cinder on a hillside, Shauna. It's not as dangerous as it sounds. I can sit down like on a sled if I want. I don't have to stand like on a snowboard or surf board."

She lifted a brow and clenched her hands into fists. "Really? And where are you going to do this?"

"Nicaragua. Cerro Negro."

"That's a live volcano! There are poisonous gases, and it might even erupt!"

"I'll be wearing protective gear." His eyes grew wider as if he were trying to figure out a way to deflect her anger, and he held his hands out in a protective stance.

She put her hands on her hips and glared at him with every bit of disdain she could muster. "For a little while there, I thought you'd changed, but you haven't. Not really."

She turned on her heel and ran for her room.

Music blared from the jukebox in Harvey's Pier, and Zach winced. The place was packed tonight, and he didn't see a single open booth or table. He was in no mood to go home after Shauna's tirade. All he wanted was to forget everything for a few hours.

He started to leave to head to another place down the road when he caught a glimpse of Valerie sitting at a corner booth. She saw him at the same time and waved him over.

He slid into the booth across from her. "Hope you don't mind me crashing your party. Where's Richard? Harvesting apples?" This time of year her husband worked long hours. Valerie was used to doing things on her own, and Richard never seemed to mind.

"It's no party, believe me." Valerie ran her finger around the top rim of her glass of iced tea. "I'm here drowning our sorrows. I don't even want to talk to Richard tonight." Her usually serene blue eyes were stormy.

He'd rather focus on someone else's troubles than his own. "What's going on?"

"We're being investigated." She gave him

a quick look, then went back to studying the iced tea. "This is between you and me, okay? Richard knew azinphos-methyl had been phased out and banned, but he thought the allowed pesticides didn't work as well so he went back to using it. And he's been acting funny — all secretive and weird. He told me he's got it covered, and no one is going to find out, but I doubt that's true. The EPA tests for these things, you know?"

"Yeah, this could be bad." The algae bloom in Clarence's picture wasn't far from their apple orchard. Could the pesticide be the cause? It wasn't for him to run down, though. Valerie wasn't one to sit back and let the ship sink. She'd handle it.

She took a sip of her tea. "Why are you here and so down in the mouth? I thought you'd be home playing house with Shauna."

Her words were like nails on a chalkboard. Did everyone in the world think he had only invited her to stay with him in order to woo her?

Valerie must have seen his ire surge because she held up her hand. "I know that look. I'm not insinuating you're sleeping with her or anything. You look upset, and I was just trying to help."

The server, a brunette in her late teens, popped over to take his order. He paused to

213

ask her to bring a root beer and fish tacos. The pause gave him a chance to cool off.

Valerie tipped her head to one side as soon as the server left them alone. "Well?"

"Shauna heard about the volcano-surfing trip. I thought the top of her head was going to blow off."

Valerie smiled and leaned back. "I knew she'd rein you in."

"Sheesh, Valerie, I'm not a horse. I have every right to have some adventure in life. Just because you like to play it safe doesn't mean I have to. And the same thing goes for Shauna. She's just a friend, that's it! She had the gall to ask me if I was trying to lure Alex into an adventure that would lead to his death too." He took a deep breath and let it out. "I wouldn't do anything to hurt him."

Her smile faded, and her eyes went somber. "Alex doesn't have a male role model, Zach. He's got his mom and his grandma. And now you. If he sees you modeling risky behavior, he'll think that's what a real man does."

"Sometimes it is," he shot back. "Men like to do all kinds of things. There are plenty of dads who played football in school, but their boys don't do it. You're both reading way too much into this."

214

"I might have agreed with you once, but you've changed since Jack's death."

"Here we go again," he muttered. "All right, so I like extreme sports. It's not a crime." In spite of his protest he shifted uneasily. Maybe she was right. It was a miracle of God's grace that he had all his limbs.

Was he trying to punish himself? He would have said no just last week, but Valerie had given him plenty of food for thought. And he would never want to do anything to coax Alex into trying anything risky. Zach would have to think about it.

CHAPTER 20

Alex kept up a steady stream of dialogue from the backseat on the way to the church Sunday afternoon. Shauna couldn't have talked to Zach if her life depended on it. She'd been too rattled by everything last night. How could he continue to do such crazy things when Jack had died because of his love for adrenaline? She had kept to her room until time to leave for the funeral so she wouldn't have to talk to him.

Only a few other cars were in the church parking lot when Zach parked the truck. Shauna let Alex out the back, then took his hand and went inside the old brick building. Organ music played, and she paused at the entrance to the sanctuary. Two closed caskets sat at the front of the church, and her gut tightened.

Zach motioned for her to go ahead into the main room. "People are starting to pour in. Do you want to stand by the casket to greet people or just have a seat in the front row?"

"I'm not their daughter. I think it would feel weird to act like I'm a family member. Let's just have a seat."

He nodded and guided her toward the front pew. What would people think if they knew she was their heir? Would there be jealousy? Probably. And why not? What right did she have to all Clarence and Lucy had worked their whole lives to earn? It felt wrong, but it was what they'd wanted.

She prayed for strength to endure the service without breaking down. People began to enter the church. Longtime friends, business acquaintances of Clarence's, members of the book club Lucy had started, and even some friends of Darla's filed past the caskets. Many stopped to speak to her, but luckily no one acted like she had any special right to grieve more than they were. Maybe they should have sat at the back. She would like to have seen everyone who came, just in case the killer was here.

Interior designer Ellie Blackmore stopped to hug her. "I've been praying for you." They'd been friends ever since Ellie and her brother remodeled Shauna's kitchen.

She thanked her, then hugged more people who stopped to say hello. As the service was about to begin, Shauna twisted in her seat and looked back. The sheriff and his wife were in the rear pew, and he nodded to her as if to reassure her that he had everything under control. She let her gaze wander around the sanctuary. Karl and his wife were just one row back. Nora's face was swollen and red with tears. He had a welt on his arm that looked like a bee sting, and his face was red and blotchy too. But he'd come to show his love in spite of what appeared to be an allergy attack.

All of Zach's employees were here, and she sent a timid smile to Valerie and her husband, Richard. Even Marilyn had shown up, but her eyes narrowed when her gaze landed on Zach. She could have sat with them, but being close to Zach would have been too much for Marilyn to handle. Kristy Gillings was back by the sheriff, and she sent a quick wave Shauna's direction.

Shauna hadn't thought her dad would attend, but he stumbled through the door. He'd even changed his clothes into an ill-fitting brown suit that was way too baggy on him. She motioned for him to join them, then scooted over so he could sit beside Alex.

"Thanks for coming," she whispered.

"I liked them too." Her dad's voice was too loud in the space, and several people looked their way.

She touched his arm. "The service is about to begin." He reeked of beer, but at least he'd made the effort.

As the pastor spoke of Clarence's and Lucy's faith in God and the way they cared about others, Shauna felt a prickle on the back of her neck. She desperately wanted to turn and see who was staring at her. The killer's presence was as tangible as a touch, and she suppressed a shudder.

Zach glanced down at her with a question in his eyes, but she huddled to herself and didn't say anything. He'd have no more way of identifying the killer than she did. Over two hundred people were here to say good-bye to the Glennons, and any one of them could be the evil smiling behind a mask.

The organ played at the end of the service, and she jumped up to turn around. Felicia beckoned to her. A sense of urgency flickered in Felicia's dark-brown eyes, so Shauna threaded her way through the crowd.

Before Felicia spoke, the sheriff joined them with a thunderous expression. "Felicia, I told you to let me handle this."

Felicia gave him a charming smile, then turned back to Shauna. "The state cops are coming to talk to you and Zach today."

The sheriff put his hand on his wife's arm. "They'll be fine, honey. I already warned Shauna they were going to be investigated. In fact, I saw a squad car pull up a few minutes ago. You might as well get it over with."

Shauna's pulse galloped, and she looked out the windows toward the parking lot. The state police car was easy to spot. Two policemen stood watching the front door. She motioned to Zach. "We'd better go talk to them. I'll have Marilyn take Alex home." She stepped to her mother-in-law's side and explained what was going on.

Marilyn went white. "They can't suspect you!" Her gaze flickered to Zach, who stood behind her.

"They're talking to everyone." Shauna hurried out into the sunshine ahead of Zach.

The policemen straightened as the two of them descended the church steps. The older one, a man in his forties with wings of gray at his temples, beckoned to them. "Ms. McDade, we'd like to speak to you. You too, Mr. Bannister."

Zach put his hands in his pockets. "The sheriff told us you were out here. That's why we came out."

Vaguely aware of people filing past,

Shauna stepped closer to the policemen. "I know you have to look at everyone, but neither of us had anything to do with their deaths. We loved them."

The older man's pale-blue eyes held no emotion. "You're their heir, isn't that right, Ms. McDade?"

"Yes, but I didn't know about it until my attorney told me. They'd never said anything about it."

"Hmm." He crossed his arms over his chest. "You were the last to see Mr. Glennon. I'd like you to go over everything that happened."

She'd been over and over it so many times. She sighed, then told him everything she'd seen and heard. The other policeman pulled Zach off to question him as well. She didn't think either of them were going to prove their innocence.

Kristy Gillings, dressed in a brown blazer and a matching skirt that stretched tightly across her hips, came across the churchyard. "The state police questioned you?"

Shauna nodded at the attorney. "They heard I'm the beneficiary. They were just asking me about my relationship with them."

The wind whipped Kristy's graying hair around her head. Her lips flattened, and she stared at the policemen. "Don't ever talk to them without me present. It's too dangerous."

"You don't think they seriously suspect me?"

"Innocent people are convicted every day. You're an easy target. I'm going to speak with them and warn them not to speak to you alone again." Her head high, she stalked toward the detectives.

The church bell tolled overhead, and tears burned her eyes. The killer was going to get away with it because the police weren't looking in the right direction, and there seemed to be nothing she could do. What if their focus stayed on her? They could lock her up and leave Alex without a mother. She had no doubt Marilyn would take custody of him in a heartbeat, but what kind of life would that be for her little man to be raised without his parents?

He'd followed her for several days hoping he could get her alone so he could find out where she'd hidden his property. Monday afternoon his patience paid off, and he'd kept a discreet distance behind her as she'd driven out to her house. Once she was inside, he sneaked into the two-story outbuilding and up to the second floor. The place smelled of dust, grass, and lawn mower.

The window looking out toward the house was the perfect place to observe. The big windows flooded the interior with light, and he trained his binoculars on them. First he'd see if she'd hidden it anywhere, and if she didn't lead him to it, he'd use a little . . . persuasion. He grinned at the thought.

His cell phone rang and he glanced it, his lips tightening. Getting away from her was going to taste as sweet as honey. She'd never see how it was her own fault, of course. She was dull and unexciting. Their sex life was practically nonexistent, and he'd had his fill of the way she looked past him. He'd become unimportant to her long ago.

Shauna shook her head at the destruction before heading down the hallway. Losing sight of her for half a minute, he picked her up again in the bedroom window. The dismay on her face sent a surge of pleasure through him. Maybe she'd think twice about sticking her pretty nose in other people's business next time. He watched her pack some things in tubs. She didn't seem to be searching for anything hidden, though, so now might be a great time to make her give it up.

He climbed down the loft ladder, then

pulled a ski mask out of his pocket and jammed it over his head. He skirted the side of the house and headed for the back door. Some idiot had locked it even though he'd knocked out the glass. He reached inside and clicked the latch, then entered the kitchen.

He paused and listened. Faint noises came from the master bedroom, and he reached down his leg to release his knife from the sheath. His fingers grazed the leather. Empty. Where had he left his knife? Retracing his steps, he went back through the door and along the side yard. It wasn't in the barn, so he returned to his vehicle. At first glance he didn't see it, then he ran his hand under his seat. The sharp edge nicked his finger, and he bit back a yelp, then grabbed the handle.

He walked the other direction this time just in case she'd looked out the window and saw him retreating. He needed to catch her by surprise. His long stride ate up the distance to her truck, and he paused as he passed. He could hide in the backseat and grab her when she got in. After pausing to consider that option, he shook his head. Better to grab her in the house.

He slipped noiselessly through the back door again and listened like before. Perfect.

She was still in the bedroom. He went to the living room and hid in the closet.

Zach would have a fit if he knew she was here. Shauna glanced out her bedroom window at the windswept yard and driveway. Another vehicle hadn't passed this way since she arrived, and she'd parked her truck in the garage so no one knew she was here. After hearing Zach talk to Alex last night, she had an irresistible urge to go through Jack's things. She'd had two hours before she needed to get home so the truck had practically driven itself here.

This pull she felt toward Zach had to stop, and the best way to put an end to it was to remember what she had with Jack. Nothing could replace that. It had been a once-in-a-lifetime love, something most never even experienced once, let alone a second time. It wouldn't be fair to another man to constantly compare him with Jack.

Not even a good man like Zach.

She turned from the window and surveyed the bedroom. It was still a disaster with clothes strewn all over the floor and the contents of the drawers upended and trampled. Stuffing from the mattress littered the carpet like snow, and nausea burned in her throat when she opened her closet. She hadn't been able to put Jack's things away, and the intruder had yanked all of his clothes off hangers and left them on the floor. Many had knife cuts in them.

She shivered and looked out the window again. Something made her shudder, but she hadn't seen anyone on the drive out here, so her fear was groundless. It was probably from the destruction all around her.

She pawed through the clothes and found Jack's favorite blue sweatshirt. She held it to her nose, and her eyes filled at the familiar scent of his cologne. It was a zip-up hoodie, and he often slipped this on to run outside, then hung it back up when he came in. But a year later it was beginning to lose its familiar aroma. What would she do when it was gone?

Maybe she should pack most of the clothes away in a plastic tub for Alex to keep. Sealing them up might preserve the scent of Jack's cologne. She'd kept two tubs in the closet in the spare room, but she found them upended in the middle of the floor. She carried them back to the master and began to fold his shirts and jeans and tuck them away.

Shoes went in the other tub, then miscellaneous things like his hunting and climbing clothes. By the time his side of the closet was empty, both tubs were filled to the top. She couldn't bring herself to put away the sweatshirt. It was her solace in the middle of the night, and her comfort when grief swamped her. It might never leave this closet.

She hugged it to her chest and felt something hard in the pocket. Frowning, she thrust her hand inside. Jack's iPhone lay in her hand, an item she thought had crashed on the rocks when he died since it had never been found. Her heart sped up as she stared at it. It was like holding a piece of her husband in her hand.

She settled on the edge of the ruined bed and tried to turn it on. Dead, of course. Carrying the phone with her, she went to the office and plugged it in. She moved torn papers from the chair and settled at the desk, then waited a few minutes to power it on while it continued to charge. He'd never set up a password, just like she didn't have one on her phone, so the icons flashed up right away.

It felt a little like Christmas as she stared at it. Where should she go first? Pictures, messages, or e-mail would be a little like talking to him. She touched the Messages icon, and a small picture of her was at the top of the list. A message from her was the last one he'd had up.

Her eyes welled when she read it. *Where are you? I'm getting worried.*

That had been the last message she'd sent before she got the call from Zach. But why hadn't she heard it go off here since he didn't have his phone with him? She checked the phone and found the sound turned off. Hitting the back arrow, she looked to see what other text messages he'd gotten in that last week. One from his mom, several from coworkers, then an odd number she didn't recognize. It didn't even have enough digits to be a phone number, and it had no name attached to it.

She opened it with a touch. There was only one message.

Meet me at the old fishing shack. If you want your wife and son to live, you'll have it with you.

Her breath caught in her throat. What kind of warning was this? She stared hard at the date. Two days before Jack's death. What was this all about, and could it have anything to do with the person who was after her now? Her head spun as she tried to wrap her thoughts around this threatening message. And it *was* threatening. There was no other way to take it.

What could it all mean? Her heart continued to thud in her chest. The ruin of the life they'd had together was in the destroyed possessions scattered all around her. Was that why the intruder had done this — to show her he could take Alex's life the way he'd taken Jack's?

She dropped the phone as if it had grown fangs and hugged herself. What should she do? The sheriff ought to know for sure, so she would have to come clean about being here in the house alone. She rose and gathered up the phone and charger.

She froze at a noise outside the office. It sounded like someone crunching glass underfoot in the kitchen. She bolted down the steps and ran for the front door. Was the closet door opening? She didn't wait to find out but slammed the door behind her, then threw herself into her vehicle. Her hands shook as she started the truck and backed out of the driveway. She'd tell the sheriff first, then confess to Zach she'd been to the house.

A headache began to throb at her temples. Who had been in there?

CHAPTER 21

Zach stood outside Rings and Things and looked in the windows. Several shoppers stared down into the display cases. The young woman assisting them had to be Dorothy's daughter, Penelope, but he saw no sign of the older woman.

They had a couple of hours to kill in Vancouver while waiting to transport a patient, and he'd convinced Valerie to help him scope out the situation here. After apologizing to Shauna, he couldn't stop thinking about how much she wanted to have answers about her family. Maybe he could get some from Dorothy.

"So what am I supposed to do?" he asked Valerie. He'd been planning to just walk in and ask to see Dorothy, but Valerie didn't think that would work.

She rolled her baby blues. "I'm pretending to be your wife so you can buy me something special. I want it designed by

Dorothy so we'll ask to speak with her back in her office."

"Good grief, all the cloak and dagger. Why not just walk in and ask to talk to her about the Duval family?"

"She won't see you. You said even the sheriff had trouble getting her to meet with him. What chance do you think we'd have if you just asked? Zero, zilch."

"And you think she'll actually answer our questions after we lie to get in? She'll toss us out the door. Look, let's just go in and ask to see her. I'll say it's regarding a personal matter."

Valerie shrugged slim shoulders. "It's your funeral."

He yanked on the handle and opened the door for her. As they stepped onto the plush plum-colored carpet, an older woman entered through the side door. She carried a velvet tray holding several pieces of jewelry that matched the vivid hues of the flowing caftan she wore.

Zach moved to intercept her before she got within earshot of the customers and her daughter. "Ms. Edenshaw? I'm Zach Bannister, a friend of the Duval family." She tensed, and he reached toward her. "This isn't about the murder. I know you really have nothing to contribute to the investiga-

231

tion. This is personal."

Her dark-brown eyes studied him. She nodded and jerked her head toward the door she'd just come through. "This way."

He shot a triumphant grin toward Valerie, who shrugged. Dorothy led them through a labyrinth of wooden shelves to a workroom in the back. A table held gold chains, gemstones, and soldering irons. The hot smell of solder burned his nose.

She stopped and set the tray of jewelry on the battered table. "Let's get this over with so I can return to work. This is a busy time for me, gearing up for the holidays."

"And I'm sorry to bother you. How well did you know Lewis and Theresa Duval?"

Dorothy's eyes flickered away from him, and she said nothing. Then she sighed and met his gaze. "As persistent as everyone seems to be, it's probably going to come out. I'm surprised it's been secret this long." She held his gaze with an air of defiance. "I knew Lewis better than Theresa. We were having an affair."

He blinked as the impact of her words soaked in. "I'll be honest — I wasn't expecting that. Shauna thought your daughter seemed angry and defensive when she was here."

"Oh, she is. She was five years old when I

started seeing Lewis, and when we broke up, I-I experienced some depression." A sigh escaped her lips. "I have to admit I neglected Penelope quite a lot for about twelve years. She grew to hate Lewis and any mention of his name. I can't blame her, really. My depression and neglect ruined her childhood."

"Lewis is a drunk. I think you were lucky to escape him."

Dorothy blinked, and her mouth gaped. "I haven't spoken to him in years. Not since a year or so after Theresa died. He thought God took Theresa as punishment for our affair. Silly, I know. It was a bad time. We relied on state assistance for a while. I finally got a big break on a jewelry piece I'd been working on for over a year, and my career was reborn."

He could see why Lewis would be attracted to Dorothy. Though she had to be in her fifties now, she was slim and attractive with flashing dark eyes, high cheekbones, and lustrous hair. In her younger days, she would have turned male heads everywhere she went.

"Is that all?"

"Just a couple more questions. Did Theresa know about you?"

"She found out just before she died. I

guess she followed Lewis to our house."

Her matter-of-fact tone held no trace of regret or guilt. He pushed away his disgust. "You called Shauna, Brenna. Why?"

She looked away and turned to move a few gemstone pieces around. "Just a slip of the tongue."

"Do you know what happened to Connor and Brenna?" He knew it was a long shot. She'd probably just say they died in the earthquake, but he wasn't convinced. "And how did you know Brenna's name? Shauna named her, and the baby was never found."

"Lewis told me about the baby being born." For the first time a hint of regret twisted her lips. "I don't think anyone really knows what happened to them, not even Lewis. He didn't even try to find them."

The shock of her words hit him like a tsunami. *They were alive.* "The state took them?"

"I assume so." She wrinkled her nose. "Awful, isn't it? He said they'd be better off in a home with a mother and father instead of a burned-out shell of a man who didn't know how to raise one kid, let alone three."

"Why did he keep Shauna?"

"She was old enough to tell her name. They called him, and he had to go pick her up. She kept saying her brother and sister were dead, so they had Lewis go to the morgue and take a look at the other children. He claimed he didn't see them."

"So they might have gone into the foster care system."

"That's the way I heard it." She glanced toward the door.

"Thanks for speaking with me, Dorothy. You realize I'll have to tell Shauna about this conversation."

She nodded. "It's past time for the truth to come out."

The question was, how was he going to tell Shauna about it?

The scent of popcorn hung in the air, and Shauna popped a handful into her mouth. She'd been waiting for the moment to tell Zach about Jack's phone, but he'd been strangely preoccupied all through dinner. Alex had finally fallen asleep after four stories. It was now or never.

She pulled the fuzzy throw off the back of the sofa and wrapped it around her legs. Weasley climbed onto her lap. Apollo's head was on her left foot, and Artemis twitched and yelped in his sleep by the fireplace. "Um, there's something I need to talk to you about."

He put down his laptop, but his distracted

235

expression didn't change much. A lock of dark hair draped over his forehead, and his blue eyes almost seemed to look past her. She much preferred it when those eyes were looking at her and really seeing her. What did that say about how important he was becoming to her?

She stroked the cat's soft fur. "I went to my house today."

His eyes snapped into focus. "What? By yourself?"

"I know. I know. I shouldn't have done it, but there was no harm done. I wanted to — well, it doesn't matter what I wanted to do. I found this." She pulled Jack's iPhone out of her pocket and held it out to him.

Zach's eyes widened. "That's Jack's phone. I recognize Alex's baby picture on the cover." He started to reach for it, then drew his hand back. "Wait, I thought this was lost when he fell. Where did you find it?"

"I thought it was lost too, but it was in the pocket of his hoodie." She turned it on and flipped it around so he could see the message. "Read this."

He took the phone and stared at the screen, then frowned. "Whoa, that's a threat."

"You have any idea who this could be? Or

what it's about?"

His face troubled, Zach shook his head and handed back the phone. "I thought Jack told me everything, but he never mentioned anything like this. Could it have been sent to the wrong person?"

"I thought about that, but I reviewed all the messages." She scrolled down and found another one. "He answered this one. The person sent him a text asking him if he was going to be late. And Jack answered he would be fifteen minutes late." She turned the phone around so he could read it for himself.

"This has to be someone he knows. You should show it to the sheriff."

"I did already. I took it straight to Everett when I left my house. He wanted to keep the phone, but I told him I wanted to go through it some more. But I gave him permission to dig into our phone records to see who might have sent it."

"I'm surprised he let you keep it."

"He didn't have any authority to take it without my permission. No crime had been committed. Though this guy threatened Jack, his death was an accident."

Zach nodded and reached for the phone. "Mind if I look at this?"

"Nope, go ahead. I hoped you'd have an idea."

She watched him scroll through the phone, reading messages, checking out e-mails. His eyes grew misty as he flipped through family pictures. "He loved his family so much."

Her throat tightened, and knowing she couldn't speak, she nodded.

Zach paused at a picture. "Hey, this is a video. Mind if I watch?"

She shook her head and leaned over to watch with him, though she wasn't sure she'd see much with tears flooding her eyes.

Jack's face came into view. *"Hey, babe. I plan to delete this if I come back from that climb alive, so if you're watching it, I didn't make it. They're watching me, and I can't get in to see the sheriff without them knowing. You need to tell Sheriff Burchell to check out Jupiter. It's not what it seems. I'm not going to say more because I don't want to put you in their bull's-eye."* He swallowed hard. *"No matter what happens just know I love you and Alex more than anything. I'm trying to make things right, to do the best I can to protect you. Turn to Zach. He'll protect you with his life, you and Alex both."* He looked off to the side of the screen. *"Gotta go. Bye."*

Shauna couldn't move, couldn't do anything more than sit with her mouth agape, her heart racing in her chest. This was real. Whoever had sent that text to Jack had been dangerous. So dangerous he'd thought they might kill him. But Jack had died in an *accident,* hadn't he?

She finally dredged up the strength to look at Zach. His face was pale, and he was breathing hard.

"Exactly how did Jack die?" she whispered.

He didn't seem to hear her as he stared down at the phone. "I-I don't understand this. Jupiter. Does he mean the planet?"

"I don't know." Her pulse still rocketed in her chest, and she couldn't take a deep breath. "He's basically saying someone might try to kill him on that climb. You've got to tell me every single thing that happened that day. All of it. Don't leave anything out."

She clenched her hands together and listened as he told her about that horrific day.

CHAPTER 22

One Year Earlier

The day couldn't be more perfect for climbing. Mount Olympus, at nearly eight thousand feet, was the highest in the Olympic Mountains.

He and Jack had always found the ascent treacherous. Shauna had dropped them off in Glacier Meadows and would pick them up in two days. It had taken two hours along the Crystal Pass path to reach the West Peak block, where the true summit glistened with snow.

Zach's breath fogged in the cold air as he shucked his backpack and took out his climbing gear, then shot a grin at Jack. Jack's turquoise eyes were always smiling, and more often than not, his auburn hair was in need of a trim. Since he'd married Shauna, she kept his neckline in a little better shape. Marriage had been good for Jack, and he loved being a daddy to little Alex.

The two climbed this peak every year on

Zach's birthday, but this year it looked like it might not happen because Shauna had a flight and needed Jack to pick up Alex. But luckily, her booking was canceled yesterday. Jack always put his family first, and sometimes Zach felt a little jealous. Silly, for sure.

"A little windy today." Jack squinted up to the snow-covered peak. He'd been a little somber and distracted today, which was unusual.

The temperature hovered around fifty. Even in summer, the peak seldom shed all its snow and ice, but they'd come prepared with jackets and ice picks. No other climbers were on the slope today, so they should have a good day without having to worry about other people dislodging boulders or ice.

They put on their boots and attached their crampons. Jack set out climbing rope and ice screws. He was ready before Zach. "Looks like we're the only ones out here so we should have a good time."

Zach pulled on gloves. "How about we make this interesting? First person to the top chooses where we eat lunch. Loser has to pay."

Jack's grin flashed back at him, and he finally seemed to be himself. "You're going down, buddy. This is my day. I can feel it in my bones."

"Uh-huh. It's my birthday, so that makes it *my* day."

"True. So maybe I'll let you choose, old man, and I'll buy anyway."

Both men moved into position. "Ready, set, go!" Jack called.

Zach drove the crampon on his right foot into the ice, then reached for fingerholds higher up. Jack was already a foot above him and moving fast, the rat. Zach tried to pick up the pace, but Jack seemed to have better toeholds and boulders to grip.

"Stupid crampons," Jack said. "I just lost the one on my left."

"Let's call the challenge. I've got more in my pack," Zach said.

"I've got good leverage here. I'm going on up. Catch me if you can," Jack called back.

Zach's lungs labored as he tried to catch his friend. He paused, then peered up. Jack was already at least five feet ahead of him. The climb was reaching the more difficult part. "Tie off, buddy! You're getting too high."

Jack's response came faintly. "I will in a minute. There's a ledge up here."

Jack was fifty feet up, higher than Zach liked to free-climb. Frowning, he worked on catching his friend so they could tie off together. He got to within ten feet of Jack when a mix of ice and rocks tumbled past his shoulder.

"Heads up, Jack!"

More rocks tumbled down the rock face, and he frowned. Zach hadn't seen anyone else out here, so the climb should have been free of this kind of danger. He searched above Jack to see if any other climbers were dislodging the debris. Nothing but blue sky.

Another rock slide started about twenty feet above Jack's head, and this one included chunks of rock and ice as big as their heads. "Jack, look out! Tie off! Tie off!"

Jack paused and looked up, but before he could drive screws into the rock face and tie off, the largest of the boulders struck his shoulder. His left hand slipped free from its grip, and he tried to hang on with his right, but another boulder struck his head.

"No!" Zach screamed as his friend fell away from the face of the mountain. He made a futile attempt to grab Jack's arm as he plummeted noiselessly toward the ground, but he missed. The thud when Jack hit the rocks below sickened him.

He'd surely broken some bones. Zach climbed down as fast as he was able, taking chances and nearly falling himself several times, but he had to get to Jack. He reached the bottom and ran to his friend's inert body, where he threw himself down beside him.

He touched Jack's neck. "Jack, where does it hurt?"

Jack's eyes were closed, and a trickle of blood flowed from the corner of his mouth. Zach pressed his fingers harder against his neck, searching for a pulse. Not even a faint thump under his fingers. "No, no." He rolled him over and put his ear on his chest. "Come on, buddy, stay with me." Cell phones didn't work here, so any resuscitation would have to be done by him.

He leaned down to check Jack's breathing, but there wasn't even a whisper of an inhalation.

His friend was gone.

Tears leaked from his eyes as he tried CPR, but after half an hour, there was still no response. He crumpled to Jack's chest and sobbed. This was all his fault. He never should have challenged him to the race.

Shauna couldn't sit still as she listened to Zach's recounting of the day Jack had died. She paced the oak floors with Weasley in her arms and the dogs on her heels. The word pictures in her mind of that day were in vivid color and all too real. In those minutes she smelled the cold, crisp air instead of the warm, acrid smoke from the fireplace. Jack had been strong even at the end, plummeting to his death without a sound.

When she wheeled around to face him, Zach's head was down, and his voice had fallen to a husky whisper. His cheeks were wet, and compassion welled like a warm flood in her chest. She'd discounted for too long how much he'd loved Jack. She'd been too immersed in her own pain to notice his.

She cleared her throat and swallowed the lump there. "What could have caused the rock fall?"

"Maybe melting snow and ice, but neither of us were expecting much trouble. There was so much rock scree tumbling down that I looked hard to see if anyone up there had dislodged it."

"Was there a place for someone to hide?"

He swiped his eyes with the back of his hand. "Well, sure. Boulders and outcroppings would have provided good cover. I wish I'd thought of all this sooner. I would have checked the top of the slope for signs of a pry bar. It's much too late now."

She pointed at the phone on the sofa. "His message lends credence to the possibility someone wanted to kill him."

"Maybe. But if I hadn't challenged him to a race, we would have been tied on. The rocks falling wouldn't have dislodged him."

"But one struck his head. The autopsy ruled he died of blunt-force trauma to the head. That big rock probably was what killed him."

She'd fought so long to blame him that arguing for his exoneration felt odd, though she knew it was right. Facing the truth meant looking at everything from a different angle. "What about that whole Jupiter thing? I don't understand what Jack meant."

"Maybe the sheriff will." Zach glanced at the grandfather clock. "It's a little late to call him tonight, but we need to follow up with him tomorrow. I'll copy everything on this phone tonight because the sheriff will confiscate it when we tell him." He frowned again. "Jack was trying to warn you about something."

"I wish he'd spelled it out better."

Zach reached for his laptop and lifted the lid. "Let's see what kinds of hits we get with Jupiter."

He settled in the armchair and began to type. This search could go in myriad directions. There was no telling what Jack had meant.

"Jupiter was the Roman god of sky and thunder, and he was the head honcho to the Romans."

"I hardly think Jack would be thinking of

a Roman myth."

He shrugged and looked back at the computer. "There's a company named Jupiter that sells musical instruments. Jack played the trombone in high school."

"Keep looking. That's not it."

"Projection equipment, a hotel, a lighthouse."

She put down the squirming cat. "Wait, the hotel. That's in Portland, and we went there for our anniversary a couple of years ago."

He stopped and clicked on a link. "They've got an art gallery that showcases emerging artists, but nothing is jumping out at me that might lead anywhere."

She agreed it didn't feel right. They'd only been there two nights and hadn't interacted with anyone. "This is hard. I think I need some hot spiced cider. How about you?"

His nose stayed planted at this screen. "Yeah, I'll have some."

As she warmed the water and prepared the hot drinks, she ran through any kind of Jupiter reference she'd heard of. She carried the hot mugs back toward the fireplace. "Hey, didn't you guys have a friend who pitches for the Jupiter Hammerheads?"

He took one of the mugs, and a bit of color came to his cheeks. "Yeah. Harry

Richards. We went to college together, but he really wasn't a friend. More like a constant thorn in our side. He was here a few weeks before Jack died. They got together for coffee, which surprised me. Jack usually didn't give Harry the time of day."

She sipped the spicy cider and felt a surge of energy. Maybe they were on to something. "Would you have a way of contacting him? Maybe he'd tell you what they talked about."

Zach set down his mug and grabbed Jack's phone. "I bet this has his number." He scrolled through the phone, then stopped. "Here it is. It's really late in Florida, though, so I'll have to call tomorrow."

"At least we have some sort of lead."

"Maybe. It might not mean a thing."

She stared into her cup and tried to think of any other Jupiter reference Jack might have mentioned, but nothing came to mind. It was pushing eleven o'clock as well. Maybe after some rest, they could figure this out.

She glanced up. Zach stared at her with an intent expression that made her mouth go dry. Surely that was longing she saw in his eyes, but if it was, what did she do with it? Ever since she'd heard him talking to Alex about heaven, her feelings had undergone a seismic shift. She relived the sensation of the rough stubble on Zach's cheek under her lips.

He didn't glance away and neither could she. In that moment, she saw into his soul and knew he saw into hers. There was a *knowing* that was impossible to explain, but it also felt immensely disloyal to Jack. Hadn't she promised to love him forever?

She bolted to her feet. "I need to get to bed."

"Shauna, wait!"

She ignored the plea in his voice and fled to her room, where she shut the door and locked it behind her. If he'd approached, she couldn't have helped throwing herself against his chest. All the guilt in the world wouldn't have kept her from kissing him. What was she going to do? She had to stay here until it was safe to take Alex home, but how did she resist the irresistible?

CHAPTER 23

Zach used a poker to separate the logs so the fire would die, then stood and paced the floor in front of the fireplace. This had to stop. One more moment and he would have kissed her. Guilt held his gut in a painful grip. What kind of friend put the moves on his best friend's widow? Scum of the earth, that's what he was.

And he hadn't even had a chance to tell her what he'd found about her siblings. That was one conversation he wasn't sure how to bring up, but the greater importance of Jack's warning had pushed everything else out of the way.

But he would have sworn he'd glimpsed the same yearning he felt in her eyes.

He slapped his hand against his forehead and moaned as he dropped onto the sofa. The cat was quick to leap into his lap, and the burning in Zach's eyes started at once so he pushed him off. "No you don't."

Weasley stalked off with his tail held high.

Sleep would be a long time coming tonight, so he might as well kill a little time before he faced the restlessness. He'd normally take his time to clean the kitchen, but Shauna had already left it spotless. Even the thriller he'd started a couple of weeks ago wasn't likely to hold his attention when all he wanted to do was bang on her door and tell her how he was feeling.

But doing that would be disloyal to Jack.

He grabbed Jack's phone and plugged it into his computer. He downloaded all the information including the pictures, texts, and videos. This was one more piece for them to go through.

Was it really possible that someone had sent those rocks hurtling down on Jack's head? And even if it were true, the connection to Clarence and Lucy seemed slim. More like nonexistent. But Theresa's necklace seemed even more unlikely to be connected to anything, yet something was going on. The tentacles of all this seemed entwined, but it was going to take some time and investigation to untangle them.

His cell phone rang on the table beside him, and he grabbed it before it woke Alex. He lifted his brows at the name on the screen. Why would Lewis be calling this late?

"Hey, Lewis, everything okay?"

"Fine, jus' fine." Duval's words were slurred.

Great. He'd been drinking. "Glad to hear it. What can I do for you?"

"She called me today."

"Who called?"

"Dorothy. Said you came to see her. That true?"

"Yes, it's true."

"Why you pokin' your nose into my business?"

"Lewis, I had no idea you and Dorothy had a relationship. I was trying to find out what happened to your other kids." Should he reveal that Dorothy told him Lewis had left them in the state's care?

Zach gripped the phone and shook his head. No sense in talking to Lewis when he was this drunk.

"Tol' you what happened to the kids. They're dead. Pokin' around like this won't get anyone nowhere."

"It might help Shauna find closure."

"That girl needs to move on with her life and quit yearnin' for what's dead and gone." His voice hardened. "I'm warning you to quit pokin' around in my life or you're gonna find yourself facing a shotgun —"

His voice cut off, and Zach glanced at the screen. Lewis had hung up on him after that warning. Why was he so upset about Zach investigating Shauna's siblings? It's not like he was afraid of losing Shauna's attention. The two barely spoke because Lewis found a bottle much more engaging than his family.

He heard a sound and looked up to see Shauna standing in the hall. She'd put on a long red gown and her hair hung around her shoulders.

She laid her hand on her throat. "My dad had a relationship with Dorothy?"

Shauna felt as though every bit of her body was vibrating. She wet her lips. "That was my dad, wasn't it? What's going on?" Not daring to even breathe in case it drowned out his answer, she locked gazes with Zach.

He sighed and patted the seat beside him. "Sit down, and I'll tell you all about it. I was going to talk to you tonight, but the news about Jack pushed it aside."

Her knees didn't want to seem to support her as she moved on bare feet to the sofa and sank beside him. "Tell me. You found Brenna? Where's Connor? Do you know?" Apollo moved over to lay his head on her foot, and she reached down to rub his head.

He held up his hand. "Whoa, Flygirl, it's not what you think."

She hadn't heard Zach use that old nickname in ages. "Then what's going on?"

He took her hand. "Your dad had an affair with Dorothy. You were right about Penelope being angry. Dorothy went into a depression when they broke up, and Penelope hated your dad for the neglect that followed."

She clung to the solid comfort of his hand. Affair? Her father was a horrible man. She'd always known it, but this confirmed it. He'd been married with kids and had another baby on the way, yet had been a total jerk. "Did Mom know?"

"Dorothy says she found out just before she died."

"Poor Mom. She probably wasn't sure what to do. All she knew was staying home and raising us. She didn't work outside the home, so she probably thought she was stuck. She had no parents of her own to turn to, no family."

His expression alarmed her. His deep-blue eyes held a mixture of pity and fear. Was he afraid she was going to cause a scene with Dorothy?

Shauna laughed, a sound that shocked her with its bitterness. "Some dad I had."

"That's what I told Dorothy when I saw her today. I'm sure she already knew he wasn't much of a father." He stared intently at her. "Especially not after what he did about your siblings."

"What do you mean? You found out something about my siblings?"

He nodded, and his fingers tightened around hers. "Now, keep in mind this is coming from Dorothy. She might have an ax to grind, or she might be mistaken. She says he left them in state care and didn't try to find them. Several children were left unclaimed, and the state assumed their parents died in the quake. Dorothy thinks they were adopted out."

A great pressure built in her chest until she couldn't breathe, couldn't think. She tried to wrap her head around the words, but they made no sense. Her dad wouldn't just walk away from his own children, would he? No one could be that terrible, not even a drunk and an adulterer.

Alive. Her Connor and Brenna are alive.

Tears rushed to her eyes, and she tried to leap to her feet, but Zach held her in place. He gripped both hands and half turned her to face him full on. "Shauna, don't jump to conclusions. We don't know for sure. It might not be true."

"But it gives us a place to look."

"It does. We can check with the county and see if there are pictures of the unclaimed children. Maybe they will release the whereabouts of the kids who were adopted and who went into the foster care system. But even then, it isn't going to be easy to find them."

Nothing could dampen the overwhelming joy bursting out of her chest. Her siblings were out there somewhere, waiting for her to find them. Or maybe they weren't. Maybe they didn't even remember her. Connor had been two, so he might have some dim memories, but Brenna had been just a newborn. She might not even know she had siblings somewhere in the world.

Shauna brushed the tears from her lashes. "I don't know what to do first."

"First we have to tell the sheriff about Jack's video. We need to bring justice to Clarence and Lucy. Finding your siblings can wait until you and Alex are safe. First things first."

She wanted to argue with him, but he was right. Her number one priority had to be keeping Alex safe, but everything in her wanted to travel wherever she had to in order to find the rest of her family. The

thought they might be alive changed everything.

"What about Darla's death? Maybe we
can start there."

She nodded and reached for her phone. "I
know it's late, but I've been wanting to talk
to Darla's best friend, Alyssa." The number
was on her contact list because she'd looked
it up several days ago.

The call was answered almost immediately. "Hello?"

"Alyssa? This is Shauna McDade. I hope
I didn't wake you."

"No, I was up watching a movie. What's
up?" She had been instrumental in getting
Darla off drugs and had been devastated by
her death.

"I have something to tell you that might
shock you, and I'd like you to keep it to
yourself."

"Of course."

"Darla's death was not accidental."

"What do you mean?"

"The sheriff hasn't let the media know,
but he's investigating her death as a homicide."

Alyssa gasped. "I *knew* she hadn't gone
back to heroin!" A long pause followed.
"She'd been acting odd for weeks and had
mentioned finding some strange things at

one of her jobs."

"Jobs?"

"She was working through a temp service and didn't say which job it was. Or what the things were, for that matter. I know she talked to Jack about it all. I urged her to tell me too, but she didn't want to get me involved."

Shauna's fingers tightened on her phone. "We recently found some evidence about Jack's death. It might not have been an accident."

"Wow." Alyssa's voice went soft. "Maybe I should be glad she didn't tell me."

"I think so too. Listen, if you think of anything that might help us get to the bottom of this, would you let me know?"

"Yes, for sure. I'll think about it. Thanks for telling me. I felt like I'd failed her, you know?"

"It wasn't your fault, Alyssa. Get some rest. Talk to you soon." Shauna ended the call and told Zach what she'd said. "She said Darla was talking to Jack."

"Wow, that ties the two of them together. We might be on to something."

She nodded. "We need to tell the sheriff."

CHAPTER 24

Zach wrapped his fingers around the mug of hot coffee Felicia had handed him and looked around the sheriff's living room. Shauna had gone off to the kitchen with Felicia for some kind of confab while they waited for Burchell to finish his shower. The sheriff was normally in the office by eight, but when Zach called the office this morning, he'd been told the sheriff had taken a vacation day.

The coffee was strong and hot, and he took another sip, then heard footsteps on the stairs. The house shook a bit, and he jumped to his feet. Another mild earthquake.

Sheriff Burchell, his hair still damp and wearing a T-shirt and jeans, came toward him with a frown wrinkling his brow. "Felicity said some kind of earthshaking news had come in. What's going on? Hold on a second while I grab some coffee."

Zach pointed to the mug beside an obviously new leather recliner. "Felicia already brought some."

The sheriff smiled. "She's a great wife." He scooped up the mug, then settled on the chair. "So what's up?"

"It's about that phone of Jack's."

Burchell shrugged. "Not much to go on with those text messages. Yes, the one could have been a threat, but it's pretty oblique. I ran down the number, and it's a burner phone with no way to trace it."

"It's not the text messages that are the problem." Zach pulled Jack's phone from his pocket and started the video, then handed the device to the sheriff. No matter how many times he listened to it, the impact was like an unexpected gut punch.

Burchell watched it in silence, but his brows rose as he listened through to the end. He stilled, then shook his head. "Do you still believe his death was an accident after hearing this? You were there. Did you see anything that might make you doubt it was a simple fall?"

"I'm starting to wonder. I never did understand where that slide of rock and ice came from. There were no other climbers, so it was out of the blue. So yeah, in light of this warning from Jack, I'm not sure what happened that day." Zach launched into the sequence of events as he remembered them.

The sheriff sipped his coffee, then stared down at the phone with a thoughtful expression. "Any idea what the whole Jupiter reference is about?"

"The only thing I could come up with is the Jupiter Hammerheads. Jack and I know a pitcher with them, but that's a stretch. I called him this morning and left a message. He was here a few weeks before Jack died. The two of them had coffee, but Jack never mentioned what it was all about. I'm hoping Harry can provide some answers."

The sheriff pulled out a small notepad and pen. "What's his last name?"

"Harry Richards."

Burchell nodded and jotted it down. "I'll see what I can find out. Did you ask Marilyn if she knew this Richards guy?"

"Marilyn isn't inclined to tell me much. Maybe you'll have better luck."

Burchell nodded again as his wife and Shauna joined them. Shauna carried a plate of cinnamon rolls, and Felicia set a coffeepot on the table in front of Zach.

Zach reached for a cinnamon roll. It was still warm and smelled amazing. "You just whip these up this morning?"

Shauna took a roll and sat beside him.

"Felicia had them ready to put in the oven. It's the anniversary of when she and Everett met."

Zach couldn't watch her like he wanted to with her beside him instead of in front of him. He had been unable to keep his eyes off her ever since they got up this morning. Sleep had been elusive last night, and he knew she'd been restless too because he heard her in the kitchen around three. It had been by sheer will alone that he hadn't gone in to talk to her then.

It was best they weren't alone together. She was entirely too tempting with her green eyes flashing and those all-too-kissable lips. Not that he'd ever tasted them, but he'd dreamed about it plenty these past few days.

I'm in big trouble.

He forced his attention back to the sheriff, who was talking about possible Jupiter connections. "Yes, we talked about all those. Nothing really seems to fit. If only he'd given us more information before he ended the video."

The sheriff consulted the phone again. "This was recorded two days before he died."

Shauna nibbled on her cinnamon roll and nodded. "Which is why we're here. What if his death is connected to the deaths of Clarence and Lucy? And to the break-in at my house? This thing could go back a whole year."

"That's a stretch, Shauna," the sheriff warned. "If that's true, why did the killer wait a year to kill them and target you?"

Zach leaned forward and jabbed his finger at the phone. "Listen to it again, Everett. The coroner ruled Jack's death accidental, so what if the killer thought with Jack dead, he was safe, but then Clarence found out something? And whatever he found out flushed the guy out."

The sheriff's lips turned in a skeptical twist. "Lucy too? They were separated. I don't think they are connected." He started the video again and let it play through. "But I do think it's possible someone rolled those rocks down on Jack deliberately. I'll poke around into the few months leading up to his death and see if anything turns up. I don't have enough personnel to be handling all these separate investigations, so it's likely going to take some time. The state is asking lots of questions, which is taking up manpower too. My first priority is to follow the trails around Clarence and Lucy first. Their deaths are the freshest, and I have the best chance of solving them."

Zach wanted to throw his roll against the wall. "Everett, if they're all tied together and you have separate teams investigating them, clues are bound to be missed. Connections won't be made like they should be. Can't you give your detectives all the information and see where it leads them?"

Shauna set down her coffee. "Please, Sheriff. What could it hurt? There's something else too." She told him about talking to Alyssa. "So that ties them together."

Burchell stared at them for a long moment, then shrugged. "Okay, I'll make sure my lead detective has all the details, but I think you're looking in the wrong direction."

The spicy aroma of seafood curry in Marilyn's kitchen made Shauna's mouth water. After talking to the sheriff, she'd gone directly to fly a client to Vancouver, and lunch hadn't been on her agenda today. It was already nearly four, and her empty stomach clenched painfully. She sat at the breakfast bar, then listened to the distant sound of Alex's game from his bedroom.

She needed to talk to Marilyn before Alex finished his video game, so food would have to wait a while. Marilyn stirred the big pot of curry with a wary expression. Things hadn't been the same between them since

Shauna had moved in with Zach, and the video on Jack's phone wasn't likely to change things for the better. Her mother-in-law didn't react well to stress.

"Marilyn, I need to show you something."

Marilyn tucked a strand of auburn hair behind her ear. "What's wrong now?"

"It's about Jack. I found his phone." Shauna pulled her phone from her jacket pocket. "The sheriff kept Jack's phone, but Zach copied everything first. There's a video from Jack I think you need to see."

It would do no good to try to explain it first. Jack's mother had formed her opinion of what had happened long ago, and only hearing from Jack himself would make her listen to any other explanation of his death. "You'd better sit down."

Marilyn came around the side of the counter and held out her hand. "You sound very ominous."

Shauna pulled up the video and started it, then handed her phone to Marilyn without another word. Marilyn's hazel eyes filled with tears as the sound of Jack's voice echoed in the kitchen. Her mouth dropped open as she watched the video. She started the video again and let it run through a second time before she spoke.

The color had leached from her face, but

she couldn't seem to tear her gaze away from the frozen image on the screen. "He expected to be killed. This is proof that Zach killed him. You need to show the sheriff."

She must not have listened well. "That's not what he's saying at all. He told me to turn to Zach for help. If he feared Zach, he wouldn't have done that. Someone was coming for him, but it wasn't his best friend. His death wasn't an accident. I talked to Zach last night about the day Jack died. The rock-and-ice slide happened out of nowhere. I think someone deliberately started it to kill Jack. I have to find out who did it. I think Jack's killer is after me now. I think he killed Clarence and Lucy. Darla too."

Marilyn said nothing as she started the video and watched it to the end a third time. She finally put the phone on the counter. "Everyone loved Jack. Who would want to kill him? And what makes you think his death is tied in with the other deaths?"

Shauna couldn't explain her conviction, even to herself. "Jack is dead. So are Darla, Clarence, and Lucy. I found out that Darla discovered something upsetting and went to Jack about it. What if they uncovered something illegal and were killed to keep it quiet? Maybe Clarence found evidence after Darla died. It all fits."

Marilyn pressed her lips together and went back to stir the curry. "Town scuttlebutt says Clarence was involved with something illegal that got him and Lucy killed. People think he was trafficking drugs. Why else would Lucy move to that neighborhood?"

Hunger forgotten, Shauna leaped to her feet with her fists clenched. "Clarence and Lucy were fine people, good Christians with impeccable integrity, and you know it. I don't care what rumors are flying around. I knew them better than anyone, and they both hated drugs, especially after Darla's death."

Could Jack have found out evidence involving drug trafficking, though? He might have told Clarence about it. "Can you think of anything in the couple of weeks before Jack died that made you wonder if he was worried about something?"

Marilyn's brow creased as she stared off into space, then shook her head. "He'd been busy with the annual audit so I didn't see him much for several weeks. He seemed quiet, but he usually was during tax time."

Remembering the same thing, Shauna nodded. "He didn't get home until after nine the week he died." Jack had owned an accounting business and often conducted audits for companies as well as prepared individual taxes. "What if he found evidence of wrongdoing during an audit?"

Marilyn scooped up rice into a bowl and added several ladles of curry to it, then handed the steaming food to Shauna. "That doesn't seem like enough to get him murdered."

"Unless the person was afraid he'd turn him in to the police. Staying out of jail is quite a motivation." The oven dinged as the timer went off for the bread. "Do you remember Harry Richards?"

"Jack's friend who plays for the Jupiters?"

"Yes, that's the one. He had lunch with Jack, and we wondered if he's the Jupiter connection Jack mentioned. Did he tell you about their lunch?"

"Just that he saw Harry and he was doing well. Jack didn't mention anything they talked about."

A dead end. Shauna spooned up some curry and closed her eyes when the spices hit her tongue. "This is so good."

"I haven't made it since Jack died."

"I know." His mother's curry had been his favorite dish, and Shauna had never been able to duplicate it. "I have his computer in storage, and his filing cabinet is in the garage. I could go back and see what he was working on the month before he died."

"Isn't the sheriff inquiring? You don't need to be inserting yourself into the investigation when someone is already targeting you. If you back away, things should settle down and you can go home."

"I don't think the sheriff is looking into Jack's death just yet. And I think his death is the start of all of this. I can't rest until I know." Shauna slid off the stool and went to call Alex for supper.

If she had to dig out the truth by herself, that's what she'd do.

CHAPTER 25

The roar of plane engines was over for the day as Zach locked the door behind his crew and went to his truck. The stench of airplane fuel hung in the air under a clear sky. It was a little after three. Now might be a good time to reach Harry Richards. He pulled out his phone and found the number he'd entered from Jack's phone. When he was dumped to voice mail, he left a message asking Harry to call him.

He'd barely slipped his phone back into his pocket when Harry returned the call. "Sorry, Zach, I didn't recognize the number. I haven't heard from you in ages. How are you doing?"

"I need to talk to you about Jack, Harry." Zach launched into the events of the past year. "What did you and Jack talk about over lunch? Did he seem worried or anything to you?"

Harry went silent, and the sound of a

distant ball field came through the phone. "He seemed a little quiet and wasn't his usual self. I asked him once if everything was okay. He hesitated, and I thought for a second that he might tell me what was wrong, but then I got a phone call. By the time I got off, he had to go. Do you really think he was murdered?"

"Yeah, I do." As the words rolled off his tongue, Zach felt the weight of his guilt roll off. He hadn't killed his best friend. It was going to take some time to fully process that revelation. Someone out there had looked down on Jack clinging to the rock face, then had deliberately rolled boulders down on him.

"I hope this doesn't sound offensive, but you and Jack weren't exactly good friends. Why did you have lunch in the first place?"

Harry went silent a moment. "Well, it's a little embarrassing to admit. I was seeing Darla Glennon, and I wanted to ask him about her. He'd been friends with the family for a long time. She'd been acting kind of weird, distracted and nervous. I thought maybe she was seeing someone else. I only got to see her a couple of times a month because of the distance, so it seemed logical."

"What did Jack say?"

"He said Darla had some trouble, and he was trying to help her. According to him, she really cared about me, and this issue would be over soon because he had a handle on it and was going to take care of it."

Zach's grip on the phone tightened. "He had a handle on it?"

"That's what he said. Of course, it doesn't matter now. Once she died from that drug overdose, I figured out what he meant. He'd probably convinced her to go to rehab again, but she didn't go soon enough."

Zach wished he could tell Harry the truth, but he bit back the words. "I'm sorry, Harry."

"Thanks, but life happens. I've moved on."

So Darla had gone to Jack for help, just as Alyssa said. He clenched his hands into fists. "I'm going to find out who did this and why. Does the word *Jupiter* mean anything to you? Other than your team's name?"

"Jupiter. Well, the only other thing that comes to mind is the planet, but you probably already thought of that."

"Yeah, we did. Nothing else?"

"Let me think a second." Harry fell silent, then cleared his throat. "There's the Mount Jupiter Quadrangle out in the Olympic Forest."

Zach frowned. "I don't think I've ever

heard that term."

"I worked for the forestry department in the summers during college. We divided the forest into quadrangles, and I worked out of the Quilcene Ranger District. Most people wouldn't know much about the quadrangles."

"Do you think Jack did?"

"Sure. He worked there one summer. He knew the lingo."

Zach had forgotten. "It's worth looking at. Where is that quadrangle?"

"I'll send you a map. What's your e-mail?"

Zach rattled off his e-mail address. He had to be careful not to get too excited. A forest quadrangle was hardly likely to give them any clues. The forest quickly reclaimed what man disturbed, and Jack had been dead a year. "Thanks, Harry. I'll check it out."

"I just e-mailed the map. Let me know if there's anything else I can do." Cheering in the background intensified. "I have to go. My break is over."

Zach clicked over to his e-mail. He opened the attached file from Harry, then enlarged it until he found the Mount Jupiter Quadrangle. Some of the peaks were familiar, but he'd never hiked or climbed in that area on the western slopes of the Olympic Mountains. There didn't seem to be any landing strips, but Shauna could fit her chopper into some of the clearings.

The quadrangle was big, though, and it would be like looking for one particular blade of grass in a ten-acre yard. But they had to try. He put his phone down and started the truck. There was satisfaction in having something to investigate. He'd felt blocked at every turn, but this might lead to something.

The two men from China met him in the small building hidden in the woods. The older one, a portly gentleman in his fifties, spoke impeccable English. "We'd like a demonstration that this device really can trigger an earthquake. This will show us if it can work on any other sites."

He wanted to roll his eyes. Hadn't he already given them decades' worth of proof? "I don't want to tip off the authorities to what's going on here."

"We cannot buy this information without a demonstration."

He suppressed a sigh. "Very well, but it will be on the small side. This is my home too, and I have friends and family here."

The Chinese guy shrugged bulky shoulders clad in a black Armani suit. "The size does not matter to us, just the proof we are not spending five hundred million dollars unwisely."

The guy had a point. He was about to fork over a fortune big enough for a comfortable life. "Okay, let me show you how this works."

An hour later, he exited the locked room and smiled at them. "The earthquake should start within the next few hours."

"That's as precise as you can be?" Armani Man's frown deepened.

"Think you can do better? Be my guest. No one else knows how to do this." Which was only a small lie. The only other person who understood how to work the machine wasn't talking, and he didn't think Duval was likely to spill his guts to anyone.

Armani Man's brow smoothed, and he waved a hand sporting a diamond ring worth enough to buy a beach estate. "You are correct. You're the only game in town. We shall go back to our hotel and await the quake. If it begins on schedule, we have a deal."

The two men exited the building, and he watched them slide into the backseat of a black limo. The chauffeur was Chinese too, probably brought over with them on their private jet. The group he was dealing with was a paranoid bunch, but that was probably necessary in this line of work. As soon as the trail of dust settled behind the big car, he went back inside and reviewed the procedure he'd just executed. Every step had been perfect.

He checked his watch and smiled. Within the next hour, they should have all the proof they needed. His phone vibrated, and he dug it out of his pocket, pausing a moment to enjoy the way her beautiful face filled the screen.

"It's done," he said before she could ask. "They wanted proof, so I triggered a small earthquake."

"They agreed to the half billion dollars?"

"They did."

She gave a whoop and his grin widened. "Get some new bikinis, baby."

"I never dreamed blackmailing the old man would be this lucrative. I've got some property all picked out to buy. I'll show you when I see you."

"Sounds good. Love you."

"Love you too."

He ended the call and pocketed his phone. Life was about to get really interesting.

CHAPTER 26

The Yellow Submarine had been a town favorite since Shauna was a kid. The small café's signature meal was grilled clam toasts with lemon and green olives served with a side of Italian roasted potatoes. Shauna caught Felicia's dubious glance at the dishes in front of them and smiled. "You'll be addicted with one bite. It's better than it looks."

Felicia, dressed in jeans and a blue T-shirt, seemed unaware that she had the attention of every male in the café. Most of the women were looking her way too, but their faces lacked the appreciation in the male glances.

She picked up a wedge of toast and took a bite. "Delicious! Thanks for bringing me. I came once by myself but didn't know what to order. The woman who waited on me just seemed to want me to leave and didn't have any suggestions."

"I'll introduce you to some people when we're done." Shauna straightened when she recognized a wide set of shoulders outside the display windows. "There's Zach."

She started to wave, but he walked on past the door and crossed the street to intercept his copilot, Valerie. The blonde looked stunning this morning with her hair in a messy bun. Had there ever been anything between the two of them?

She forced her attention back to Felicia, who was looking at her with a knowing glance. "What?"

Felicia's smile widened. "You're in love with him."

"Of course not. He's just been a friend forever."

"Girlfriend, I recognize that lovesick expression so you might as well quit covering it. He's nuts about you too, so you don't have to be afraid."

Heat washed up Shauna's face. "You're mistaken on both counts."

Amusement lit Felicia's dark eyes. "I'm never wrong about these things. I realize you're in the middle of trying to figure out a murder, but I'd be using this time at his house to see where your relationship might go."

"We have no relationship! I mean, not that

kind." Her tongue tripped over itself, and she reached for a piece of toast to cover her confusion.

"What's the problem, anyway? He loves you and you love him. Is it your son?"

"No, Alex loves Zach and Zach loves him." Shauna wanted to plant her face in her hands. "Zach was my husband's best friend. It would be disloyal to Jack."

Felicia nibbled at a triangle of toast. "So your husband was a jerk who would want you to be unhappy the rest of your life?"

"Jack was a wonderful man! He only wanted the best for us."

"Then why would you think loving Zach would be disloyal? If Jack was so wonderful, he'd want you with a man he loved and trusted, wouldn't he? I heard that video too. He told you to turn to Zach if he died. So why are you running away?"

She's right. Shauna sat back in her chair and exhaled.

Felicia took another bite. "I wouldn't have pegged you for a coward either, but you're sure acting like one. Hiding away in your house, afraid to move on and be happy again. What kind of life is that for you or for Alex? You're only in your early thirties. Do you plan to spend the next fifty years alone? Alex will grow up and move out before you can blink."

Good grief, the woman was blunt. Shauna wiped her fingers on her napkin. "You're practically a kid yourself. How do you know so much about life?"

Felicia's smile was sad. "I've had to become a student of men and what makes them tick since I was fourteen. I was on my own by sixteen and swimming with the sharks of the world. When I met Everett, I knew I would be safe. He saw me for who I am and not for just what I looked like. Zach looks at you that way too."

"Zach and I share a common history built around love for Jack. I'm not sure how to even get past having Jack at the center of everything." Shauna heard the tremble in her voice and swallowed it down. "I mean, I'm not sure how to do it. He's part of who I am."

"Moving on doesn't mean forgetting Jack. He'll always be part of you. Our experiences, good and bad, shape us and form us. That's all part of our growth. I wouldn't be who I am without having spent some time in a foster home or without those nights crying alone in my hotel room. My foster parents were great, by the way. The nights in the hotel room weren't."

Maybe she wouldn't be giving up Jack if

she moved on with her life. She'd gotten a little caught up in what people would think, which was silly when she stopped to think about it.

Felicia devoured another wedge of clam toast. "You were right — this stuff is pretty good," she mumbled with a full mouth. "So what's it going to take for you to move on? I can see you're still hesitant."

Shauna's attention went out to where Zach still stood talking to Valerie. "Maybe once the murders are solved, I can think about it."

"What if they're never solved? Life doesn't always fit into our neat boxes."

"I have to find justice for Jack. Lucy, Clarence, and Darla too."

"Have the courage to admit you want justice for you, not for them. Justice this side of heaven is a myth. It's not our job anyway. Real justice belongs to God."

Shauna held up her hands. "Okay, okay, I give."

Zach turned and headed back toward the restaurant. Her cheeks went hot when he yanked open the door and stepped inside. Felicia was right. Shauna loved him, and she couldn't deny it. The smile that lifted his lips when he saw her made her pulse leap.

When the trembling started, she thought at first it was because the revelation was so earth-shattering. Then glass began to break around her, and someone screamed out, "Earthquake!"

It was only after she was crouching under the table with her hands over her head that she realized the screaming was coming from her.

The earthquake threw Zach down, and every time he tried to get up, he hit the floor again. When the earth steadied, dust and debris littered the space. The café's ceiling was mostly gone. He scrambled up and headed the direction where he'd last seen Shauna.

Screams and cries blasted him from everywhere, but he had to reach Shauna. He climbed over the debris to where she crouched with Felicia under a table. Shauna's eyes were clamped shut, and she rocked back and forth as she continued to cry out. She didn't appear injured. At least, there was no blood.

Broken glass bit into his knees as he got close enough to pull her into his arms. "It's okay, Flygirl. You're safe. It was a small one." He guessed the earthquake had been under seven but more than five since it had caused the ceiling to fall and glass to break. "I've got you. Look at me."

She cracked open one eye, and the wailing stopped. "Cowboy?" Her voice trembled.

The old nickname meant more to him than he'd ever let on. He pulled her close. "It's over. There might be an aftershock, but we're okay."

Both green eyes popped open. "Alex!"

"He's at school, and it's a concrete building. I'm sure he's fine. I'll call now and check." He pulled out his phone but got an out-of-service message. "The cell tower must be down. We're only four blocks away. We can go right over and check on him." He moved out from under the table and held her hand to help her up. "Careful of the glass."

People were crying around them as they picked themselves up from the floor, but he didn't see anything more than a few cuts and scratches.

Felicia looked a little dazed too. She had a cut on her hand oozing a little blood. "Wow, that was intense. I'd better go find Everett and see if he needs any help." She stood and brushed debris from her jeans. "You okay, Shauna?"

Shauna's face was as pale as the fallen

plaster. "I'm terrified of earthquakes, but I'll be okay. I have to make sure Alex isn't hurt. I'll call you later." She clung to Zach's hand and pulled him toward the door.

He went willingly, but turned her away from her truck. "The traffic is already bad, and the lights are out. It will be faster if we walk."

She nodded and took off to the north at a run. Praying for the safety of the children as he ran, he jogged beside her as they jogged around debris on the sidewalk. It was only a few minutes before he saw the school. "Looks intact." He pointed. "Look, the kids are all outside in the soccer field."

"There's Alex!" She waved and called her son's name.

Alex turned and ran to meet them. "Mommy, did you feel the earthquake? It was so cool!" He leaped into her arms.

She hugged him to her, and her gaze locked with Zach's over Alex's shoulder. The naked fear on her face made him step forward and encircle them both with his arms.

"We're all okay. Let's make sure everyone is all right, and we'll go home and check on things."

She nodded and stepped back, then took Alex's hand. "Was anyone hurt at school?"

"No, we were outside for recess. The teachers wouldn't let us go back inside." He sounded disappointed. "I wanted to see if any ceilings came down." He stared up at his mother. "You've got white stuff in your hair."

She brushed at her long, dark hair. "The ceiling came down at The Yellow Submarine."

Alex frowned. "Did you get hurt?"

"No, no, I'm fine."

She waved to the teacher and mouthed that she was taking her son. The teacher nodded.

Zach wanted to see if he was needed in town, and Alex was never going to keep up. Zach stopped and held out his arms. "How about a piggyback ride?"

"Yay!"

Zach lifted him and set the boy on his shoulders. "Hang on to my hair, kiddo. We need to move along."

Alex's small fingers were quickly entangled in his hair, and Zach set off at a faster pace.

Shauna jogged alongside them. A bit of color was coming back to her face. After what she'd gone through as a kid, he didn't blame her for that meltdown. Her concern for Alex had quickly gripped her enough to push away her fear. As they neared the town center, he saw Felicia tending to small cuts in a triage line with a couple of nurses. Everett and his deputies scurried from building to building making sure everyone was out and accounted for.

Zach lifted Alex from his shoulders. "Stay here with your mom a minute."

Everett saw him coming. "Shauna doing okay?"

"Yeah, she's fine. The kids at the school were all out for recess so no injuries there. The school looked in good shape."

"Good, good." Everett looked past Zach's shoulder. "No fires as far as I can see. You might be on the lookout as you take them home. I'm telling everyone to go to their homes and check for gas and water leaks. I think we're okay, though. It could have been worse."

"I thought for a minute the big one they've been talking about might have started."

"Yeah, well, today is not that day, thank the good Lord." Everett clapped him on the shoulder and turned away.

Zach rejoined Alex and Shauna. "The sheriff wants everyone to go home and check for damage. Let's take your truck. Mine is blocked in by emergency vehicles."

She nodded and fished her keys from her pocket. "I'll let you drive."

He opened the back door and she climbed in the back with Alex. She wasn't going to let him be far from her. It took half an hour to navigate through vehicles parked in the streets, and he found his gaze straying to her in the backseat as she kept up a happy chatter with Alex. The smile didn't reach her eyes, though, and Zach knew the trauma of the day would hit her hard after Alex settled in for the night.

Zach planned to be there for her, no matter what she needed.

CHAPTER 27

With the dogs on the floor beside her, Shauna sat on the back deck in red pajamas with her legs curled under her. Stars spread across the sky in a twinkling canopy that reassured her all was right with the world. If God kept the stars spinning, he could keep this round ball spinning in space no matter how much the earth shook.

Every nerve ending Shauna possessed vibrated with stress. Even the hot apple cider Zach brought her failed to settle the jitters.

Zach shut the back door behind him and came out with some huckleberry tarts she'd made the day before. He grabbed a throw from the back of the chair and tossed it over her. "You might stop shaking if we get you warm enough. If you'd come inside, I'll start a fire. I got Jack's files and his computer. We can take a look at them."

She caught the scent of cinnamon in his

hair as he moved past her. "I wanted to be outside to see the stars." Admitting she was afraid felt like weakness. "I'll come inside in a minute."

He settled into the chair beside her and stretched out his legs with a contented sigh. "I checked on Alex to see if he wanted to come out with us, but he was asleep."

With us. The phrase sounded so comforting and homey. Would there be an *us* when this was all over? Shauna could admit to herself that she hoped so.

"Thanks for checking. I looked in on him before I came out too." She took a sip of her cider to avoid looking at him. With the way she was feeling right now, she knew her emotions would be all over her face.

She rubbed her forehead. "It's all such a jumble. Maybe I'm wrong and the murders are not related. Marilyn thinks I'm not thinking clearly about it. Do you think I'm wrong?"

"No. I think it's all connected somehow. I was remembering something that might be important. I saw Darla talking to Jack outside the coffee shop the day before she died. She looked upset, and he was trying to calm her. At the time I didn't think much about it and assumed she had man trouble and was pouring her heart out to him. Jack had a sympathetic way about him. You always felt your secrets were safe with him. And I talked to Harry. He said Jack mentioned Darla had come to him with a problem, and he was trying to help."

"So others saw it too, not just Alyssa." His compassion was one of the things she missed most about her husband. "He always thought of Darla as a little sister." She watched a small plane, its lights blinking, move overhead among the stars. "What if he told her about the danger he was in?" But if so, why hadn't he told his own wife?

Zach craned his neck to look at the airplane too. "Or she came to him with the danger she was in. That might be why she died first, then the murderer went after Jack, knowing he knew too much."

She tried to think through the possibilities, but there were so many directions to go that she felt like someone in a rudderless boat bobbing in the waves with no idea how to get to shore. "Did Harry have any idea about the Jupiter reference?"

He told her about the rest of the call, and her pulse sped up at the mention of the Mount Jupiter Quadrangle. "Maybe that's what Jack meant!"

"But what could Jack mean when he said things aren't what they seem at Jupiter? At first I was excited to have a lead, but the more I thought about it, the more I wondered how a wilderness area could be what he was talking about."

"We have to at least take a look."

Zach exhaled and raked his hand through his hair. "But where? I've got a map, and the area is big. We don't even know what we're looking for."

Her initial rush of enthusiasm collapsed in a rush of disappointment. "Maybe you're right, but can't we at least fly out there and see if anything looks out of place?"

"Sure. I found some clearings where you can probably land your chopper. Want to go tomorrow?"

"I have a charter that will be done by one. We can go after that if you're free."

"Sounds good."

His intent gaze didn't leave her face. What was he thinking? "Have you heard if anyone was hurt in the earthquake?"

"A few minor cuts and scratches were reported, but nothing major."

"We all know a tsunami is possible after an earthquake. That's why the school was built of concrete in the first place. What if a big wave had swept up and caught them off guard?"

He took her hand and squeezed it. "But it

didn't. This one wasn't the big one we're expecting."

"How could they know that, though?" The thought of a massive wave sweeping away her child, her life, made tears pool in her eyes.

"You can't let fear rule your life, Flygirl."

"When you've suffered one traumatic loss, you keep waiting for the other shoe to drop. It's hard not to be watching for it."

"None of us knows what the future brings. We only know we are safe in the Lord's arms. This life isn't the end, though it often feels like it. You know Jack is more alive now than he's ever been. And when any of us pass on, we will be experiencing more life than we can even imagine now."

Her head knew he was right, but her heart quailed at ever experiencing more loss. It was just too hard.

She realized her hand was still in his, and he was tracing circles on her palm with his thumb. The tingle shooting up her arm surprised her, but she couldn't bring herself to pull her hand away.

All she would have to do was lean over and press her lips against his. She saw the longing in his eyes and knew he was thinking the same thing. Pressure to do just that built in her chest until she knew she'd either have to kiss him or flee from the temptation.

She bolted to her feet. "I'd better get to bed. Good night, Cowboy."

He didn't call after her, but for a fleeting moment she wished he would. The nickname had started when Jack first introduced them. He was a bit of a hotdogger when flying, and she'd dubbed him with the name when he landed after a particularly hair-raising flight.

The stars were bright overhead as he got into the long limo the Chinese men had sent for him and settled back on the plush leather seats. In just a few days he'd have more money than he'd ever imagined. Dreams of a different life had floated through his head all afternoon since the earthquake hit.

Vindication. Even he had doubted this would come about, but it was especially sweet when he knew he'd have her by his side the rest of his life.

It was all in his grasp.

The limo stopped at a lookout over Rainshadow Bay. Another limo, a white one, idled by the guardrail. He couldn't see through the dark windows, but he knew his buyers were ready and willing to cough up the money. The driver got out and opened the door for him. The back door of the white limo opened, and the older Chinese guy beckoned for him to join them.

He stepped across the gravel and slid into the seat facing the two men. The limo smelled of new leather and expensive male cologne. "What did you think of my little show?"

The older man sipped a finger of whiskey. "Impressive. When can you deliver the deed and the drawings?"

"I want half the money wired to my bank in Switzerland. Once I have that, I'll meet you with the deed, the drawing, and the keys. You'll wire the rest of it while I wait, and as soon as I verify the transfer, you'll have it all."

The younger man, slim and sleek as a snake, leaned forward with a menacing twist to his lips. "You sound as though you do not trust us. We do not do business that way."

"Then I'll sell it to the Russians. They're willing to do it my way." He stared him down until the man blinked and leaned back against the seat with a shrug to his associate.

The older man stared at him, then nodded. "Very well. But we know how to deal with someone who double-crosses us. There is nowhere you can hide to escape us, and I will personally make sure your death is not an easy one."

He kept his smile pinned in place and gave no indication of the chill running down his back. "Threats aren't necessary. I have no intention of going back on my word."

"The money will be in your account in two days."

"Two days? How about tomorrow?"

"Two days."

The man's implacable tone told him it was all about a show of power. *Fine, let the guy throw his weight around a little.* "Very well. Once I verify the money is there, I'll call you and arrange where and when to meet."

The younger man nodded to the driver, who got out and opened the rear door.

Back in his car, his smile faded. Everything hinged on getting his property back. The two men would demand the drawings of the construction before they paid the money. Where had Shauna hidden the necklace? He had to get inside Bannister's house, but everything he'd tried had failed.

Maybe it was time to snatch the kid. She'd trade everything she had for him.

Debris blocked much of the sidewalks in

town and even lay tumbled along the sides of the street. Zach managed to find a parking place in front of the sheriff's office.

Burchell stood in front of the window looking at the chaos. He turned to greet Zach. "It's a mess. We have volunteers coming at nine to begin the cleanup."

"I came in to help, but I wanted to check and see if you have an update on the murders." Would the sheriff even tell him since he didn't trust Zach?

Burchell swiped at his hair, which had too much product to move. "I found a witness who saw a man enter Lucy's apartment the night of her death. He's doing a police sketch as we speak. A top-notch forensic artist, Gwen Marcey, is in town doing training. So far, the guy doesn't match your description."

"What about Clarence's killer?"

Burchell's brows drew together. "A bunch of C-4 was stolen from a crew constructing a road through the mountains. I suspect it was used to kill Clarence, but I have no way of confirming that. The company had a camera set up, and they turned the films over to me. I have a deputy going through them, but it will be a miracle if we uncover anything. The camera snapped pictures every fifteen minutes."

Four pictures per hour wasn't great odds. "That's all you've got to follow on Clarence's murder? What about the box of stuff he sent with Shauna?"

"That's a dead end. We've checked out the Edenshaw woman, and she didn't know Clarence. We found no evidence that she's even been in the area." He beckoned for Zach to follow him to his office, then shut the door behind him and went around to the other side of his desk. "I've gone through everything in the box. The key seems to be to a safety deposit box, but it doesn't open anything here in town. The pictures don't seem important either."

Zach hadn't had a chance to look at the pictures much, but he was going to study them all tonight. And he'd made a copy of that key. Maybe he could figure out what it opened. No one knew Clarence better than Shauna. "I have a couple of things to tell you." He launched into what he'd found out from Harry Richards. "So I think Darla went to Jack about something dangerous, and he was going to help her. Whatever she knew got her killed. Then the killer went after Jack."

The sheriff's dark brows drew together as he listened. "You might be on to something, Zach. I've had no clues to Darla's murderer,

297

but this could change that."

"When did you decide I'm not really a suspect?"

Burchell's grin held no humor. "Call it intuition. I think the murders are tied together, and you wouldn't have told us your suspicions about Jack's murder if you were involved. And Jack told Shauna to turn to you for help. This is something bigger than one murder. I just don't know what yet."

The speakerphone on the sheriff's desk squawked. "Sheriff, Karl Prince is here to see you. He says it's about Clarence's murder."

The sheriff's black brows rose. "Send him in." He stood from behind his desk and stepped to the door to open it.

What information could Karl have about the murder?

CHAPTER 28

Zach hung out drinking freshly roasted coffee at The Rainshadow Brewhouse and watched for Karl to exit the sheriff's office across the street. Big drum roasters squatted in the west window, and the aroma of roasting coffee sent him to the counter for a refill. The cleanup crews were beginning to form in the streets, but he had enough time for one more cup.

The aroma of coffee mixed with the cinnamon rolls just coming out of the oven. This was his favorite hangout in town. The coffee shop had been around for ten years or so, and the brew was always strong and roasted to perfection. The building had once been a bar in the late 1800s, and it boasted wide plank floors, tin ceilings that soared to sixteen feet, and a polished wood bar top with its original mirrors behind it. The character in the place always made him feel like putting his feet up on the heavy wooden tables and watching TV.

The bell on the door tinkled, and Jermaine entered with his wife. Zach waved to them and pointed to the empty chairs at his table.

Michelle joined him, and Jermaine went to the counter to order. They'd been married five years. She made a line of organic skin-care products with lavender oil from her farm. Judging from her beautiful Asian skin, it worked well. Her glossy black hair hung in a braid over one shoulder.

Michelle pulled out a chair and settled in it. She wore a flannel shirt over slim-fitting jeans tucked into work boots. "Did you come in to help?"

"Yeah, you two also?"

She nodded. "Jermaine had been looking forward to a day off, but it was not to be."

Jermaine, dressed in work clothes and boots, handed his wife a cup. "Venti mocha with whip. That will give you the energy to get through the day." He sat in the chair beside Zach.

Zach took a sip of his coffee. "Did you suffer any damage from the quake at your house?"

"A crack in the living room ceiling was about all I found," Jermaine said.

Michelle was studying him with a knowing expression. "What's this I hear about you and Shauna?"

"What are you hearing?"

"That the two of you are getting pretty cozy." Her eyes smiled at him over the rim of her coffee cup.

"Well, we've always been friends."

"Not always," Jermaine put in. "I've heard some pretty heated words since Jack died."

Zach wanted the world to know he wasn't responsible for his best friend's death, but now wasn't the time. The sheriff had been adamant about keeping the details of the murders quiet. "She got over that. We're getting along okay."

"You've always had a thing for her," Michelle said.

His fingers curled into his palms. "What do you mean by that? She was married to my best friend. I never made a move on her. Ever."

"I didn't mean you made a pass, goof ball, but you've always watched her with a lot of admiration."

"Well, yeah, she's been my friend ever since Jack started dating her. I approved of her for Jack."

"Are you saying you're not attracted to her and never have been?"

Michelle had him there. "I'd have to be blind not to have noticed she's beautiful, kind, and a good person."

She sat back with a satisfied expression. "You didn't see me, but I was in town during the earthquake yesterday. I saw the panic on your face, and the way you focused on making sure she was safe. Looked like love to me, my friend."

His face burned, and he took a gulp of coffee. "I'm just helping out. I owe it to Jack."

Jermaine's pale-green eyes held amusement. "Tell yourself whatever you want, boss, but I'll bet you there will be a wedding ring on your finger within a year. Want to take that bet?"

Zach shifted his gaze across the street to the sheriff's office. Karl stepped out the door and headed toward the coffee shop. "Here comes Karl, and I need to talk to him." At least he wouldn't have to face the inquisition any longer.

Zach stepped out into the brisk wind and dodged a wheelbarrow full of rubble, then held up his hand toward Karl. "Hold up there a minute, buddy. Got time for a coffee?"

Karl stopped near a pile of shattered glass from a demolished car. "I have an appointment at the office in a few minutes, so I'll have to take a rain check."

"I heard you had information about Clarence's murder. I'm trying to keep Shauna and Alex safe, and I was hoping you'd share with me whatever you know."

Karl's light-brown eyes softened. "Ever the protector. I don't know much, really. I came across a box of Darla's belongings in a compartment in the trunk. I thought there might be something important in her things so I brought it to the sheriff."

Zach frowned. "In your car? I don't get it."

"I had bought her old car for my granddaughter to drive back and forth to school. The Camry was in good shape and didn't have that many miles on it. Alyssa had a flat a couple of days ago, and it was the first time she'd opened the trunk. There was a box of stuff in it. She and Darla were good friends."

"Did you look through it?"

Karl nodded, and a lock of his thick salt-and-pepper hair fell over his forehead. "There was a denim jacket and snacks." He hesitated. "There were also needles and some white powder. I thought it might be heroin or some other kind of drug. I guess it proves Darla went back to the drugs. Sad."

Would this new evidence take Darla's death out of the investigation if the powder proved to be heroin? Zach didn't know what to think.

Storm clouds built in the west behind the mountains, but the storm was far enough out that Shauna would be able to return to the airport before it hit. She sat on a log near her chopper and listened to the birds chirp in the trees surrounding the clearing. The distant voices of her clients mingled with the tinkle of running water in an unseen stream.

She couldn't get the picture of Zach last night out of her head. It only would have taken one of them leaning toward the other for them to have kissed. Her burgeoning feelings for him still felt disloyal to Jack, even though she'd told herself over and over again he would want her to move on with her life. It was one thing to know something in your head and another thing to really believe it in your heart.

Guy and his two associates stepped out of the woods, and she rose to head toward the helicopter. "Just in time. That storm looks nasty. I'd like to be back to Lavender Tides before it hits."

Guy's frown didn't lessen, but he nodded. A lock of golden-brown hair lay plastered on his damp forehead. "We're done here for now, though I'd like you to fly over the western part of the Jupiter Quadrangle."

She stopped in her tracks and turned. "What did you say? The western part of what?"

"The Jupiter Quadrangle. We're on the southeastern part of the Mount Jupiter Quadrangle. I think the runoff is coming from something in the western part."

"Jupiter Quadrangle. Funny term." Her pulse throbbed in her throat. When Zach had mentioned it last night, he wasn't sure if it was connected, but here was a prime opportunity to find out.

Guy pulled a creased and dirty map from his back pocket. "The forestry department has the area divided into quadrangles." He unfolded it and turned it toward her. "We're here." He pointed a muddy finger at their location. "I would have guessed you'd know all that."

"I don't use forestry maps to fly."

"Why the questions then? You seem pretty intense about it."

She wasn't about to explain her husband's last words about checking out Jupiter. "I hate being caught flatfooted about directions." She turned back toward her helicopter and jogged over to climb in and start the rotors. A few fat drops of rain hit the windshield, and she wasn't sure they would get back before the force of the storm hit. The low, churning clouds had moved faster than she'd anticipated.

She motioned to Guy and the other two men. "Let's head out."

They climbed into the chopper, and she lifted off as soon as she could. Winds buffeted the bird, but she kept the chopper level and veered west.

The area was heavily forested, so it was going to take a lot of hiking to see anything important. Was she even on the right track? From the air she saw nothing that didn't seem to belong, just endless treetops and rocky hillsides.

Guy pointed out a steep hillside on the very edge of the area. "The runoff might be coming from there."

The place looked familiar, then it clicked. The Baers' orchard. She'd have to mention it to Zach. Lightning flickered across the sky. "We need to get back."

Lightning continued to flash and rain wrapped the helicopter as she headed for the airport. Perspiration dampened her forehead by the time she set the chopper on the pad. She ran through the cold rain to the office and waved to her passengers as they pulled out of the parking lot in Guy's big truck.

Zach looked up when she burst into the office and shook the rain off her head. He held out a mug. "I just poured the coffee and haven't had any of this yet. You need it more than I do."

She curled her fingers around the mug and took a gulp of warming coffee. "Thanks. Hey, I learned something today." She dropped into a chair and told him about the runoff. "It's in that Jupiter Quadrangle."

Zach poured another mug of coffee from the rolling cart behind his desk, then returned. "Harry sent me a map. Let me take a look." He pulled it up on his computer. "Yeah, I see what you're saying. The hillside is right there." He stabbed a finger on the spot.

She took another sip of coffee and studied the map on his screen. "Did Jack have any forestry maps? I never asked how he knew where to go on his hikes and climbs."

"I think I have a box of his climbing stuff in one of the lockers. Let me see what's there." He set down his mug on the battered desk and went to the back storeroom.

Shauna warmed her hands on the mug and tried not to raise her hopes. Even if Jack's comments referred to the Jupiter

Quadrangle, it was a large area to explore. They still had no idea what it might mean, or even if it was the same Jupiter he referred to in his video.

Zach came back through the door with some maps in his hand. "Bingo! There's a Mount Jupiter one here, and it's got several areas circled."

She jumped up and looked over his shoulder as he smoothed out the creased map onto the desk. "Any idea why these areas would be marked?"

"They are all areas we've climbed and hiked, but there might be more to it than that. I can check them out."

"How about we land and hike them together?" She watched pleasure spread over his face. Even though the invitation had popped out of its own accord, she didn't regret it. Something was happening between them, and she wanted to see where it would lead.

CHAPTER 29

Shauna glanced out Marilyn's kitchen window into the backyard to see Alex's legs dangling from the tree house Jack had built him. He'd be occupied for a while. The aroma of oyster stew made her mouth water, and she settled on a bar stool near the stove.

Marilyn stirred the stew, then put down the spoon. "You want to stay for dinner?"

Shauna glanced at the clock above the sink. "We can't stay. Zach is barbecuing tonight, and I told him we'd be home by six."

Marilyn's lips compressed into a straight line. "I see."

At least Shauna didn't have to endure a tirade about Zach's guilt, but it was probably going to take time for Marilyn to put all her anger to bed. "I wanted to talk to you about something."

"You've heard something about Jack's death?"

Shauna shook her head. "No, nothing like that." Though she knew every waking thought should be focused on finding the murderer and getting him behind bars, she couldn't keep her thoughts from straying to her missing siblings. "You know about my brother and sister. Through this investigation we've learned they are likely still alive." She told Marilyn about her dad's affair and how his mistress claimed he'd let the children go into foster care.

Marilyn's hazel eyes widened as the story spilled out. "I know you want to believe all this, Shauna, but have you stopped to think this woman might be telling you this to cause you pain? Maybe she wants to punish Lewis for deserting her. There's no proof of what she's told you."

Shauna hadn't thought of any of that. "No, there's no proof." Could Marilyn be right and it was all lies? She didn't want to believe that. She wanted to cling to the hope that she'd find her siblings again someday.

Marilyn tucked a lock of her short auburn hair behind an ear. "If it were me, I'd try to corroborate the story. Talk to some people in Child Protective Services. Some of those working then might still be there, and even if they aren't, some records should exist."

"I don't have time right now, not until I know we're safe, but you're right. I should start by verifying Dorothy's story."

It had been a mistake to talk to Marilyn about it. All the hope Shauna had been feeling leaked out like coffee from a cracked cup. She studied Marilyn's expression — the flattened lips, the furrowed brow, and the way she didn't look Shauna's way. "Do you want me to be unhappy forever, Marilyn?"

The older woman's head came up, and her narrow shoulders stiffened. "Of course not, Shauna. Why would you say something like that? I'm simply trying to make sure you don't have unrealistic expectations."

"It's not just about my siblings." Shauna slid off the bar stool and paced the travertine floor. "When you think of my future, what do you see?"

Marilyn stared at her. "Is this about Zach?"

Shauna's chest hurt as she recognized the wariness in Marilyn's face. Until the last few days she would have said her mother-in-law felt unconditional love for her. Now she wasn't so sure. "No, this is about me. Do you love me because I was married to Jack or for myself? What would it do to our relationship if I got remarried or if I found my siblings and had another piece of family to love and depend on?"

Marilyn's eyes flashed. "You're marrying Zach, aren't you? Just like I thought. The next thing I know you won't even come around with Alex anymore. You don't need me now, do you?"

"That's not what I'm saying at all!" Shauna crossed the room and tried to embrace Marilyn, who stood ramrod stiff with her arms crossed over her chest. "Don't you want more out of life for me than an empty house after Alex is grown?"

Marilyn jerked away. "I've had an empty house for many years, and I'm perfectly happy that way."

"But maybe I'm not. I'm still young, Marilyn." Shauna dropped her arms to her sides. "I'm not buried with Jack. Even if I finally am able to move on to a new life, I won't abandon you. You're my family." Shauna's vision blurred with tears, and she reached toward Marilyn, who stared back without making any welcoming move.

The back door flew open, and Alex rushed into the room carrying a tattered bouquet of lavender. "Mommy, a man gave these to me for you." He thrust them under Shauna's nose.

Her eyes began to burn, and her sinuses swelled. She stepped away as a headache pulsed at her temples. "What man, Alex?"

"I didn't see him, but men always give the flowers, don't they? He left them in the driveway with this note for you." With his other grimy hand he produced a white envelope with her name typed across the front.

Her head was pounding in earnest, and she plucked the note from his hand. "Take the flowers outside, sweetheart. I'm allergic to lavender."

His expression fell. "I forgot. I'll throw them away." He retreated through the door and shut it behind him.

She hated that she'd had to disappoint him. Who would have left these flowers? With one finger under the flap, she ripped open the envelope and pulled out the single sheet of paper inside. Her breath caught at the message.

There's nowhere to hide. Give me what I want or the kid might get something a little more deadly. Like peanut butter.

She felt faint and grabbed the edge of the countertop. Who knew about her allergy, and more importantly, who knew peanut butter could kill her son?

He watched the kid from the shadows of the tree line. Through the window he could see Shauna in the kitchen with her mother-in-law, and they seemed to be in a heated discussion from their tense postures. Maybe he could grab the kid and get away before they even noticed. He had to make sure the boy didn't cry out and alert them, and that might be difficult with him in a tree.

Alex was sitting in the doorway of the tree house, and his sneakered feet swung back and forth. He was dressed in jeans and a Seahawks sweatshirt. The weathered boards indicated it had been there for a while, probably built by his dad.

He'd come prepared to make sure the kid couldn't identify him if it all went wrong. He glanced toward his vehicle parked on the narrow fire road and nearly hidden by the bushes. Careful to stay hidden in the shadows, he walked back to his car and hit the button on his fob to unlock the trunk. He quickly donned the Halloween costume he'd bought two hours ago, then went back to his lookout spot. He rustled the trees to make noise.

Alex turned toward the sound. His eyes widened, and his mouth dropped open.

"Spider-Man?"

"That's right. I've been watching you because I really need a new sidekick. Fighting crime by myself has gotten pretty hard."

Alex scrambled down, the rope ladder swaying with the speed of his descent. A smile stretched from ear to ear as he jumped from the final rung and ran toward the trees. "What's my name going to be?"

"Alex the Smart, because I know how bright you are. You can help me figure out the best way to trick the bad guys."

Alex's smile vanished, and his turquoise eyes went somber. "Daddy always told me to think about what I'm going to do. That way I won't get in trouble." He looked back toward Marilyn's house. "And I should always talk to Mommy first."

An idea arced through his head. Maybe he could talk the kid into fetching the key. "I have your first assignment, but you can't tell your mother. She might accidentally say something and then the Joker will get word of it."

Alex's brows drew together. "The Joker is Batman's enemy. Is he around here? Is Batman with you?"

He cursed his inadequate knowledge of superheroes. "That's right. Batman and I are teaming up against the Joker. That's why

I need your help. Will you help me? If so, let's shake on it."

Alex grasped his outstretched hand and shook it. "I wish Daddy was here. He loved Spider-Man! I have all his old comics. I can't read them yet, but Mommy says she's keeping them for me until I'm older." He looked back toward the house. "What do I need to do? And when do I get my costume?"

"I'll have your costume when you prove yourself. Only it's just like in the movies. It's a secret." He knelt and told the boy what he was supposed to look for and where it might be once he was back at Zach's house.

Alex's brow furrowed. "Are you sure I can't tell Mommy? She might see me looking for it."

"You can tell her after the Joker is in jail. You'll hear about it on TV. And I'm sure she won't mind once she realizes how it was used for good. She'll be so proud of you."

Alex puffed out his chest. "She says we should always look for ways to do good and help others."

"I need you to get it tonight. After your mom goes to sleep, I'll wait in the backyard, and you can bring it out to me."

Alex's lip trembled. "But I might fall

asleep. I always go to sleep before Mommy."

The kid had a point. Most five-year-olds were in bed by eight. He'd watched Zach's house most nights, and the lights were rarely out before eleven. "How about if you hide it in the backyard tomorrow morning before you go to school?"

"Where?"

The kid was beginning to get on his nerves. "You know the yard better than I do. You tell me."

Alex took a step back at his sharp tone, and tears flooded his eyes. "I don't think I want to be your sidekick. Not if you yell at me."

His fingers curled into fists at his side, and it was all he could do to keep from grabbing Alex by the throat. He forced a smile. "Sorry, this is very important. People could die if we don't help them. What you're doing will save them."

Alex fiddled with the cord on the neck of his sweatshirt. "Okay, I could hide it in the flower bed by the mums. I take Zach's dogs out before breakfast, and I can put it there."

"I knew you were the smart one." He ruffled Alex's hair. "You're a good sidekick. I'll bring you your special costume on Saturday night."

But he had every intention of being on an island with a mai tai in his hand then.

CHAPTER 30

Shauna was pale, and her eyes drooped. She wore red pajamas and lay curled in a ball on her bed with an ice pack held to her head. She looked limp and exhausted in the dim hall light shining through the open door. She hadn't touched a bite of dinner and hadn't moved since Zach got home. He'd fed Alex and put him to bed before checking on her. The dogs were standing guard outside her bedroom door.

He pitched his voice low. "What can I do? Rub your neck or something?"

"Jack used to press on the acupressure point between my thumb and first finger." Her voice was weak. "You might try that."

He moved to the side of the bed and settled beside her. "Here?"

She nodded. "Press as hard as you can. It's tough on your fingers so stop when it's too much."

Nothing would be too much if it helped

her. He pressed his thumb into the spot and saw the pain on her face begin to ebb. "It's already helping?"

"It usually helps right away. The trick is keeping it from coming back."

His thumb was feeling the pressure, but he was determined to keep it up until they were sure the headache was gone. Holding her hand like this wasn't as romantic as he would've liked to have made it — not when her head was thumping like a jackhammer.

"Has lavender always affected you like this?"

"I loved it when I was a little girl."

"What changed?"

She opened her eyes. "I hadn't really stopped to think about it. My mom used to put lavender in my bathwater, and I thought I was a princess when she did. I hated being around it after she died because a bottle of lavender water shattered in the earthquake, and the entire area reeked of it. Every time I smelled it, I thought about that day. I don't think I smelled lavender again until my thirteenth birthday. After a lot of cajoling, my dad had agreed to a birthday party, and one of my friends brought a bunch of lavender. I had an instant headache."

Her mouth sagged open a bit, and her eyes

grew wider. "I wonder if it causes a head-ache because of the trauma?"

"It's possible." The color was returning to her face as he watched, and her eyes were a bit brighter.

"I think you can stop now. I feel much better."

He released the pressure from his throb-bing thumb but didn't pull his hand away. "I can do it longer if you think it will help."

"I'll let you know if the pain comes back." She scooted up higher in the bed. "Not many people know about my aversion to lavender. The school and the church know about Alex's peanut allergy, so that's a big-ger pool of people. But who could know about both?"

He pulled his phone from his pocket and touched the Notes screen. "Let's make a list and cross-check it."

She adjusted the pillows behind her head. "Okay. Let's start with who knows about the lavender. Marilyn, you, and a couple of old school friends are all that come to mind." She rattled off the names of two women who still lived in Lavender Tides. "I still have lunch with them once in a while, but they're unlikely to have anything to do with this. Jermaine and Michelle, of course."

Marilyn. "This happened at Marilyn's. Do

you think she would have done this to scare you?"

"I can't see her ever threatening Alex, and basically that note was a warning that Alex might be a target. I don't think it's her."

He heard the quiver in her voice and knew she was trying to convince herself as much as she was him. "She's been feeling left out. I know she'd never hurt Alex, but she might want to feel needed."

"S-she did try to convince me again to move in with her."

He wanted to feel relief that Marilyn could be behind the implied threat, but it didn't sit right, even though he'd argued for it. "Whoever left this note wants something you have. We still don't even know what that is."

"I'd give it to him if I knew what he wanted. Life needs to return to normal. Alex is coming to depend on you too much. He'll miss you when we move back home."

You don't ever have to leave. He clamped his teeth down against the words and swallowed hard as a tsunami of emotion choked him. He loved her. When had that happened? When he wasn't looking, his admiration had morphed into something much, much stronger.

"Is something wrong?" she asked. "You

322

look, I don't know, alarmed or something."

He picked up her hand again and laced his fingers with hers. "I'll always be here for Alex. And for you."

Her dark hair fell across her pink cheek as she looked down at their linked hands. "I-I know you will. But it's too easy to lean on you. I've got to face this and get my life back."

He leaned closer and used his other hand to tip her chin up. "What would you say if I told you I want to be part of that life?"

She wet her lips and stared into his eyes. He'd always loved her eyes, such a vivid green with flecks of gold. His gaze went to her lips, so full and kissable. He stroked his thumb over her plump lower lip, then pulled her close and lowered his head. Her lips were soft and pliable, fusing against his as if they were made for him. Her arm crept around his neck, and he pulled her onto his lap to deepen the kiss.

The taste of her, the feel of her in his arms imprinted a sense of destiny in him. He refused to feel guilty. Jack was gone, and he was here. Shauna was here. He pushed away his thoughts and kissed her again.

She finally pulled back and put her hand against his chest. "You make my head spin, Cowboy. I don't know where we're going with this."

"I don't either, but I want us to find out together." He drank in her beautiful face and knew he'd do whatever was necessary to win her heart.

Zach tossed and turned, trying to get some sleep, but the kiss replayed over and over in his head. The sheets tangled through his bare legs until he finally kicked them off and got out of bed. Still dressed in shorts and a T-shirt, he went toward the kitchen to snag the last muffin Shauna had made. When he stepped into the living room, he heard a noise and stopped. A tiny beam of light moved through the space, and he caught the dim outline of a small figure.

He flipped on the overhead light. "Alex, what are you doing?"

The little boy whirled around to face him. "I-I wasn't doing anything." He was in his Superman pajamas.

The doors on the end tables stood open, and several items from inside were on the floor. "What are you looking for?"

Alex stared down at his bare feet. "I can't tell you. It's a secret."

Zach squatted in front of him. "You can tell me anything, kiddo. What's going on?"

Alex looked up and locked gazes with him.

"I'm going to be Spider-Man's sidekick, but I have to give him the key to prove I can be a good helper."

"Spider-Man?" Zach touched his forehead. Was he sick or just sleepwalking? "You should get back to bed. It was just a dream."

Alex shook his head. "No, it wasn't a dream. He came to see me at Grammy's house this afternoon when I was in the tree house. He's going to bring me a costume and everything."

Zach frowned and stared into the boy's clear turquoise eyes. It could only have been a dream, but Alex seemed adamant he was telling the truth. "What did Spider-Man want you to do?"

"Bring him the key so we can stop the Joker."

A key? Zach stood and lifted the boy in his arms. "The Joker is Batman's enemy. He wouldn't have anything to do with Spider-Man." But his spine prickled at the word *key*. There was a key in the box Clarence had given to Shauna.

"That's what I told him, but Batman is working with us too. I didn't see him, though."

Zach turned and headed back toward Alex's bedroom. "Sounds like a big problem." The boy's bulk, so trusting and warm, felt right in his arms.

"It is. I have to leave the key outside for him in the mums. Could you help me look for it?"

"I think you'd better get to sleep before Mommy hears you up and around. You've got school tomorrow."

Alex stiffened in Zach's arms. "But I won't get to be his sidekick if I don't bring him the key!"

"I'll look for it while you're in bed." Zach pushed open the door and nearly tripped over a train set in the middle of the floor. He hopped on one foot and recovered his balance, then set the boy down on the bed. "Hop in there, kiddo. We'll talk about it tomorrow."

"Okay." Alex crawled under the covers. "Bring me the key if you find it."

Zach tucked him in. "I'll do that." He brushed a kiss on Alex's cheek, then retreated to the hallway.

What if there was something to this? First lavender was left with a warning, and now Alex was looking for a key. The whole Spider-Man thing sounded like a dream, but what if it wasn't?

Curled up with an afghan on the sofa, Shauna still looked a little pale from her headache the night before, and Zach handed her a cup of coffee. "You sure you're up to going to the Quadrangle today?"

"Yes, I'm fine." She sipped her coffee.

Alex yanked on the doorknob. "Can I go out and play, Mommy?"

She glanced at her watch. "You've got about half an hour before we need to leave. Just stay in the yard."

"Thanks." He twisted the doorknob but couldn't get it to open.

"Here you go." Zach opened the door for him, and the boy vaulted out. He wished he had half the energy Alex did.

Coffee in hand, Shauna yawned and headed for the kitchen. "Any pancakes left?"

"Yep." He slid a stack of still-warm pancakes toward her, then handed her the maple syrup.

"Thanks."

The dogs were squirreling around his feet. "I think I'll take them out while you eat and get ready." He called Apollo and Artemis. When he stepped out onto the back deck, he didn't see Alex. The access door from the garage gaped open, so he went that way across the large expanse of yard. Dust motes danced in the air inside the garage, but a glance around convinced him Alex wasn't in here.

His pulse kicked up a notch as he went back outside. "Alex?"

It was then he saw the back gate standing open. His long stride became a sprint, and he darted for the opening down the hillside to the bay below. He spotted a shock of auburn hair glinting in the fading sunlight. The boy stood with Zach's boogie board at the top of the rocky slope that ran down to the beach, which was just a small sliver with the tide rolling in.

Zach's gut clenched. Alex intended to ride the board down the slope. "Alex, don't move!"

The boy turned with the board in his hand. "Zachster, there's another boogie board in the garage. We could ride down together and surf right out onto the waves."

Time slowed and morphed back twenty years. A kaleidoscope of images played out in his head of all the times he'd coaxed Jack into going along with some crazy idea. He hadn't been interested in surfing until Zach talked him into it. The thought of skydiving made him want to puke until Zach told him he needed to learn to be a real man, one without fear. But did he want Alex to always try to measure up to the crazy things Zach did?

No, he didn't, but history would repeat

itself with Jack's boy if Zach didn't stop it.

He stepped forward and grabbed the boogie board from Alex's hand, then snapped it in two across his knee. "I was wrong, Alex. A real man doesn't have to prove it by doing dangerous things. A real man is like your daddy — someone who took care of his family, loved his neighbors, and cared about people in need. I remember when we were in grade school, your dad bought lunch for an immigrant kid from Croatia, then asked your grandma to start making him a big lunch every day so that he could share it with the boy."

Alex's eyes widened, and Jack's innocence and goodness shone out in them. "You're just like your dad. Don't try to be a tough guy. Be kind and good like your father. He was a real man. I'm going to work on being more like him too."

Alex nodded solemnly. "Okay. Does that mean you're not going to go volcano surfing anymore?"

"No, I'm not. I'm going to stay here and take care of you and your mom. It was a stupid thing to want to do in the first place, and I'm sorry you heard about it."

The feel of Alex's trusting hand in his made a boulder form in his throat. Why had he been so blind for so long?

"I'm hungry," Alex announced.

"There's chili on the stove, and we can make popcorn later."

Zach turned toward the house and caught sight of Shauna standing five feet away. Tears swam in her eyes.

"How long have you been there?"

She sniffled and swiped at her cheeks. "Long enough."

He released Alex's hand. "Run on ahead and check on the dogs. I'll be right there."

"Okay, Zachster."

Shauna smiled as her son darted past her. "Zachster. It's so cute to hear him call you that."

"You used to call me Cowboy. I always liked it." Zach paused in front of Shauna. "I'm sorry, Shauna. You were right. I was going to lead Alex in the wrong direction. I realized that I've been seeking a new thrill to prove to myself that I wasn't afraid, when the reality is, I'm scared most of the time. Scared of not measuring up to the man my dad was. His escapades were legendary, and I read all the articles he wrote for the travel magazine. I wanted to be just like him. I don't want to do that to Alex. I'm so sorry."

Her mouth softened, and she put her hand on his arm. "It's all right, Zach. Now let's begin our exploration."

A weight fell off his shoulders, one he hadn't even realized he was carrying.

He didn't like skulking around Zach's house in the daylight, but he had no choice. He waited until it seemed likely that most neighbors would be gone to work, then parked down the street and set off at a brisk walk along the sidewalk as if he knew where he was going and didn't want to be interrupted. The tree-lined street was quiet, and he didn't see anyone out or movement through any windows.

He wore a ball cap low over his forehead, and he hoped the nondescript jeans and T-shirt would suggest a meter reader of some kind if anyone happened to glance out their windows. Just to be on the safe side, he paused at Bannister's house and walked with purpose along the side to where the electric meter was situated. The trees of the property hid him from the street, so after looking around, he climbed the privacy fence and dropped into the backyard.

A ferocious volley of barking started immediately, and he scrambled back to the top of the fence, then stared down into the snarling faces of two rottweilers. *Great, just great.* The kid could have left the key, and he'd never know it with these two guarding the yard.

He dropped back onto the ground outside the fence and walked around to the back. All he really had to do was open the gate to let the dogs out. The gate was padlocked from the inside, though, and the dogs had tracked with him and were snarling on the other side. Maybe he could break in through a side window, open the back door to let the dogs in, then go around and shut them inside.

He retraced his steps to the side of the house, took a handkerchief out of his pocket, wrapped it around his hand, then broke the window and unlocked it. As the tinkle of glass echoed in the air, he looked around to see if anyone poked a head out of a neighboring house. Nothing stirred.

Moments later he was inside a bathroom. He hurried down the hall and through the living room to the kitchen. The dogs were going crazy in the back, but they were over by the side near where he'd broken the window. He opened the kitchen door and whistled, then raced back to the bathroom and shut the door.

Once he heard them snarling on the other side, he exited through the window, rushed to the backyard fence, then climbed over it. He shut the door that led into the kitchen and grinned.

Success felt sweet. He hurried to the flower bed and pushed back the mums. Nothing under the foliage but dirt and mulch.

All that work to get in here, and the kid had failed him. Maybe he hadn't been able to find the key, or maybe Shauna had found him searching. His chest grew tight until he remembered that the kid thought he was Spider-Man.

The only thing he could do now was to snatch the kid.

CHAPTER 31

The noise in the chopper faded to a dull throb with her headset on. Shauna spoke into the microphone and gestured to Zach. "I'll put us down there. I didn't realize until now that Dad's cabin is in the Mount Jupiter Quadrangle."

The sun shone out of a beautiful September sky with the temperature hovering around seventy. Sitka spruce vied with big-leaf maple for space and created a canopy over the understory of sword fern and stair-step moss. A grassy clearing opened up below, and she executed a perfect landing, then shut off the engine.

Zach removed his headset and reached for the backpack of food, water, compass, and binoculars. "I wish we could have brought Alex. He would have enjoyed this."

She dragged her gaze from the way his muscles flexed in his navy T-shirt. "I didn't want to risk walking into something dangerous." She'd looked forward to the day with Zach, even though she tried not to admit it to herself.

He nodded and opened his door. "Better to be safe."

She opened her door and ducked beneath the blades. Zach met her by a small brook rushing over gleaming stones. The water was clear and melodious as it mingled with the sounds of birds chirping.

"Where should we start?"

He shouldered the backpack and pointed to the west. "Let's go that way. We should reach your dad's cabin around lunchtime, and we can stop in and say hello."

It bothered her that her dad's cabin was in this area. Could he have had anything to do with whatever Jack saw? Jack often stopped to check on her dad so he was in this area a lot. "I suppose we should ask Dad if he knows what Jack might have been referring to."

Zach shot her a quick look. "You're worried he might be involved?"

"Aren't you? It seems likely Jack stumbled onto whatever danger he found near Dad's cabin. It's not very far."

"The quadrangle covers a lot of area. He could have run into whatever it was while hiking up Mount Jupiter or in the Brothers

Wilderness. The location of your dad's cabin is likely just a coincidence."

"Maybe." She intended to grill her dad about it, though. Over the years she'd learned whatever depths she suspected he might sink to were never really as far as the man could go. She wanted to love him, but it was hard to look past all the ways he'd disappointed her.

They set off through a mat of wildflowers that released a sweet aroma as they stepped on the blooms. There were no trails through here. It was as if they were the first to ever walk the area. It would take days to hike in from the nearest fire road, and not many would have the fortitude to come this way. They reached the end of the clearing and moved into the shade of the giant trees. Lichen and moss were underfoot, as well as smaller shrubs.

Zach kept consulting his compass and directed them this way or that way to stay on track. The trees thinned out again, and they stepped into another clearing, one too steep to set her helicopter down in.

She paused and wiped the perspiration from her forehead. "Now which way?" When Zach didn't answer, she glanced at him looking to the south. "What?"

"It looks like a road has been cut there. A

wide one with pavement that's all broken up now. It seems like it hasn't been used in decades."

She saw it then. "A fire road maybe?"

"Maybe."

She followed him to the road. It meandered around a small pond before disappearing into the trees again. "It has to have been abandoned awhile. Saplings and vegetation are taking it over. Let's follow it and see where it goes."

The rough road made walking faster. There were no fallen trees to clamber over or rocks to avoid. The road began to widen and ended next to a small building. It was still shady even in the clearing, and Shauna stared overhead.

She touched Zach's arm. "Look, there's some kind of green covering over this area. Someone is trying to hide this."

Zach's gaze roamed over the building. "Hard to tell what's inside. There aren't even any windows."

She walked to the metal door and looked it over. "It has both a regular lock and a padlock. Whoever put this here really doesn't want anyone poking around."

"Let's walk around and see if we can figure out what this is doing here." Zach set off to the right of the building.

Shauna hung back and examined the locks. It would take a huge bolt cutter to remove the padlock, but the other lock was a dead bolt that would only open with a code. She finally trailed after Zach and found him with his ear pressed against the building. "What's wrong?"

"I hear some kind of noise, but I can't figure out what it is."

She pressed her ear against the building too and heard a rumble and a hum. "Machinery of some kind?"

"Yeah, but what? And why is this place so hidden?"

"We can check with environmental organizations and see if they have any idea. Or the sheriff might know. How far are we from my dad's?"

Zach gestured to the left. "Only about a half an hour walk that way, I think, so he might know something about this place."

"He might, but it's hard to say if he's even sober enough to carry on a conversation. We can go ask, though."

A brightly colored bird flitted through the trees, then chirped a happy song as they walked under the canopy of branches and pushed through the understory. Zach glanced at Shauna walking beside him. She looked adorable with strands of dark hair escaping from her ponytail to rest against her pink cheeks. He wanted to take her hand, but it still felt a little presumptuous. She hadn't said anything about the kiss last night, and he hesitated to bring it up.

She caught him looking at her. "What?"

He stopped and shrugged out of his backpack. "Just getting some water." He pulled two bottles out and handed one to her.

Her lips twitched, and her green eyes lit with amusement. "You're sure that's all it was? Your expression was . . ." Her cheeks went redder.

"You look very pretty today. It's hard to stop staring at you." Holy cow, could his compliment be any lamer? *Pretty* was hardly the right word. *Ravishingly beautiful* was more like it, but that kind of effusive talk got tangled between his teeth and his tongue.

Her white teeth flashed in a smile that accentuated the dimple in her left cheek. "I don't mind if you look." She caught and held his gaze.

He couldn't stop himself from sidling closer. "Do you mind if I touch?" Without waiting for permission, he cupped her cheek, then leaned forward and brushed her lips with his.

The enticing scent of her breath brushed over his face. Her arms came up around his neck, and she leaned into the embrace. He deepened the kiss and took his time plumbing the sweetness of her response.

How had he fallen in love with her so fast? But maybe it wasn't all that quick. He'd loved her as a friend for years. It hadn't taken long for those feelings of friendship to morph into something else. Breaking the kiss, he stepped back.

Her beautiful eyes looked a little sad as she dropped her hands. Did she think he was rejecting her? He reached for her again, but she turned away and uncapped her water.

She took a swig before aiming a smile his way that looked pasted on. "We'd better get going."

He couldn't let her think he was pushing her away. "Shauna, the way I feel about you is moving so fast it's giving me vertigo. This isn't just some casual hook-up for me. I hope you know that."

Her smile faded for a heartbeat before she nodded. "It's scaring me too, Zach. I-I thought I'd never be truly happy again, but maybe I was wrong. Being with you makes me want to laugh and live again."

"You deserve that." The need to tell her how he felt trembled on his lips, but it was too soon. She'd think he was totally crazy. He smiled and took her hand. "Let's go talk to your dad."

They'd only taken one step when something whizzed by his head and struck a nearby tree. As pieces of bark flew out, he grabbed her and pushed her to the ground. "That was a bullet!"

He threw himself on top of her and covered her body with his. Another bullet plowed into the ground four inches from his head. This was no hunter with a stray shot.

Someone was trying to shoot them.

He lifted his head and looked around for a boulder or something to hide behind, but only trees held any kind of concealment.

He spoke in her ear. "Let's get behind that big pine to our left. I'll see if I can find where the shooter is. Let's roll that direction together."

He clutched her tightly and began to roll toward the tree. More bullets tore into the dirt where they had lain just a few seconds before. They reached the tree, and he released her. "Crawl around to the other side."

Once she was safely behind the bulk of

the pine tree, he scooted around himself, then stood and peered in the direction he thought the shooter had been.

He heard only the wind through the branches and the birds chirping. Another bullet smacked into the tree, sending chips of bark against his cheek.

"You're bleeding," Shauna said.

"It's nothing." If only he had his rifle. They were as easy to pick off as cans on a post. "I'll try to circle around and jump him from behind. Stay hidden behind the tree."

Her eyes were enormous in her face. She grabbed his arm. "Don't go! He'll be able to shoot you."

"I'm going to run from tree to tree. I'll be fine." He brushed a kiss across her lips. "Just pray."

"I am."

Another bullet dug into the side of the tree. "When he spots me moving, I want you to run across to that other large tree." He pointed out a Sitka spruce to their right.

When she nodded, he made a big show of leaping from behind the tree and running for a smaller pine. A bullet bit into the ground by his feet. He paused long enough to see Shauna dart to the spruce tree before stealthily crawling to a large bush.

No more shots rang out, and he moved to

the next tree. He was having trouble sighting where the shooter crouched, but Zach continued to circle back to where the last bullet had come from.

He found a crushed patch of wildflowers and weeds as well as some spent casings. The one clear shoe print he found looked to belong to a smaller man, maybe one the size of Jermaine. The bullet casings might come in handy to the sheriff, so he pulled out a handkerchief and picked them up before returning to Shauna.

"He's gone for now. Let's get to your dad's." The old man wouldn't be much help, but he had enough firearms to outfit a small army.

CHAPTER 32

His phone rang, and his gut did a slow roll at the number on the screen. "Just the call I was waiting for."

"The first half of the money is in your bank account. We want to be on our way home by this time tomorrow. We will meet you at seven tonight."

"Excellent! However, I already have a commitment for tonight. Make it eight tomorrow."

A long pause followed on the other end of the call. "I have warned you not to play games. If you have any thought of double-crossing us, put it out of your mind or your wife will be looking for another husband."

A shudder made its way down his back. These guys wouldn't mess around, but he couldn't do it tonight. "I intend to deliver the plans and deed as promised, but it will need to be at eight tomorrow. You'll still be on your way home in time."

"Very well. But if you're late, you won't like the consequences."

"I won't be late." He ended the call and climbed into his vehicle.

If he couldn't get Shauna to cough up the key, what was he going to do? But if he had the kid, he held all the cards. She'd do anything to protect Alex. He liked kids — he really did — but he had no choice.

Setting his jaw, he drove to Marilyn's house and parked in the trees where he'd hidden his vehicle last time. Through the foliage, he looked in the backyard but didn't see Alex. Maybe he was in the tree house. Careful to stay in the shade of the trees, he skirted the yard and softly called Alex's name.

No response. He moved closer to the house and tried to peek in the windows. He caught a glimpse of Alex sitting at the bar with Marilyn doing something in the kitchen. Great. Now what? He could wait and maybe the kid would come out to play, or he could take both of them. While he really didn't want to deal with two hostages, having Marilyn along might work in his favor. She could help keep Alex calm. If he had to dispose of Alex, he might be able to make it look like a murder/suicide by a grieving mother. It was well-known in town that Marilyn hadn't dealt very well with the loss of her only child.

Marilyn had a cabin up in the forest she rarely used. He'd been by there last week and had stopped to look around. The place was overgrown with weeds, and the lock on the door was rusted shut. He didn't think anyone had used it in at least a decade, maybe two. It would be a perfect place to stage the disposal. He couldn't bring himself to call it murder when he had no choice.

This was all Shauna's fault. If she hadn't poked her nose in, the Chinese guys would have their plans, and he'd be sitting on a beach with his lady, enjoying life.

He heaved a sigh and went back to his vehicle to put on his Spider-Man costume. No sense in revealing his identity until he had them safely locked up. He pulled on the face mask and took a pistol and rope from the glove box before heading to the backyard again.

When he reached the tree line, he saw Alex outside on the porch. Perfect.

The boy looked up as he approached and scrambled to his feet. "Spider-Man! I'm sorry, but I couldn't find the key. I don't know where it is. Zach saw me looking and made me go back to bed."

He kept the gun and the rope behind his

back. "It's okay. I have another plan, but we'll have to take your grandma with us. She won't understand at first and will probably be upset, but I don't want you to try to help her, okay? It would be dangerous for her. We have to take her to a safe place. The Joker is coming here any minute, and we have to get her away."

Alex's brow furrowed. "Why would the Joker come here? Grammy just stays home and gardens. She has chickens and things. She doesn't even go to town very much."

"Who knows why a super villain does what he does. All I know is that we have to take your grandma and get to safety. Can you call her out here?"

"I guess so." Alex went to the back door and opened it. "Grammy, Spider-Man is here to see you."

Marilyn's voice was too far away to make out every word, but she said something about silliness. He grinned and curled his finger around the trigger of his gun. She wouldn't think it was so funny when this was all over.

Marilyn appeared in the doorway. She wiped her hands on the apron she wore over her gray slacks and blue sweater. "What on earth are you yammering about, Alex? Is this some kind of game?" Her eyes widened when she spotted him, and her hand fluttered to her mouth. "Who are you?"

Alex rushed to her side and took her hand. "This is Spider-Man, Grammy. We have to get you away to somewhere safe. The Joker is on his way to snatch you."

"Spider-Man isn't real, Alex." Her voice went hard, and her brown eyes narrowed. "This isn't funny. Quit confusing the boy, and take off your mask."

He pulled his hands from behind his back and gestured with the pistol. "I'm afraid I'll have to tie you up. Turn around. And don't try anything funny unless you want to risk the kid."

The color drained from her face. "Don't hurt him. I'll go with you. Just leave him here."

"Turn around."

She swallowed, and her Adam's apple bobbed. "Just don't hurt him." She turned her back to him.

He grabbed her left arm and pulled it behind her, then wrapped rope around her wrist before yanking her other arm back. "My truck's this way. Come along, Alex."

He'd get them stashed, then call Shauna. It was all going to work out.

The cabin looked deserted, but Shauna

knew she'd find her dad passed out in his ratty recliner. She pushed open the unlocked door. "Pop?"

The stench of rotten meat hung in the air, and she grimaced, then pointed to the hallway. "His arsenal is in the spare room. It's usually locked, but the key is on top of the gun cabinet."

Zach nodded and rushed down the hall while she continued on to the living room. The slight snore and the gentle movement of her dad's chest told her she was right. He was fully drunk. She went to the kitchen and made a pot of strong coffee. He had to be coherent enough to talk. They could take his truck and drive to the helicopter, but she needed answers from her dad. She should dump the remains of rotting steak outside, but there was no time for that.

Zach came back down the hall with a rifle and a Glock. He loaded both weapons, then slung the rifle over his shoulder. "I'm going to keep a lookout for the shooter. He might have followed us."

It was only by the grace of God they hadn't been injured or killed. The shooter had meant business, and she shuddered at the thought he might be out there stalking them.

The coffee began to perk and mask the

putrid smell of the house. She found bread and cut off a small moldy corner, then made a turkey sandwich for her dad. By the time she was done with that, the coffee was ready, so she poured a cup, added a cube of ice to it so he could drink it down, then carried both to the recliner.

"Pop." She shook his stockinged foot. "Wake up."

He jerked with one eye at half-mast. "Wha-up?" The eye closed again.

She shook him again and spoke louder. "Pop, you have to wake up. I need you. Someone wants to kill me."

He blinked and opened both red eyes. His bleary gaze couldn't seem to land on her and stay. "Tha' you, Shauna?"

"Yes, Pop. Here, have some coffee." She lifted the cup to his lips and helped him take several swallows. "Have some more."

He obediently drank down more of it, and keeping an eye on Zach stalking from the front to the back windows, she broke off pieces of the sandwich and fed it to him.

Fifteen minutes later he had downed all the coffee and most of the sandwich. His eyes were a little more focused, and though he still slurred his words, she thought he might be sober enough to answer her questions.

She carried the plate and cup back to the kitchen and poured more coffee for him, then dragged a kitchen chair in to sit beside him. The sofa was too far for him to focus.

She gave him the cup, and he managed to hold it with only a little tremble in his hand. She sat beside him. "Dad, do you know who owns that metal building about two miles east of here? The one with no windows and two locks on the door?"

Something shifted in his eyes. He looked away and took a sip of his coffee. "Wha's this all about, Shauna?" He put down the cup on the table beside his chair and leaned back with his eyes closed. "Don't be nagging me, girl. Let a man get some rest."

Was he deliberately slurring his words more than he had a minute ago? "Pop, open your eyes and look at me."

He blinked at her sharp tone, then opened his eyes. She leaned forward. "Someone shot at us just now." She pointed to Zach. "He's standing guard because we think that person might have followed us here."

Her father reared up and started to stand, then fell back into the chair. "Get me my gun! I'll teach him not to come onto my property."

"Teach whom? Do you know who wants me dead? Listen, a lot is going on." She

351

launched into a condensed timeline of the murders and how the killer seemed to be stalking her. "Your grandson is in danger too. We both are. Zach is doing his best to protect us, but it's hard when we don't know where to look to figure this out. Jack was killed too, and he left a video telling us to check out Jupiter. We think he might have meant the Jupiter Quadrangle, so we brought my chopper and started searching."

He was gazing somewhere past her shoulder as though he didn't know she was in the room. "You found the doomsday machine, didn't you?"

She considered him carefully. "Doomsday machine?" Was he hallucinating? Did he understand a single word she'd just said? She sighed and rubbed her forehead. Once upon a time he'd been one of the finest engineering minds in the country. It was sad what alcohol had done to him. Maybe they should just take his old truck and leave before that guy opened fire again.

"Killed your mama. Wanted nothing to do with it then," he mumbled.

"What killed Mom? What are you talking about?" She took the coffee mug and held it to his lips. "Let's get more caffeine in you."

He knocked it away, and the cup clattered

to the scarred wooden floor, spilling its contents. "I told him I wouldn't help him, but he kept pestering me and pestering me. It was my fault everyone died, and I couldn't fix it." He bolted to his feet and stumbled past her to the hall and into the bathroom.

She heard him retching and sighed. "He's not making any sense," she told Zach.

The silhouette of his expression was grim as he studied the front yard through the window. "We need to talk to him when he's sober. In the meantime, I think we need to get back to the helicopter and hightail it out of the forest. We can bring the sheriff back to check out the building."

"If it even has anything to do with the shooter. We don't know for sure."

"We weren't far from there when he opened fire. I think he knew we found the place and was trying to make sure we never told anyone."

She nodded. "I think you're right. I'll grab Pop's keys, and we can take his truck. Do you think it's safe to leave him here alone?"

Zach shook his head. "We'd better take him with us. We can sober him up and try to squeeze some sense out of him by the time we reach the chopper."

Seeing him standing there so strong and focused made a warm sensation curl in her belly and float up to her chest. She could count on Zach, and she loved that about him.

CHAPTER 33

The path back to Marilyn's cabin was full of potholes and blown-down limbs. He tried to avoid bottoming out in the craters, but several times the undercarriage smacked down in a deep dip. He'd tied up Marilyn, and she sat with a clenched jaw in the backseat without saying much.

She blinked when foliage scraped the side of the car. "Are we going to my cabin?"

"Yep. Seemed like a good place to hole up for a while."

She lapsed back into silence and looked out the window. He glanced into the rear-view mirror to try to decipher her expression. Was she planning on trying to escape? Her face was closed and her mouth set.

Alex was right behind him. "I want my mommy."

He felt a pang. Maybe there was a way around disposing of them. If he could pull this off without them realizing who he was, he might be able to head for the airport and leave them to walk out of the forest on their own.

It was a nice dream, but in his heart of hearts, he knew it was unlikely he could spare their lives. Not and live in any kind of security.

He spied the cabin ahead and slowed the vehicle, then pulled it into what was left of the driveway overgrown with azaleas and pine trees. He stepped out of the vehicle into knee-high weeds, then yanked open the rear door. "Let's get you both inside."

When Marilyn struggled to maneuver because of her bound hands, he grabbed her forearm and hauled her out. She yelped, then clamped her lips shut.

He motioned to the boy. "Come on, kid." Holding his stuffed bear, Alex climbed out and stood, blinking back tears.

The bolt cutter in the trunk should make short work of the door. He motioned to the porch. "Be careful. The floorboards are rotted, and you might go straight through." He grabbed the tool, then walked to the door and cut the bolt. It fell to the buckled floor with a clatter, and he shoved at the door. It resisted opening, and he put his shoulder into it. With a squeal from the rusty hinges, it finally opened.

He stepped out of the way and gestured to Marilyn and Alex. "After you."

She wrinkled her nose and didn't move. "The place isn't habitable. There isn't even a bathroom, just an outhouse that is probably filled with black widow spiders."

He hadn't thought of checking any amenities, but he shrugged off her concerns. It wouldn't matter soon. "Inside."

She stumbled over the warped threshold and entered the cabin. He motioned to Alex. "After you, boy." He waited until the kid entered, then stepped into the space himself. The furnishings had been nice once upon a time, but raccoons had evidently called the place home for a while. The leather sofa lay in shreds. Mice or rats had destroyed a rocker upholstered in orange by the window, and droppings of some kind littered the scratched walnut tables.

Sad to see it in such disrepair. He kicked a pile of rubble out of the way. "Why'd you leave this place for the animals?"

"Jack and I quit coming after my husband died. It was never the same without him." Her voice trembled, and she bit her lip.

Alex grabbed one of her bound arms. "Grammy, I want to go home. This place is scary, and there's nowhere to sit."

"I thought of that. There are chairs in the

trunk, and I'll grab them. We won't be here long, just until your mom gives me the key."

"You keep talking about a key, but I have no idea what you are talking about. I doubt Shauna even has what you want."

The stupid mask was making his face as hot as a furnace. "She has it. Clarence gave it to her."

Her mouth dropped open. "You killed Clarence?"

He shrugged. "He was poking his nose in where it didn't belong. I didn't want to do it, but I had no choice."

"There's always a choice between right and wrong."

Where did she get off lecturing him? She didn't even know who he was. "I'll grab the chairs."

He went back through the creaky front door and grabbed the three chairs he'd packed in the trunk, then returned to the house. She had moved from the front window to the back door, which she was struggling to open with her tied hands. "I nailed it shut from the outside when I was here last week. You can't get out that way."

There was no way out at all. He unfolded the chairs. "Sit."

Marilyn eased down onto the seat of the one closest to her. "I need to use the bathroom." Her lips twisted with disgust. "Can you check the outhouse for spiders?"

"Yeah, fine. Come with me." He grabbed a dilapidated broom from the corner and herded Marilyn and Alex out through the front and around to the back of the house.

He lashed her hands in front of her with the rope, then tied the other end to the handle of the outhouse. "Just want to make sure you don't do something stupid like try to run off." He didn't think she'd leave her grandson, though.

The outhouse door creaked when he opened it and he peered inside. Tons of cobwebs crisscrossed the inside of the space, and several spiders scurried away. The webs looked like black widows had taken over the space, just as Marilyn had predicted.

He backed out. "I don't think you'll want to use this. No amount of knocking down cobwebs is going to clear out that nest of spiders."

She blanched and looked away. "I-Is there a bucket or anything like that around?" Her voice held an edge of desperation.

He spied one half hidden by weeds near the back door. "There's one." He knocked out the bugs inside and took it around to the back of the outhouse. "I'm going to untie your wrists, but I'm keeping Alex with me. If you try to run away, I'll have to hurt him."

She bit her lip and nodded. "I won't run."

Lewis's junker truck wouldn't start no matter how much Zach fiddled with the battery cables. He resisted the urge to kick the tire and yell with frustration. He had to get Shauna to safety. He rummaged in the lean-to shed for tools to work on it but found only carpentry items like a rusty saw and a hammer with a cracked grip.

Now what? He listened to the chirping birds in the trees and considered the options. One last time he climbed in the truck and turned the key. Nothing. They would have to hike out of here, and dread curled in his gut at the thought of a sniper stalking them.

He walked back to the house. Shauna still plied her father with coffee, and Lewis looked a little more alert.

He stopped by the recliner. Shauna appeared to be cooler and more collected than Zach felt. "The truck won't start."

Her dark brows winged up. "Did you try cleaning the cables?"

"Yep. The engine won't turn over. We'll have to walk out of here, and we don't know if that sniper is still out there." He slapped his palm against his forehead. "I'm an idiot. I should have called the sheriff as soon as I got here." He lifted the phone beside Lewis from its cradle and held it to his ear. "No dial tone."

"I told them to shut it off. I was tired of getting sales calls," Lewis mumbled.

Shauna rose from the chair and carried the coffee cup to the kitchen. "We need to find a cell signal and call the sheriff."

"We haven't had a signal since we landed the helicopter."

"So we're back to square one and walking out on foot." She turned to her father. "Pop, you're going to need to come with us. Can you walk?"

" 'Course I can walk. I'm not an invalid." Lewis wasn't slurring his words any longer, and his rheumy eyes looked a little clearer.

"Wait here a second." Zach went down the hall to the gun cabinet in the bedroom and selected two more rifles and two more pistols. Lewis was a crack shot when he was sober, so all they could hope for was that he was coherent enough to help. In spite of his flaws he'd want to protect his daughter.

Zach grabbed boxes of ammo too and returned to the living room, then handed Lewis and Shauna a rifle and a pistol. He stashed the ammo in the backpack. "We'd better get going if we want to reach the helicopter by dark."

Shauna loaded a rifle, then shouldered it before tucking a pistol into the waistband of her jeans. "I'm ready. Come on, Pop."

Lewis lurched out of the chair and reached for the rifle. His hands steadied as he loaded both weapons. "Tell me again what's going on."

Did he even remember Shauna asking him about the building? Zach went through the sequence of events again. "Any idea who is shooting at us, Lewis? Who would want to keep us away from that building?"

Shauna touched her dad's arm. "You said something about it being your fault. What did you mean?"

A truculent expression settled on his face. "I don't know what I said. I don't remember. Let's go." He set off for the front door and let it bang open behind him.

Shauna looked at Zach and sighed. "I think he knows something, but I'm not sure what it's going to take for him to tell me."

"Maybe when the bullets start whizzing, he'll spill it."

"Maybe." But she didn't look convinced. "He's a stubborn old man."

Zach embraced her with one arm and dropped a kiss on her forehead. "I'd much rather you stayed here where there's a little bit of protection, but I can't fly the chopper out of here for help. I don't want anything to happen to you, Shauna."

She laid her hand on his cheek. The soft feel of her skin made his pulse jump, and he turned his head to kiss her palm. Her smile came then. "Nothing's going to happen to me."

"I'll hold you to that." He reached over and opened the door all the way for her. "Stay alert."

"Alert is my middle name." She gave him an impish grin and went out the door.

He let his gaze linger on her sweet curves as she walked away. Now that he'd finally admitted to himself how he felt, the thought of losing her was a knife in his guts. He stepped onto the porch and closed the door behind him.

He'd do everything in his power to protect her.

CHAPTER 34

Now what was he supposed to do to make sure they didn't escape while he got to an area with cell phone service? Marilyn had been subdued after he brought her in from the toilet break, and Alex sat on his grandmother's lap with his bear clutched to his chest. All he really had to do was make sure Marilyn couldn't get away.

Ah, he knew what to do. "Alex, come here."

The boy looked up and shook his head. "I want my grammy."

"You're going to come with me for a little while." He stepped to the chair where they sat and dragged the kid from the old woman's lap. The boy cried and reached for his grandmother.

"Stop it." He yanked the kid back. "Marilyn, I'm going to lock the door. You better not try to climb out the window or escape in any way. If you're not here when we get back, you'll be visiting a fresh grave beside Jack's."

Her hazel eyes widened and her mouth trembled. "Don't hurt him."

"It's all on your shoulders, lady. Do what you're told, and he'll be on your lap in half an hour. I won't be gone long. I just need to call Shauna and arrange to exchange you and the boy for the key. This will be over soon if you cooperate."

She gave a jerky nod. Her auburn hair was a tangled mess, and her blue sweater had smears of mud on it. The gray slacks had a tear where she'd caught it on brambles in the woods. A pang of pity surprised him, and he shoved it away.

He'd grabbed her purse on the way out of her house so he dug around in it until he found her cell phone, then took Alex's hand. "I've got a candy bar in the glove box for you." The boy kicked and screamed, but he ignored the kid's temper tantrum and dragged him out the door to the vehicle.

He opened the rear door and pushed the kid inside. "Buckle your seat belt, and you can have the candy bar." He had a satellite phone he could use, but he wanted to make sure Shauna would answer the call.

Alex sniffled but buckled his seat belt.

It was a little ironic to even care about the

seat belt when things were likely to take an unpleasant turn in a few hours. He got the candy bar from the glove box and tossed it into the back. "There you go. We'll be back in a jiffy."

"You're not really Spider-Man. You're not nice at all."

"So I'm told. Just shut up and eat your candy." He drove off along the bumpy road and kept checking Marilyn's cell phone. No bars.

He finally got one bar and pulled onto the shoulder to call Shauna's number. The call rang, then stopped. He cursed and drove back onto the road. A better signal couldn't be too far down the road.

He glanced the rearview mirror and saw Alex's mouth smeared with chocolate. "Pretty good stuff, huh?"

Alex swiped the back of his hand across his lips. "Grammy says she knows who you are. The sheriff is going to put you in jail for pretending to be Spider-Man and kidnapping us. You need to let us go before you get in more trouble."

He froze. Marilyn knew who he was? How could she know? He was using a stolen SUV and wearing a mask. She couldn't possibly identify him.

"Who did she say I was?"

"She didn't tell me, but she knows. I want my mommy!" Alex wailed and hugged his bear.

Great, he would have to listen to that caterwauling until they got back to the cabin. "Cool it, kid."

But Alex cried even harder. Gritting his teeth, he drove farther down the road. There had to be a cell tower around here. Maybe he should climb a ridge and see if he could pick up a decent signal. The kid would be a problem, though. He'd be better off driving until he got a couple of bars.

He watched road signs, but they were in the middle of wilderness. It had taken over an hour to reach the cabin, and it might take that long to find a signal. He spotted a high ridge with a fire tower poking out of the trees. Maybe he could get a signal there.

He parked in a scenic overlook and got out, then opened the rear door. "Let's go, kid."

"Where are we going?"

"We're going to see a fire tower, up there." He pointed.

"Cool!" Alex scrambled out. "My friend Brandon climbed one once. I'll be able to tell him I got to climb one too."

The climb up the ridge would take a little time with a kid in tow. He set his hand on

Alex's head and steered him toward the path. "Let's hurry so you can see your grandmother soon."

"Okay." Alex scampered up the pine-strewn path and paused several times to make sure he didn't get too far ahead.

This kind of hike was for kids. He was huffing and puffing, and Alex still had enough energy to pick wildflowers and examine a caterpillar or two. They were nearly to the top of the ridge. If the coverage was still poor, he'd have to head for town, but that would mean removing his mask. The kid would be able to identify him.

It probably didn't matter. He would have to do whatever it took to escape.

The small hairs on the back of Shauna's neck stood at attention as she walked between her dad and Zach. Someone was stalking them, but he'd failed to shoot or make his presence known in any way. Zach took point, and her dad paused often behind her to check out the landscape, but neither of them seemed to feel the alarm dogging her steps.

She checked her phone. "Still no signal."

"And you won't get one for quite a distance," her dad said. "Probably not until the clearing where you landed your bird."

She stopped and looked back at her dad, who seemed sprier by the minute. "I can't believe you stopped your phone service. How am I supposed to call to check on you?"

His grizzled jaw jutted, and he narrowed his eyes at her. "Don't need anyone checking on me. I'm a grown man, Shauna. Can take care of myself."

She bit her lip and didn't answer. Going over all the ways he failed to take care of himself was a waste of breath. "Someone's out there."

He shrugged. "Sometimes in these woods you can get the heebie-jeebies, and there's no one there at all."

She heard the snap of a broken twig. "Get down!" She threw herself to the ground at the same instant a shot rang out. The bullet dug into a tree near where she'd been standing.

Zach turned and fired. She heard the sound of someone running away, and Zach rushed after the sniper. Shauna turned to check on her dad and found him jogging after Zach, so she joined in the chase as well. They came to a stream running through a small clearing and stopped.

Zach tipped his head and listened. "I

don't know which way he went. The dude is fast."

Her dad stopped and examined the ground. "I think we made a wrong turn. I don't see any recent tracks through here."

Zach's hand came down on her shoulder, and she welcomed the warm reassurance with a smile. "You weren't hit, were you?" he asked.

She shook her head. "I think he ran off because he realized we were all armed. Three against one. He probably thought he could pick us off easily, then abandoned the idea when you returned fire."

"Probably, but let's play it safe and get to the helicopter as soon as possible." He took her hand as if it was the most natural thing in the world.

She curled her fingers into his warm grip, and they turned back toward their destination. Something major had shifted between them today, and it was going to take some time to adjust to these new, crazy feelings.

Her dad eyed her, then stared at Zach. "What's going on with you two?"

A surge of color ran up Zach's neck, but he held her dad's gaze. "We've always been good friends, and we realized maybe there could be more than that between us. You okay with that?"

Her dad shrugged. "She's the one to make that decision."

The laconic disinterest in his voice pierced her. He'd long ago given up any desire to be part of her life, to voice any opinion about what she did or where she went. She'd hoped for that to change, but it was never going to be any different.

Zach's fingers tightened on hers, and she clung to the gentle encouragement in his grip. He and her father were polar opposites. Zach would always be a steady influence on her and Alex. He'd always have an opinion on anything that concerned her. She and her dad were strangers and always would be.

They were within five hundred yards of the helicopter when her cell phone rang. She stopped. "Looks like we have a signal!" She glanced at the screen. "Hey, Marilyn, sorry we're late. I'll tell you about it when we get back."

"This isn't Marilyn, so listen carefully." The man's voice was pitched in a way to disguise his identity. "I have Marilyn and your boy. If you want them back, we'll make an exchange."

Her heart seized, and she gripped Zach's hand. "Who is this? What do you want?" Zach's expression had gone somber. He stood close to her, and she held the phone out from her ear a bit so he could hear.

"Clarence gave you some stuff, and I need one item back immediately. If you don't do exactly what I say, you'll never see your boy and Marilyn again."

"Don't hurt them!" Terror roughened her voice and squeezed her chest. "I'll do whatever you say. But the sheriff has all that stuff."

"He doesn't have it all. He gave an item back to you."

Realization washed over her. "The necklace, you mean? I have it. Where can we exchange it for Alex and Marilyn?"

"Take it to the lookout point at Rainshadow Bay. There's a plaque on the point. Tape it to the back, then call me when you're done. Once I have it, I'll release them."

"That's not good enough! I want to meet. I'll give you the necklace, and you can give me Alex and Marilyn."

"You have one hour to deliver the necklace there, or the deal is off. Don't call the sheriff, or you'll never see them alive again."

"How do I know you really have them?"

"Hang on. Here, Alex, tell your mommy you want to go home."

Her mouth went dry. "Alex? Talk to me, baby."

"Mommy? Spider-Man isn't nice. He tried to make Grammy use the outhouse with the black widows. I want to come home."

"I'm coming to get you, Alex. Stay strong, sweetheart." She could barely force the words past the tightness in her throat.

The distorted voice came back on. "Satisfied? Do what I ask if you want to see him again."

The call ended, and her fingers went numb. The phone would have fallen to the ground, but Zach caught it. Her eyes burned, and she struggled to hold back the sobs. Crying wouldn't get her boy back. "I have to do what he says."

Her dad sidled closer. "Someone has my boy?"

She nodded and told him what the man had said. "I'm so scared."

"I always knew it would come to this," her dad said. "I'm the only one who can fix it."

He plunged off into the forest, and she quickly lost sight of him. Zach pulled her into an embrace. "We have to call the sheriff."

She buried her face in his shirt. "We can't! He'll kill them."

"We don't have a choice. This gets bigger

373

by the minute. We have to protect Alex and Marilyn, and we can't do that by walking into a trap." He kept one arm around her as he called the sheriff on her phone.

CHAPTER 35

Shauna couldn't breathe, couldn't think beyond flying the helicopter out of the clearing. The chopper made its way through blue skies punctuated with puffs of white clouds, but her hands did what they had to do while her heart urged her to get to Alex, to scoop him into her arms and never let him go.

Who was this maniac who killed her friends and targeted her own family? And why had her dad run off like that? She had no way to contact him to find out what he'd meant about fixing it.

Zach's voice spoke in her ear through the headset. "We'll find Alex. Stay calm, Flygirl."

She gave a jerky nod. "We shouldn't have called the sheriff. The man said not to."

"We can't fight him on our own. You know that."

It felt wrong to go against the kidnapper's orders. What if he had someone inside the sheriff's office? What if he'd tapped her cell phone in some way? There was so much that could go wrong. She prayed for God to keep watch over Alex and Marilyn as she pushed the chopper as fast as she dared for the airport.

Two sheriff's department squad cars were in the parking lot when she set the helicopter down. Zach leaped out when the skids touched the ground. The wind blew his hair, and he ducked down to run out from under the rotors. Shauna did the same as soon as she had everything shut off.

She rushed up to the sheriff, who appeared very somber. "Any idea who has my boy and Marilyn?"

Sheriff Burchell shook his head. "Marilyn lives in the middle of nowhere, so there are no witnesses of the kidnapping. I have two deputies at her house right now going over the premises to see if they can find any evidence."

"I've got to take the necklace and leave it for him like he demanded. I've barely got enough time to get there by the deadline."

"Where is the necklace?" the sheriff asked.

She tugged it out from under her shirt. "I like wearing it. It makes me feel closer to my mother, but it's nothing compared to Alex's life. And Marilyn's."

"I have several deputies masquerading as tourists around the pull-off. They've been instructed to follow him and see if he leads them to Alex and Marilyn." Everett reached into his car and pulled out a roll of duct tape. "Use this to tape the necklace to the back of the sign like he said, then leave immediately."

"This feels wrong," Zach said. "What's to ensure he returns Alex and Marilyn once he has the necklace? I don't think you should do it, Shauna. Once he gets the necklace, he can do what he wants."

She chewed on her lip and nodded. "I tried to tell him I wasn't going to do it that way, and he said I'd never see them again if I didn't."

"Of course that's what he'd say," Zach said. "He's trying to force your hand. This leaves you no bargaining power."

"What if I tape a note to the back of the sign with an alternate plan? I can tell him we'll meet him in Rainshadow Bay, by Eagle Rock. I'll tell him I will fly him wherever he wants to go in my helicopter if he lets Zach take Alex and Marilyn."

Zach was shaking his head before she finished. "I don't like it. What's to keep him from killing you once he escapes? I'll fly him out in my plane, and you can take Alex and

Marilyn to safety." He rested his hands on her shoulders, and his dark-blue eyes held desperation as he stared into hers. "You can't risk leaving Alex an orphan. You just can't."

"It might work," the sheriff said.

A vivid image of Zach floating lifeless in the bay struck her, and she shuddered. What she felt for Zach wasn't just attraction or loneliness, but a deep, lasting love like she'd had for Jack. She couldn't bear to lose him like she'd lost Jack, but she knew he was right. Alex had only her. It would destroy him to lose her too.

She pushed away the fearful image and nodded. "Okay." A search of her purse yielded a notepad, and she wrote out the alternate exchange offer, then grabbed the roll of tape from the sheriff. "I think I should go alone. If he sees too many people milling around, he'll take off."

"Any idea why he wants that necklace?" the sheriff asked.

"Not a clue. He didn't say."

Zach pursed his lips. "I just thought of something. You know how Alex has those vivid dreams and sleepwalks? I caught him looking for what he called 'the key' last night. He said Spider-Man needed him to find it so Alex could be his sidekick and save

378

us all from the Joker." He held up his hand. "I know, I told him the Joker was a Batman villain, and Alex had an explanation for that. What if this guy tried to get Alex to grab the necklace for him, but when he failed, he took him to force you to give it up?"

Shauna took it off and looked it over closely. It was still just a Haida argillite stone with an abalone hummingbird. "But it's not a key. It's a necklace."

"It's even weirder that it was your mother's yet it's important to him all these years after she died," the sheriff said.

She glanced at her watch. "It's four thirty, and I only have an hour. None of that matters right now. I have to get Alex and Marilyn back." She clasped Zach's neck to bring his head down, then brushed her lips across his. "Pray for me."

He gripped her shoulders. "Constantly." He snagged the necklace from her fingers. "Let me keep this for now."

The drone of a small plane landing on the runway made Sheriff Burchell raise his voice. "You have no intention of letting her go in there alone, do you?"

Zach shook his head and started for the hangar with the sheriff on his heels. "Not a chance. I knew she'd object if I told her,

379

but I'm taking my ATV after her. I can run it in the fields, and I'll get there before she does."

The sheriff caught his arm. "My men are watching. I think we'd be better off trying to track down Lewis and find out what he knows. This could all go very badly if we're not careful."

Zach stopped in the hangar doorway and ran his hand over the back of his neck. The stakes couldn't be higher. "We don't know where Lewis went." But he remembered the look on Lewis's face when Shauna asked him about the strange building. He told the sheriff about it. "He could have gone there. He did head in that direction."

"I'll go with you. Can you take your plane in there?"

"There's not enough room to land." And it was impossible to get there by car. Hiking in would take too long. Zach crossed the yard and went to his office, where he pulled out a topo map and spread it out on his desk. He jabbed a finger on it. "We could take a boat up the river and get off about a half mile from the site, then hike in. We could be there in an hour."

Past the deadline. He'd be in an area with no cell service and no way to know what was happening back here. The thought forced the air to leave his lungs. What should he do? Everything in him wanted to go to Shauna and protect her.

The sheriff must have seen the indecision on his face because he put his hand on Zach's arm. "We can't sit back and wait, Zach. If we let this guy control things, Alex and Marilyn might not make it."

Alex was probably terrified and crying for his mother. The thought was a stab in Zach's guts, and he rubbed his forehead. "Okay, let's go."

"I'll drive," the sheriff said.

Zach got into the passenger side of Burchell's vehicle, and they sped toward town where Zach had a boat docked. Neither of them had much to say in the five-minute drive to the pier. Zach kept going over and over in his head everything Lewis had said. *I always knew it would come to this. I'm the only one who can fix it.*

Lewis knew exactly why this had happened and the identity of the kidnapper. But how? He barely left that cabin in the woods. How did the necklace figure in with this? It seemed an old bauble without much value, yet someone was willing to kidnap two people to get it. And how had Clarence even gotten ahold of it? There seemed no way to detangle this.

They reached the dock, and he pointed out his boat, a forty-footer he'd bought three years ago. Once they reached the pilothouse, he pulled out his phone. "You think you can captain this? I've got a hunch I want to check out."

Burchell's brows rose, but he nodded and started the engine. "I was born boating." As the boat pulled away from the dock, Zach sat at the bow and called Dorothy Edenshaw's shop.

She answered on the third ring. "Rings and Things, this is Dorothy."

"This is Zach Bannister again. I'm sorry to bother you, but we have a desperate situation in Lavender Tides." He launched into the circumstances before she could hang up on him. "Is there anything special about the necklace? Could it be used as a key in some way?"

"Not that I know of." Her voice was cold. "You keep trying to drag me into this, and I want nothing to do with it. Please, just leave me alone."

She was about to hang up. "Please, Dorothy, a little boy's life depends on us figuring this out. Doesn't that mean anything to you?" There was dead-air space, but he could still hear the faint sound of voices in the background. "I'm sure he's scared to death."

She finally broke the silence with a sigh. "Who has the necklace?"

"I do."

"Turn it over and you'll find three little ridges on it. They're spaced evenly apart on the back."

He pulled the necklace from his pocket and flipped it over, then ran his fingers over the smooth black surface of the argillite. "I feel them."

"Press against them and turn it counter-clockwise."

He followed her instructions. "The back popped off. It looks weird now." There were protrusions and indentations inside.

"There's a matching lock the protrusions fit into. When the necklace is in place, you can turn the lock."

"What lock?"

"That's something you need to ask Lewis. I've told you everything I can."

This time there was no mistaking the fact she'd ended the call. He looked at the phone to verify there was no connection, then put his phone back in his pocket. "Look at this." He showed the back of the necklace to the sheriff. "She says Lewis knows what this is all about. It's already nearly five."

The sheriff revved the engine, and the bow of the boat lifted out of the water. "Then we'd better find him."

CHAPTER 36

Shauna parked in the pull-off, then got out of her truck under blue skies and the noise of gulls fighting over a piece of bread in the parking lot. She was halfway here when she realized she'd left her weapons behind in the helicopter. An older couple glanced at her as they got back in their car to leave, and she forced a smile, then walked to the sign explaining the spot's history. Two eagles surveyed the area from atop a tall pine to her left. The overlook held a stunningly beautiful view of the blue water of Rainshadow Bay and mountains that usually took her breath away.

Today she was only interested in doing whatever she had to do to get her boy back. She opened her bag and pulled out the envelope with the note and looked at it. Was this the right thing to do? The man's threats still froze the blood in her veins, and going against his orders felt dangerous.

She had no choice, though. Zach had taken the necklace for safekeeping, so she couldn't leave it now anyway. She retrieved the duct tape from her bag and went toward the sign. The back of her neck prickled, and she looked around. Was he here watching her? Probably. He'd want to grab the necklace and get away before someone else happened to see it.

There was hardly anywhere to stand behind the sign. It looked out over a steep cliff, and the ground sloped quickly here. She pulled strips of tape loose and attached them to the envelope, then hung on to the post while she sidled around and slapped the note into place. He might have a hard time retrieving it.

Her left foot slipped as she tried to move to safer ground. For a heart-stopping moment she imagined herself plunging over the side. Her mouth dry, she clung to the post and regained her balance, then moved to a flattened area.

The door to her truck still hung open, and she slung herself under the wheel and started the engine. After shutting the door, she sped out of the lot, her tires kicking up gravel. The clock on the dash read 5:25. She'd made it with only five minutes to spare.

She shook her head. Not really. The guy didn't have the necklace, and she shuddered to think what he might do when he saw her note. This had been a bad idea. How would she live with herself if something happened to Alex?

She accelerated down the road as fast as the truck would roll. Whatever happened, she needed the necklace, just in case the guy wouldn't listen. It had taken nearly an hour to get out here, and she had to get that necklace from Zach.

She was nearly to the airport when her cell phone rang. She froze when she saw Marilyn's name on the screen. Her hands trembled on the steering wheel as she pulled onto the shoulder. "I'm here."

"You will regret this!" His voice vibrated with anger. "I have to have the necklace now!"

She pressed her hand against her churning stomach. "I don't trust you. I'm happy to give it to you, but I want my son and Marilyn in eyesight when I do. How do I know that you haven't already k-killed them?" She bit her trembling lip to keep her voice strong.

"They were fine up until now. I can't say the same for the rest of the evening."

She closed her eyes briefly. "Look, we both

want the same thing. I want you to have what you need. Please turn over my loved ones. Our offer is a good one. You can get out of the country and disappear."

"You think I'm stupid enough to fall for this? You've already told the sheriff, and deputies are all over looking for me. Zach's not going to fly me anywhere but off to jail. Besides, I already have plans in place, and your idea won't help me." His voice hardened. "I'm not taking your offer. You're going to turn your truck around and drive back to the pull-off where you will hand me the necklace. I'll give you the address of where you can find them, and then I'll be gone. One hour."

"Wait! I —" The call ended before she could tell him she didn't have it. She called Marilyn's number right away, but after four rings, it went to voice mail. She tried again and got the same result.

She pounded the steering wheel, then rubbed her burning eyes. She'd call Zach. He could meet her with the necklace. She called his phone, but he didn't answer. She left a message, then tried his number again. Nothing. Where could he be? She called the sheriff, but got his voice mail too. Dread slithered up her spine and she shuddered.

She rested her head on the steering wheel.

Maybe she should go back to meet the guy and explain what had happened. As she raised her head, her phone signaled a new voice mail, and she snatched it up. It was from Zach and had been left an hour ago. She must have missed it somehow.

His voice sounded strong and confident. *"Shauna, the sheriff and I are on our way by boat out to the building we saw. I think your dad might have been heading there. I'm sure he knows who this guy is and where Alex and Marilyn are. It will take us an hour to get there so we should be on our way back by the time you leave the meeting place. Be strong."* His voice faltered a bit. *"I talked to Dorothy, and she told me how to twist off the back of the necklace. There are three protrusions that make it into some weird kind of key. I'm sending you a picture of it to see if you have ever seen anything like it. Talk to you soon."*

Gone. He was gone and no help to her right now. She checked her text messages and saw one from Zach. The necklace didn't look the same at all, but something about it was familiar. She'd seen something this would fit into. What was it and where was it? She bit her lip and pressed her fingertips to her eyelids, but the memory wouldn't surface. She had to let go of it for now and head back to the parking lot.

How did she tell this guy she didn't have the necklace? She never should have let Zach take it from her. It left her with no bargaining power at all and a sense of hopelessness.

By the time Zach got back, she'd be meeting with this guy face-to-face, and it didn't look good.

Small twigs and branches crackled under Zach's boots as he led the way to the building they'd found. His breath came hard in his chest as they ran full-out from where they moored his boat.

The sheriff huffed from the exertion and paused to catch his breath. "Hold up there a minute, Zach. I can't keep up."

Zach wanted to put his fist through a tree, but he stopped and exhaled. "We don't have time. We have to find Lewis."

"You don't seriously think the guy is going to accept the alternate offer, do you?" Burchell's heavy black brows winged up.

"Of course not. You and I both know he has no intention of letting Alex and Marilyn go, but I couldn't tell Shauna that. We have to figure out who he is and where to find him before he disappears. Time is running out."

"You're right. Some of my best deputies

are on it, and hopefully he's leading them right to Shauna's family." Burchell motioned with his right hand. "Lead on. I'll keep up the best I can. If I fall behind, go on without me and get to Lewis."

Zach took off through the forest again. The woodland seemed determined to slow his progress. Twigs and sticks caught at his feet, and his soles slipped on moss. The aroma of pine and mud filled his nose. The building was just ahead, and his steps quickened. He burst out of the trees into the clearing and saw Lewis talking to a woman about forty feet away. Her back was to Zach, and all he could see was her long, dark hair spilling over a camouflage shirt tucked into camo pants. She had a rifle slung over her shoulder.

Neither of them saw him, so he stepped back into the shadow of the trees and looked around for Burchell. The sheriff stepped from behind a large cedar, and Zach put his finger to his lips and motioned for him to follow. They crept through the trees and made their way nearer to where Lewis stood with the woman. Something about her looked vaguely familiar, but he couldn't place her without seeing her face.

Snippets of their discussion were carried on the wind, but he couldn't make sense of anything. He was so intent on getting close enough to hear that he didn't watch where he was stepping. His right foot came down on a large twig, and the snapping sound was as loud as a gull's squawk.

The woman jerked around, and her gaze locked with Zach's. Dorothy's daughter. Penelope's mouth grew pinched, and her eyes hardened. In an instant the rifle was off her shoulder and aimed at him. Zach leaped behind a tree as the rifle cracked. The bullet plowed into the bark beside Zach's cheek.

She'd been the one shooting at them.

Burchell yanked his revolver out. "Sheriff! Drop your weapon!"

Another shot rang out, then he heard tussling and shouts. He peered around the tree to see Lewis yank the rifle from Penelope's hands. Zach didn't wait to see what would happen but leaped out of the forest and ran to help. Burchell was on his heels, still shouting for them to throw down the rifle.

Penelope turned and saw them heading her way. She screamed an obscenity at Lewis, then ran the other direction. Zach cranked up a fresh burst of speed and ran after her. Alex's life depended on running her down and finding out what she knew. His breath burned in his chest. Just a little faster, just a few more steps and he'd have her.

He hadn't tackled anyone since his high school football days, but the ability came surging back — he threw himself into the air and at her legs. His right hand closed around her ankle, and she tumbled to the ground with a scream. She tried to kick his grip off her leg, but he held on and reached out with his left hand to grab her other ankle.

Panting, he got to his knees and pulled her toward him. "Where are Alex and Marilyn?" he snarled. It was all he could do to hold on to her legs as she kicked and flailed on the ground.

"Let go of me!" she spat.

"Where's Alex?" Zach demanded.

She struggled to get to her feet. Burchell grabbed her arm and hefted her up. His hand swatted at his waist. "I'm out of uniform, so I don't have my cuffs. Where are Alex and Marilyn?"

"I don't have any idea what you're talking about."

"If you're so innocent, why were you shooting at us? You shot at us earlier too, didn't you? And followed us to Lewis's cabin." Zach jerked his head toward the building. "What's this all about?"

She pressed her lips together and stared at him defiantly. Zach looked at Lewis. "You have a key to get in?"

Lewis shook his head. "She might, though."

"Hold her." Burchell began to search her pockets, then shook his head. "I'm not finding anything." He took charge of her from Zach and held her by the arm.

Zach squeezed Lewis's shoulder. "Lewis, what's this all about?"

"The Bible always says your sins will find you out." His eyes flooded with moisture. "It's true. This is all my fault. I started this, then I was too weak to stop it. My wife died, and it was my fault. Now my grandson is in danger, all because of me. I should have told what I knew years ago." He picked at nothing on his sleeve and stared at the treetops as if an angel perched there.

The man was unraveling. "Lewis, look at me. Tell me what you're talking about!"

Lewis's mouth trembled. "I can't tell you. I'm going to have to show you." He turned to the sheriff. "Can you shoot the lock off the door?"

"No!" Penelope thrashed and tried to get out of Burchell's grip. "You have no right."

"I have every right." Lewis marched for the building. "Sheriff, shoot off this lock."

Penelope let out a nearly inhuman wail and managed to tear loose from the sheriff's grasp. She dove for her rifle on the ground, then rolled over and leaped to her feet. She aimed the barrel at Burchell's head. "Throw down your weapons, all of them, or I'll shoot him." Her brown eyes seemed lit from within with a zealous glow. Her finger flexed on the trigger. "Don't make me show you."

Zach eyed her expression and saw how eager she was to pull the trigger. He threw his gun to the ground and held up his hands. "Let's all calm down and talk about this." The sheriff dropped his gun too.

Lewis hesitated, then shrugged and tossed down his weapons. "You won't hurt us."

"This is all his fault." She jerked her head toward Lewis. "Empty your pockets, all of you."

"We don't have any other weapons," Zach said.

"Do what I say!" Her finger moved toward the trigger again. "I can see the bulge in your jacket pocket. Pull it out."

"It's not a gun." Zach's fingers curled around the necklace and pulled it from his pocket. "See?" He started to drop it back into his jacket, but a slight smile curved her lips.

She waved the gun toward him. "Put it

there on the fallen tree and step away."

Zach frowned but did as she ordered.

In three steps she reached the necklace and grabbed it up with a triumphant grin directed at Lewis. "We're going back to your cabin to get what we need. Once I take care of these two."

Lewis shook his head. "They come too or you won't get what you're after. You don't know where it is."

Her eyes narrowed. "Don't play games with me, Duval. I could shoot you too."

"And then you'd really be up a creek without a paddle. They. Come. Too."

She stared at him, then gritted her teeth. "Fine. Lead the way."

CHAPTER 37

His car sat in the shadows of the forest where he could watch the parking lot. Alex had fallen asleep in the backseat. What was he going to do with the kid while he grabbed the necklace? His mother would almost certainly rush to him. The trunk might work, but he'd have to gag him, and he didn't want to do that. Alex wasn't so bad, and he was so much like his dad that it hurt to think of having to deal with him.

Was there a way around it? He dabbed lavender on his bee sting while he thought about it.

Before he could decide what to do, the satellite phone on his console rang. He snatched it up. "Everything okay on your end? I've told Shauna she can trade the necklace for Alex and his grandmother. She's bringing it to me now."

"No, she isn't." Penelope sounded gleeful. "I've got it in my hot little hands right now, and we're going back to Lewis's to collect the drawings."

He grinned, and the pressure in his chest eased. "How'd you get it?"

"Her new honey had it in his pocket."

"Zach's there?"

"And the sheriff and Lewis, but I've got everything under control. We're nearly to Lewis's house. I'll grab the plans, then set fire to the place with them in it. I'll meet you at our spot, and we can get on our way."

He glanced in the rearview mirror at the sleeping boy. "We can't let any of them get away or we'll be hounded for the rest of our lives."

"I know that," she snapped. "Just get going, okay? Let's get this over with and catch that flight to Cambodia."

"What time should you be done on your end?"

"Send your buyers to the building in the morning, and I'll turn over the plans to them in your place. You can handle things on your end, then meet me. That will give us time to take care of any loose ends and get out of town. I don't think we should meet until we're ready to leave. You got the money, right?"

"Yes, half is in my account as promised. I'll have to call them. That's not the original plan." His pulse ratcheted up at the thought of altering the plan and getting the Chinese suspicious, but he had no choice. "You did great, sweetheart. See you soon."

He sat back and exhaled. At least he didn't have to wait and confront Shauna. He could take Alex back to the cabin and make sure Marilyn was still there. They hadn't seen his face so they couldn't identify him. Alex's comment about his grandmother knowing his identity was just bravado. He could leave them confined to the cabin while he escaped with Penelope. The only ones who had to vanish were the sheriff and Zach. Lewis didn't matter. He wasn't going to say anything because he'd be implicating himself as well.

He placed the call to the Chinese. "There's been a slight change of plan. My partner is going to meet you in my place with the plans. I, ah . . . I have some things to handle on my end."

"This is not acceptable. I will not transfer the money unless you are present. We will not walk into a trap."

He spit out a silent curse. This guy meant business. There was no dissuading that implacable determination. "Fine. I'll be there too."

"See that you are."

The call ended, and he dropped the phone back onto the seat. He smiled and started the car. By this time tomorrow, they'd be safely away from any chance of arrest. And rich. Very rich.

Shauna parked in the same spot as before and sat back to wait. No other vehicles were around, so the man must not be here yet. Right now she was a hot mess, trembling and shaking like she had a fever. This was all going wrong, and she didn't know how to fix it.

She got out of her truck and lifted her face to the salt-laden breeze. Closing her eyes, she prayed for wisdom and courage. She'd never get through this alone. How could birds sing so carefree and happily in the trees when her world was crashing down? The waves rolled onto the rocks below, and she stared down the steep cliff into the water. She felt like she was at the mercy of one of those roiling waves and didn't know which side was up and which was down.

There had to be something she was missing. Surely there was a clue that would tell her who was behind all this, but what? She ran through all the events over the past few weeks. A hint of lavender floated on the wind, and her head began to throb. Wait a minute, there were no lavender fields for miles. She retreated to her truck and grabbed peppermint oil to rub on her temples.

As the pain began to abate, she realized that every time the murderer had been around, she'd gotten a headache. She stopped and looked around. Maybe the guy used lavender oil as a remedy. It was well-known to help many conditions: dandruff, hay fever, eczema, bee stings.

Bee stings. Something about that issue set alarms flaring, but no matter how much she tried to grasp the memory, it escaped her.

She paced the gravel lot and watched. Her phone confirmed it had been nearly ninety minutes since the last call. Was he not going to show up? Maybe he'd already run off. She knuckled her wet eyes and turned back to her truck. Her phone rang, but the screen read *Anonymous.* She almost didn't answer it, but then she realized he might be using his own phone this time instead of Marilyn's.

She answered the call and put the phone to her ear. "Yes?"

The weird distorted voice was loud in her ear. "I warned you not to play games."

"I'm not playing games!" When he didn't respond, she pulled the phone away and stared at the screen. The call had ended. Did he hang up or did it drop? She tried to call it back, but without a valid number it didn't do any good.

Her heart squeezed, and panic nearly dropped her to her knees. Where was her baby, her little boy? She longed to hold him and breathe in the little-boy smell of mud and hard candy. She had to get to Zach. Together they could figure this out and find Alex.

She tried his number again but only connected with voice mail. Calling the sheriff yielded the same result. What would be the fastest way to reach that building and intercept him there? The chopper would get her there in about thirty minutes, but she was an hour from the airfield. Or she could go back to her dad's. She was about half an hour from the turnoff back into the forest, and then once at her dad's, she would be about two miles from that building. If she jogged as quickly as she could, she could get there in about half an hour.

Wait a second. She was within a mile of Jermaine's place. Just over the hill. He had an ATV she could borrow for the two-mile trek. She'd be back there in minutes. She jumped into the truck and stomped on the accelerator. The tires spit gravel as she aimed the truck toward Jermaine's. In two minutes she was at his driveway.

A movement caught her eye, and she saw Jermaine mowing with a garden tractor. He wore headphones and belted out some country tune way off-key.

She skidded to a stop and jumped out, waving her arms. "Jermaine!" The scent of freshly mowed grass hung in the air.

He stopped the tractor and turned off the engine. His pale-green eyes were always startlingly vivid in his dark face. "Shauna, what's up?"

"I need to borrow your ATV, right now. I've got a hitch on my truck. Can I take it? I don't have time to explain, but Alex is in trouble."

"You got it." He pointed to the trailer already loaded with the ATV. "Back up your truck, and I'll hitch you up."

She breathed a relieved sigh, then jumped into her truck and backed up to the trailer. It could only have been a minute or two before he slapped the back of the truck, but it felt like hours.

"All clear to go. I can come with you to help if you need me."

"I just need to get to Zach." She hesitated. "You might check in at the sheriff's office and let them know I'm heading out to my dad's area to meet up with him and Zach. If they don't hear from us soon, they'd better send a deputy."

His face held concern. "I'll be praying. If I don't hear from you, I'll come too."

"Thanks, Jermaine, you're the best." She hit the accelerator and pulled away as fast as she dared with the trailer.

No other traffic was on the main road as she headed for the forest turnoff back to her dad's. She could drive straight to his cabin, then drive the ATV from there to the building. He might have returned to his cabin and could help her, though she doubted it. Still, it was worth a try.

She sped up until the trailer began to sway behind her, then she made herself slow down. Her dad's place was nearly in sight when her truck gave a cough and began to run rough. She pounded on the steering wheel. "Don't quit on me now!" It sputtered and wheezed, then the engine stopped. She tried to start it again, but it turned over without firing. What was wrong with it?

Her focus landed on the gas gauge. Below empty. How could she be so stupid?

CHAPTER 38

Perspiration stung Zach's eyes as Penelope kept prodding them to a near jog back toward Lewis's cabin. She'd lashed their hands behind their backs with vines, something he'd found harder to break than he expected. It was hard to keep his balance at such a fast pace. Lewis was six feet ahead of him, and the sheriff huffed alongside Zach.

Sunset was approaching, and gloom started to claim the forest. They'd probably make it to the cabin by dark, but just barely. Why had she been so elated to get the necklace? Penelope had to have called whoever had taken Alex and Marilyn, because she clearly didn't have them. Zach mulled over the things he'd heard her say. Something about plans, but how could something that mundane be the catalyst for murder and kidnapping? She'd kept her voice pitched low on the phone call, so he hadn't caught much beyond the blueprints reference.

He had no doubt she intended to get rid of them once she got what she was after. Only Lewis's intervention had prevented her from putting a bullet in their heads. He had to figure out how to grab the gun from her, but with their hands tied, it was going to take some coordination.

His wrists chafed from the vines, and he licked dry lips. Lewis might be their only hope. At least Shauna wasn't here. Something to be thankful for. Though finding out Lewis was part of this would be painful for her. If she ever found out.

A tree root snagged his left foot, and he went sprawling. He slammed face-first into a patch of wildflowers. He writhed on the ground until he succeeded in getting to his knees, then onto his feet.

She poked him in the back with the barrel of the rifle. "Keep moving. I don't have all night to get this done."

"Why are you doing this?"

"No talk." She shoved him, and he nearly went sprawling again so he shut up. For now.

The darkness came down as if God had dropped a giant blanket over the forest. One second he could see and the next, he couldn't make out Lewis in front of him any longer. Maybe this was his opportunity to make a dash for the trees. He shook his head. He couldn't leave the sheriff with Penelope. They would need to work together to take her down.

"Hold up. Lewis, we can't see you." She flipped on a flashlight and pinpointed Lewis in its beam. "Got you. Lead the way."

They all started walking again, more slowly now that it was dark. The wind cooled and brought some relief to Zach's face and neck. They'd arrive at the cabin in ten minutes. All he had to do was figure out how to get free, then seize a gun from Lewis's massive armory.

It sounded easy, but he needed a knife or something sharp. These vines were tougher than they looked. He'd have to stay alert. The glimmer of light through the trees guided them the last few feet to the cabin. Zach caught the glint of moonlight shining on an ax stuck in a log near the front door. If he could get away, he might be able to use it.

Lewis stepped through the front door. Zach followed him and stopped to let his eyes adjust to the light inside the cabin.

The sheriff bumped into Zach as he came through the door. "Distraction," he whispered.

Zach gave a quick nod, then turned to face

Penelope as she entered the cabin and closed the door behind her. "What are you going to do with us? You can't just murder the sheriff and expect to get away with it."

He'd thought she was attractive when he first met her, but there was nothing beautiful about her flat eyes and hard mouth now. "I can do anything I want. No one knows about me or my partner. They'll find your —" She clamped her mouth shut, and her gaze went even more distant.

She was smart and wasn't about to get drawn into revealing anything. A coiled rope lay by a pile of fishing nets and poles, and she grabbed it, then lashed their hands to the doorknob. "Lewis, show me the safe. Now."

Lewis wiped his mouth with the back of his hand. "I need something to drink."

"You need to take me to the safe." He ignored her and headed for the refrigerator. Raising her voice, she followed him and jerked the beer bottle he grabbed from his hand. "I don't need you drunk!"

He gave her a hard look. "If I'm going to betray my daughter, I need something to help me do it."

"You'll do what I say!" She hauled off and slapped his face hard enough that his head rocked back.

He passed his palm over his cheek, then snatched the beer out of her hand. He uncapped it and took a long swig. "I shouldn't have let you blackmail me. I should have been stronger."

Blackmail?

Zach tried to think of anything Lewis cared about enough to let someone force him into criminal activity. Shauna maybe? He shook his head and looked around for something to use as a knife. A beer bottle sat on the coffee table, but she'd hear it break.

Lewis took another swig. "Just take the plans and go. The deed should have been enough for you, but you're just like your mother. It was all or nothing with her too."

"Leave my mother out of it!" She raised her hand again and punched him in the chest. He reeled back, and she advanced. "You ruined my life. After you left, she was never the same. I'd come home from school and find her sitting on the sofa. No food waiting, no smiles, nothing." She kicked him in the knee, and he let out a yell as he fell. "She never came to anything at school. I felt invisible." She grabbed him by the arm and yanked him up. "Let's get this over with."

Zach stayed quiet by the sheriff. Maybe

she really would leave them here alone and they could get loose.

She should have let Jermaine come with her. Shauna struggled with the ramps for the ATV until she was panting. It was nearly dark by the time she managed to get them out and roll the machine onto the ground. It had been years since she'd driven one of these things, but it couldn't be that hard, right? Wasn't it like riding a bicycle?

She climbed onto the seat, and it all came back to her. The machine controls were exactly like the last one she'd driven. Encouraged, she turned it on and headed for her dad's, about ten minutes down the road. She tried to keep her mind on the task at hand, but fear clawed at her insides. Alex was out there somewhere without her. He was probably crying for her. She could only hope and pray Marilyn was keeping him calm. She wouldn't allow herself to think about what that man might do.

As she neared the cabin, she saw lights on in the living room. She cut the engine, then dismounted. Could they be here? If she wanted to find out what role her father might be playing in all this, it was safer to approach by foot.

The wind carried the murmur of voices to

410

her ears, and she ducked down to approach the cabin as stealthily as possible. It sounded like her father was arguing with a woman, and the voices came from his bedroom. She crept toward the window, then stood to peer inside.

A woman with long dark hair stood with her back to Shauna. A rifle was slung over her shoulder, and a pistol protruded from the waistband of her jeans. Something about her was familiar, but Shauna couldn't place her until the woman half turned toward the window. She bit back a gasp. Dorothy's daughter.

She ducked down and held her breath as Penelope stepped closer to the window. What was she doing here, and why was Pop so mad?

"Where is it?" Penelope demanded. "I don't see a safe."

"It's not exactly in a safe."

Shauna peeked up again to see her dad turn toward the closet. He opened the door and pushed aside hangers of old flannel shirts and jeans.

Penelope pushed past him. "Where is it?"

"In the back of the closet. There's a metal box in the wall this fits into." He held out his hand. "Give me the necklace."

After a brief hesitation, Penelope handed

it over. Shauna clenched her hands into fists. If Penelope had the necklace, she'd taken it from Zach. Terror tightened like a garrote around her throat. She needed Zach to help her find Alex and Marilyn. She wanted her baby so badly it was all she could do to stay put and listen. Every fiber of her being wanted to leap into the room and demand to know where they had her son. She didn't doubt that her father knew.

She couldn't examine how she felt about that — not right now. Somehow she had to hold herself together and be strong enough to rescue her son.

She swallowed hard, watching her father fiddle with the necklace until some weird prongs popped out. He crawled into the closet until all she could see of him were the soles of his shoes.

Penelope peered in to watch. "What are you doing?"

"You're blocking my light." His voice was muffled. "How'd you get this anyway? I thought it was buried with my wife."

"My partner sneaked it out of the casket when no one was looking. He was a pall-bearer. Then it went missing right around the time Darla got suspicious. We realized after she died that she had to have taken it. When Clarence came by my partner's office with some questions about Darla, he knew Clarence had found the necklace."

Shauna tried to think of who'd been pallbearers, but she'd been too young when her mom died to remember.

Penelope stepped out of the way and glanced toward the window. For a heart-stopping second, Shauna thought she'd been spotted. She ducked down and held her breath, but when no footsteps headed her way, she relaxed and peeked up again in time to see her father emerge from the closet with a roll of white papers.

He held them away from Penelope when she snatched at them. "I want my grandson or you can't have this."

Penelope yanked out her gun and pointed it at him. "You're of no use to me now."

Before he could respond, a shot rang out. Shauna stuffed her fist in her mouth as her dad fell to the old green carpet. A red stain formed under his head, and a bullet carved a hole in his forehead. Bile choked her throat, and she breathed through her nose to keep from vomiting.

Penelope grabbed the papers, then went to the bed and spread them out. Her father used to be a geologic engineer, and from the little she could see from the window, the plans appeared to be some kind of geological design.

Shauna's gaze returned to her father. She sank to her knees and stifled the sobs. She had to find Zach and the sheriff. Right now she had no weapons and no way to force the woman to give up Alex.

Keeping her head down, she ran around to the back of the house and peeked in the kitchen door. Their backs to one another, Zach and the sheriff were working to break the ropes tied to their wrists. Zach tore furiously at the knots on the sheriff's wrist, but they didn't look to be budging. Praying Penelope was still busy looking at the plans, Shauna eased open the door and stepped inside.

This was all riding on her. If she failed, Alex would die.

CHAPTER 39

"Here, I brought you dinner." He tossed some deli sandwiches he'd brought in a cooler to Marilyn, and she caught them.

Her gaze shot to Alex, who still stood by him. "Come here, Alex. I'm sure you're hungry."

Alex nodded, then glanced up at him as if to ask if it was okay.

"Listen to your grandmother." He pulled out bottles of water and tossed them one at a time to her too. "Your girl didn't come through, but I still got what I wanted. Before I go, tell me the truth. The kid says you know who I am."

Fear flashed across Marilyn's face, and she shook her head. "I just said that to help him have courage. I have no idea who you are or why you are doing this. You can let us go. We can't identify you."

She's lying.

He saw it in her face, and regret shivered

down his spine. "Eat your dinner. I have to make a call."

He went out the front door and padlocked it behind him. He slid into his car and yanked off his mask before he reached for his sat phone to call Penelope. Everything in him rebelled at the thought of what he had to do. He could dispose of Marilyn, no problem. The boy was another matter. He liked the kid and always had.

Maybe he could make it painless, though he was out of ideas on how to do that. Drugs maybe, but he had very little time to procure anything.

Penelope answered on the second ring. "I have the plans! I was just looking them over to make sure they're all here. Lewis always said he stumbled on the earthquake-induction potential by accident, and looking at these drawings, I think that's true. Lucky break for us, huh?"

"That's great!" He tried to force enthusiasm into his voice but failed.

"And now it's all ours."

"Yeah." He glanced at Marilyn's cabin. "We can get out of here tomorrow and never look back."

"What's your problem? You don't sound excited."

"It's the kid. I don't want to have to hurt

him. I can handle Marilyn, but I want to take the kid with us. I can give him to someone when we get out of here."

"Don't be ridiculous! I don't want a kid along on our trip. Besides, he can identify you."

"I don't think so. I wore the Spider-Man mask every time he saw me. I think maybe Marilyn recognized my voice, but I'm not positive. I have to do something about her for sure."

"You're such a softie. Maybe that's why I love you so much. Do whatever you think is best. Did you get ahold of the buyers?"

"Yes. They're insistent that I show up in the morning too. I had no choice but to agree. They wouldn't put the other half of the money in my account if I didn't."

"It's only seven so you should be able to dispose of your liabilities and get to Lewis's cabin with no problem. Did you buy our plane tickets yet?"

"I bought open-ended ones as soon as the first half came through. First class too."

"Whoo-hoo!" she squealed. "I've never flown first class."

He grinned. It was going to be fun to spoil her. He still couldn't believe he was about to spend the rest of his life with her. "What about your mother? Won't she wonder where you've gone?"

"Probably. I'll get in touch with her sooner or later, once all the hoopla here dies down. I think she might have suspected something was up when Shauna came sniffing around about the necklace, but I managed to placate her."

"We can make sure we get a big enough place that she can come visit."

"What about your wife? Any regrets?"

A pang struck him, but he pushed it away. His wife would survive, and his kids and grandkids would get over it eventually. "Our marriage was over a long time ago. She'll move on."

"I hope you don't say that about me someday."

"Never," he vowed. "We're going to have a great life together. I can't wait to show you the world. We'll go on a luxury cruise once we get settled."

"You're the best. Listen, I already had to shoot Lewis."

"What? I thought you were going to make it look accidental. Fire is the best way."

"He gave me no choice. He was trying to bargain for his grandson's exchange and wouldn't give me the plans. I'd had enough of him anyway."

She'd taken the opportunity to get rid of

Lewis. He suppressed a shudder. Her dangerous side was one of the most intriguing things about her. Life with her would never be dull. "So you've got the sheriff and Zach contained?"

"Partially. I'll throw Lewis to the fishes, and then I'll set fire to this place."

He frowned. "What about Shauna?"

"What about her?"

"I hate that she's going to lose Zach now too. And Marilyn." He rubbed the bee sting on his arm, which had begun to smart again. He reached for the lavender essential oil. "I mean, we had to kill Jack, which I didn't want to do. It seems cruel to take Zach too."

"You're getting all soft on me. We can't finish this too soon for my taste. Let's get on with it."

He rubbed in the oil. "It's just been a long time coming. You're right. We need to finish this and get out of here. I'll take care of things here, then head your way. See you soon."

He ended the call and got out of the car. This would take some special handling so he didn't scare the boy. He pulled his mask on again and headed for the cabin.

Zach tore frantically at the knot in the vines,

but it didn't budge. The shot he'd heard couldn't mean anything good. It had been just a single report from the pistol, followed by the heavy *thud* of a body falling to the ground. If Lewis had shot Penelope, he'd be out here right now. Which meant Penelope would be back in here any second.

A movement caught his eye, and he glanced to his right to see Shauna ease through the doorway. She had mud on her jeans and boots, and her dark hair was in a tangle. The sheriff stiffened at the same time as Zach. She held her index finger to her lips, then grabbed a paring knife from the kitchen counter on the way to his side.

"Okay?" Her voice was a faint whisper.

"Did you find Alex?"

She shook her head. "Not yet. Penelope murdered my dad. I saw the whole thing. She has to be stopped." She sliced through the vines, then slid the knife into his hand. "I have to get a gun. This puny knife is no match for her."

He flexed his wrists and palmed the knife. "I'll go after weapons. You're liable to run into her." Penelope could emerge from the bedroom at any moment.

"I'm going now. There's no time." She stepped quietly into the hall, then vanished into the gloom before he could argue.

He held his breath and prayed she got to the armory before Penelope opened the other door. No sound came from that direction so maybe she'd already made it inside to the gun room. Then a squeak down the hall told him Penelope had opened the bedroom door. Footsteps came down the hall, and he tried to quickly cut the sheriff's bonds too, but there was no time. The knife was caked with something, but he slid it into his palm and kept his wrists together behind his back so she couldn't see he was free.

The gun was in Penelope's right hand and down at her side as she emerged from the hall shadows. Her left hand held a roll of papers that had to be the plans he'd heard her mention. Blood splattered her right sleeve and boot.

Her eyes narrowed as she took in their proximity. "I figured it wasn't safe to leave you two alone for long, but you'll never untie those knots. I know how to make them foolproof." She brought the gun up and aimed it at them. "I'd be lying if I said I was sorry I had to do this. The two of you are all that's standing in the way of my perfect new life."

She's going to shoot.

Zach nodded toward the plans. "Looks

421

like you got what you wanted, but that's pretty cold, shooting a defenseless old man. Is he dead or did you leave him to suffer?" It would only take a movement of a few inches to be able to pass the knife to the sheriff without her seeing. He shuffled a bit and flexed his shoulders as if he had a cramp.

"Of course he's dead. I don't miss."

Zach slid the handle of the knife into Burchell's hand. "Why'd you kill him?"

"He tried to bargain to get back his darling grandson." Her lips curled as she said the word *darling.*

"Will you tell Shauna you killed him? She loved him once."

"She wouldn't understand. Enough of this. I'm not really going to shoot you. That would be too obvious to investigators. Walk to the bathroom."

While the sheriff worked on cutting his restraints, Zach flexed his wrists to get the blood circulating again. "You could always take us to my boat and scuttle it."

A slight smile lifted her lips, and she dropped the plans by the door and reached for a pack of matches. "I've got something much better in mind."

The sheriff shook his head. "Fire won't work. They'll find the ropes on us, along with ligature marks. They'll know it was murder."

Her brow furrowed and she blinked. "The rope will burn up, and so will the ligature marks."

"People always think that, but it usually isn't true. Just last year the police in Seattle tracked down a killer who torched his girlfriend's house with her in it. The rope remnants were the giveaway that it was murder. Plus, the bodies are rarely fully burned. Look it up if you don't believe me."

Zach had to admire the way the sheriff gave out the information. Shauna should be back any moment so the longer they could stall Penelope, the better.

She bit her lip and looked at the matches in her hand. "Fire is clean. It's always the best way."

The sheriff shook his head. "Fire leaves more evidence than most people realize."

"Enough talking. I know what I'm going to do." She motioned with the gun toward the hallway. "Get moving."

Had the sheriff managed to free himself yet? Zach would have to risk it even if Burchell wasn't able to help. Once they were in the bathroom, they'd be trapped unless they managed to break down the door. But the space was so tiny, it would be hard to generate enough momentum to crash through the door.

If Shauna came down the hall now, she'd be an easy target, so he prayed she stayed back where it was safe.

CHAPTER 40

Shauna couldn't just walk back down the hallway with the gun. Penelope had killed Pop with one shot. Shauna loaded two extra pistols, then stuffed them in the waistband of her jeans. She filled her pockets with extra ammo just in case, then eased open the door. She froze when it creaked a little.

Penelope's voice droned on in the living room, but she couldn't make out the words. From the hall, Shauna could see Zach looking toward the fireplace, but she couldn't see the woman. Shauna's gaze went across to her dad's bedroom. The door stood partly open. The big window on the south side of the room usually opened easily. He kept it open most of the year because he liked a cool bedroom.

Shauna knew every creak, every soft spot in the floor of this cabin, so she managed to get to her dad's room without making a sound. Her throat closed when his scent, a mixture of tobacco and beer, hit her in the face. He hadn't been much of a father, but she'd loved him in spite of it. Now there would never be a chance to make him love her.

But Alex was all that really mattered.

She swallowed down the pain and shoved the window up the rest of the way, then climbed onto a cedar chest positioned under the window. She dropped noiselessly into the bushes outside the window, then crept around to the front of the house toward the door that stood partially open. Her back to Shauna, Penelope had a gun pointed at Zach and the sheriff and was herding them toward the hallway. Good thing she hadn't gone that way. They would have been in her line of fire.

If only she could simply shoot her, but Shauna had to make her tell where to find Alex.

She made sure the safety was off on her firearm, then shoved open the door. "Drop your gun, Penelope!" The woman froze and started to turn, but Shauna fired a shot into the floor by the woman's right foot. "The next one will be in your head. Drop your gun."

Penelope lifted her hands in the air, but she didn't toss the gun to the floor. A sneer lifted her mouth. "Look who found some courage. I took care of your dad for you. You'll have to stand on your own two feet now."

"You don't know anything about me or my father. If you did, you'd know I was always the strong one. He came here to lick his wounds after Mom died, and he never came out of it. I know you think life has given you a rotten lemon, but you don't know how lucky you are. A loving mother, a good career. You didn't see what you had — only what you didn't."

Penelope rolled her eyes. "Loving mother, a lot you know. She hardly knew I was on the planet once your dad was through with her. Your dad deserved everything he got. I'm glad I was the one to bring justice."

Shauna gritted her teeth. "Where is my son?"

A smile curved Penelope's lips. "You let me out of here with those plans, and I'll tell you."

"I don't care about any blueprints. All I want is my son."

"Good. Hand them to me then."

Shauna didn't dare take her eyes off the woman. She kicked the white roll of paper toward her. "What's so special about them anyway?"

"Your dear old dad accidentally stumbled on a way to trigger earthquakes. That one that killed your mom was started by the deep-injection well he had near here. When he realized what he'd done, he closed the pumps."

"He could start earthquakes?" Shauna shook her head. Did Penelope really believe such a fantastic story?

Behind Penelope, Zach brought his hands out from behind his back and snatched the gun from Penelope's hand. She gasped and turned a mottled red before swinging toward him and reaching for the gun.

He pushed her back as she swiped at the hand holding the gun. "Sit down. This is over."

The color washed out of her face, and her dark eyes looked huge. "You can't ruin it for me now! We're going to live a dream life by the water in Cambodia. I won't give it up!"

She lunged at him. Her nails raked at his face, and she tried to gouge his eye with her thumb. He reeled and fell back with her on top of him.

Shauna rushed to his side. "Don't hurt her, Zach! She has to tell us where to find Alex."

The words were hardly out of her mouth

when the gun in Zach's hand went off, and Penelope sagged against Zach. He shoved her off, and Shauna saw a spreading stain on her chest.

"Oh no." She knelt by Penelope's side and pressed her fingers against the artery in her neck. No pulse.

The sheriff knelt beside her. "Is she dead?"

"Yes." Shauna's breath whooshed out. "With her dead, we don't know where to look for Alex and Marilyn."

Zach sat up and scooted closer to her. "I'm sorry, Shauna. She had the safety off. I didn't try to shoot her, but when she fell on me, the gun just went off."

"What are we going to do?" She turned to him and buried her face in his shirt. His arms around her kept her from sinking to the ground in a miserable heap.

She needed Alex in her arms. The thought of him out there in the dark with some madman nearly drove her insane. What if she never saw him again? Her eyes burned, and she tried not to think that way. They had to find him.

Something niggled at her again. She lifted her head and tried to think through the little nudges she'd had. "She said Cambodia, didn't she?"

"Yeah," Zach said. "Does that mean something to you?"

"I know someone who is always talking about how much he loves Cambodia and how an American can live like a king on the Gulf of Thailand. I just can't quite pull out the memory."

Pacing the floor, she tried to think. "Pop was a top-notch geological engineer in his younger years. The money from his patents is what he lived on. Maybe there's something in that deep-well site she mentioned. It has to be that building we found, right?"

Zach nodded. "Lewis started to take us inside to tell us about it, but she insisted we come here after the plans. I can grab that ax in the yard and we can bust in."

"I could shoot it off, but it might be safer to cut it off. I'm sure Lewis has a bolt cutter in the shed," the sheriff said. "Let me go look."

Shauna started for the door, then stopped as she felt dizzy with the revelation that struck her. "I know who the man is. Karl Prince is always talking about retiring to Cambodia, and his wife just rolls her eyes."

Zach took her arm when she swayed. "You mentioned lavender was used to treat bee stings. His wife has those bees, and he had to take over for her when she went to visit her sister."

She turned and hung on to him for dear life. "What do we do now? Go find him or go to the building?"

"The building is close. He might even have Alex and Marilyn there."

She could only pray as he led her to the door.

Zach couldn't wrap his head around Shauna's accusation against Karl. Why would a man who had everything — a successful business, a beautiful wife, and great kids — go off on this rabbit trail in his life? Zach didn't argue with her, but he wasn't sure he believed it either.

He trained the lights from the ATV on the door of the building, then got out with the sheriff, who had found a bolt cutter. The night air was cool and held the hint of rain. Zach had brought along the ax just in case as well as a flashlight belonging to Lewis.

Shauna flipped on the flashlight and walked around the building calling for Alex. There was no response.

Zach banged on the metal door. "Come here, honey, we'll get in this way."

The desperation in her eyes tore at his heart. He felt the same urgency, but he was managing to hold it in check. Barely. He put his arm around her, and they stood back to let the sheriff try to open the lock.

Burchell positioned the tool on the padlock and quickly cut through the metal. In moments the lock lay on the ground in pieces. He shoved open the door, and the odor of rusty metal and mold rushed to greet them.

Zach took the flashlight from Shauna and focused on the wall beside the door. Just as he thought, a bank of light switches was just inside on the right. He flicked the first switch, and the hum of fluorescent lights sprang to life. The dim glow brightened as the lights warmed up. The space had concrete floors. He walked across the floor to another door toward the back that was locked as well.

The sheriff took the bolt cutters, then turned and shook his head. "No padlock on this one. Good thing you brought the ax. I think it can bust through this door."

Zach nodded and hefted the ax, then brought it down against the doorjamb. It splintered but didn't open, so he chopped at it until it hung ajar in pieces.

The sheriff shoved open the ruined door, and Shauna shone the light around the space. There were pipes and a tank inside. "There's the deep-injection well." Burchell stepped closer and looked it over. "Doesn't really look all that special."

Shauna hugged herself and stepped back. "It must be worth a lot of money, though, or Karl wouldn't be willing to give up his life for this."

Zach put his arm around her. "I'm not so sure it's Karl. I can't see him killing people. Especially not Clarence and Lucy. Jack and Darla too." Zach turned her toward the door. "Let's go talk to Karl."

She stopped as they reached the door. "I just remembered something Alex said. He mentioned that Spider-Man tried to force Marilyn to go into the outhouse with the black widows. He must have them at a rough cabin somewhere. Karl has been part of our lives for a long time. He was best friends with Marilyn's husband and helped build that old cabin she never uses. I asked about using it once, and she said the outhouse was likely infested with spiders by now. What if he's holding them captive there?"

"You're reaching. The guy could have them in any of dozens of old, abandoned cabins."

She gripped his arm. "Look, it's not that far. We could check it out, right? Then if he's not there, we can continue on to Karl's house."

"She's right," Burchell said. "That old place is on our way back to town anyway. Let's give it a try."

Zach wasn't convinced the delay was worth the risk, but he was overruled. He prayed he was wrong, and they found Alex and Marilyn safe and sound in the cabin.

CHAPTER 41

He glanced at his watch. No matter how many times he told himself he had to finish this, he couldn't bring himself to do it. His face itched under the mask, and he was hot in spite of the coolness of the night air pouring in through the cabin's broken windows.

The boy was sleeping on an old cot and covered with his grandmother's sweater. Now would be the best time to do this. Once Marilyn was out of the way, he'd scoop up Alex and take him out of here with them, even if it wasn't what Penelope wanted. He could probably even sell the kid once he got away.

Marilyn sat huddled in one of the chairs near Alex's cot. She hadn't said much since he'd left to call Penelope. She probably realized he didn't believe her. There was no doubt in his mind that she'd recognized him somehow.

He cleared his throat. "I need to get some

sleep so let me take you outside for a potty break before that."

"I'm fine."

"I don't want to be awakened at midnight. Let's go."

She glanced at him, and her mouth flattened, then curved into a tender smile when she gazed one last time at her grandson. "Do what you have to, but don't hurt him. Please, please, don't hurt him."

"I'm not going to hurt him as long as you don't give me any trouble."

Her hands twisted together, and she gave a jerky nod. "I won't give you any trouble. Alex is the only good thing left in my life now." She stood and wobbled a bit, then tipped up her chin. "I'm ready."

He'd already decided to put a bullet through her head rather than lock her in the outhouse and burn it down. A quick, easy death seemed the better way. She hadn't deserved any of this, unlike her nosy daughter-in-law.

Marilyn started for the door, then turned with a pleading expression. "Don't make any noise. I-I don't want him to see it."

Smart woman. She understood the situation he was in. "He won't."

Tears swam in her eyes, but she squared her shoulders and went out the door. He closed the door softly behind them. "Around back."

She shuffled that way through the ankle-high grass. Insects chirped and wind rustled the trees. He really didn't want to do this. The other people he'd killed had actively tried to take him down. He'd always liked Marilyn, and he hated to have to kill her.

They reached the backyard, and she turned to face him. "Do what you have to do, Karl."

He winced when she said his name. "I knew you were lying."

At least he could get rid of this stupid mask. He ripped it off and tossed it into the weeds. The breeze on his skin was a little touch of heaven. Her face was pale in the moonlight, but she faced him without fear in her eyes. She was one gutsy broad.

"What tipped you off? How'd you recognize me?"

"Your voice. Even though you tried to mask it, I'm good with voices. Why are you doing this, Karl? You killed my boy, didn't you? Why would you do that?" Her question ended on a sob.

"I had no choice. Darla stole some stuff from my office, then went to him for help. They were going to turn me in to the sheriff. It was his own fault for sticking his nose into my business. I wasn't doing anything wrong."

She sighed. "That doesn't even make sense, Karl."

"Darla worked for me the summer before she died." He barked out a laugh. "Nora suspected I was having an affair and asked Darla for help proving it. When she was snooping around my office, she found the necklace and my proposal to the Russians and Chinese. She stole it all and took it to Jack. Luckily, she never told my wife. He was auditing my books and came to me with questions after I killed her. I had no choice."

He should just put a bullet through her head and be done with it, but he couldn't until she understood that it wasn't his fault. "Look, I have a new life waiting. One with a beautiful young woman. She'd guilted Lewis out of the deed to some property, and all we were going to do was sell it. That doesn't sound criminal, does it? The money from the sale will set us up for life. I wasn't about to let it all fly away because your boy poked his nose into our business."

"How could selling some property bring you that much money?"

Maybe he'd tell her the whole story. Why not? It would be good to get it off his chest.

The sheriff drove the ATV while Shauna perched between Zach and Everett. It was a tight squeeze for her, and the machine nearly rolled over in the curves because of the load, but they were nearly there. Marilyn's cabin was just through this stand of trees.

Shauna tapped Zach on the shoulder, then shouted over the wind rushing past them. "We should stop here and walk in so he doesn't hear us."

"If he's there." Zach tapped the sheriff on the shoulder and repeated Shauna's request.

The ATV rumbled to a stop, and Everett turned off the engine. The sudden cessation of sound and movement was a relief. Now that they were here, her throat was full of unshed tears tangled up with fear and dread. What if she was wrong and this brief detour cost her the life of her son? She bit her lip and pushed away the horrifying thought.

She pointed to the slight incline. "The cabin is just over that rise. Let's go."

Zach took her arm and dropped into step with her. "Do we have a cell signal here?"

"I don't think so. There wasn't one the

last time we were here."

The sheriff paused and looked at his phone. "No service. We'd better hurry." He drew his gun. "Stay behind me. We don't know what we're walking into."

They crested the hill, and she saw a dim glow of a lantern shining through the broken windows. Her heart surged in her chest. "Someone's there!" She broke into a run, but when she started past the sheriff, he grabbed her arm.

"Careful, Shauna. We don't want to rush in there and cause him to start firing bullets in Alex's direction."

She swallowed and nodded. "Okay."

"Stay close and don't make any noise."

His order was easier said than done. Gravel crunched under her feet, and her breath sounded loud in her ears. She veered to the shoulder of the road where soft dirt and vegetation muffled her footsteps.

As they neared the cabin, she heard voices. Everett held his finger to his lips, then led them across the high grass toward the outhouse looming in the moonlight. She made out two figures standing near the edge of the woods, one taller than the other. Marilyn and Karl maybe? She couldn't make out any features. They crept a bit closer, and she recognized the voice.

Her fingers dug into Zach's arm. She'd been right. Karl was behind this. She didn't see Alex, though. Where was he? Surely Karl hadn't hurt him.

They advanced closer until she finally understood what Karl was saying. He seemed to be explaining to Marilyn about how he'd fallen in love with Penelope and had concocted this plan to sell the deep-injection well and the blueprints for how it was built.

"You're telling me this well can start earthquakes?" Marilyn's voice held skepticism.

"Yep. That earthquake on Wednesday? I started it to prove to the Chinese that it works." Karl's voice was full of pride.

"How did Penelope get the well in her name?"

"Penelope went to Lewis and told him he owed her for ruining her life. He'd been drinking and told her how he'd started the earthquake accidentally. She demanded he sign it over to her or the entire world would know he was a mass murderer. He did it, but regretted it as soon as he sobered up. Nothing he could do about it then, though."

"We sold it to the highest bidder, the Chinese."

"You're disgusting," Marilyn said. "And a

traitor to your country."

"It won't be my country for much longer. I'm out of here in the morning." His voice hardened. "I thought you'd understand if I explained it, but I was wrong. Time to say lights out, Marilyn. I'm sorry." He brought up his arm, and moonlight glinted off the gun in his hand.

The sheriff took a shooting stance with his gun pointing at Karl. "Freeze! Police! Karl Prince, you're under arrest. Throw down your gun."

Karl froze. The gun dropped to the ground, and he held his hands up as he turned toward them. "I can explain."

Zach vaulted past the sheriff and tackled Karl. The two tussled in the grass for a few moments until Zach managed to subdue him.

Zach hauled Karl to his feet. "Where's Alex?"

Karl stared back defiantly and didn't answer.

Shauna wanted to leap on him and throttle the answer from him. "Where's my son?"

Marilyn rushed for the door. "He's in the cabin!"

Shauna leaped after her, quickly outpacing her to reach the door first. She burst into the cabin and saw Alex curled on the cot sleeping. Relief coursed through her, and she nearly sagged to the floor.

Her legs trembled as she staggered to the cot and scooped him into her arms. She buried her face in his neck and inhaled the smell of little boy. Her boy. Tears flooded her eyes and ran down her cheeks and onto his face.

His eyelids fluttered, then opened, and he stared into her face. "Mommy? I knew you'd find me." He wrapped his arms around her neck. "Spider-Man was really mean to me and Grammy."

She petted his hair. "I know, sweetheart. The sheriff arrested him, and you're safe now. Grammy is safe too. We're all going to go home and crawl in our own beds."

"I want to go to Zachster's," he said into her neck. "That's home now."

She looked up as Zach came through the door. "I think so too."

CHAPTER 42

The lights of the passing boats were pin-
pricks in the dark night. Shauna stood on
the hillside looking down into Rainshadow
Bay with a canopy of stars overhead. Zach's
arm was around her waist, and the dogs
were on her other side. Marilyn was inside
sleeping with Alex, and they'd come out
here to talk where there was no chance of
Alex overhearing.

She laid her head against his chest. "I still
can't believe it. Karl Prince of all people."

"Greed and lust can really change a man."

"And my dad." She cleared her throat.
"I'd heard of deep-injection wells triggering
earthquakes, but I had no idea it could be
done deliberately."

"It sounds like your dad stumbled onto
the right depth and pressure accidentally.
Guilt ruined his life. He should have told
someone and faced up to it."

"He should have done a lot of things. Like

found his kids and taken care of all of us." Her eyes burned, and her throat tightened at the thought of all she'd lost. "He ruined our lives."

His warm fingers touched her chin, and he tilted her face up to look into her eyes. "He didn't ruin anything, Flygirl. You're still here. So is Alex. So am I."

"Jack's not." Her voice trembled.

"No, he's not. We never can understand why bad things happen to good people like Jack. But all that you've gone through has made you strong."

He turned her slightly so she was looking out onto the water. The waves caught the glimmer of the moonlight as they rolled to the shore. "Look at the view from here. If we were down on the shore, we wouldn't be able to see how the two boats maneuver to avoid each other. We can see the lighthouse and the Dungeness Spit. From up here, we can see lots of things we couldn't if we were in the middle of the waves."

She got where he was going. "Now that it's all over, we can see how God took care of us through this. He let us find Alex in time."

"Exactly. God never said bad things wouldn't happen, but he's promised to work those things for good in our lives. I think he's done that. You know the truth about what happened. God has provided for you every step of the way too."

His words struck a chord deep in her heart. The future looked bright for them. She could lay down her fear and trust again. Love again.

She cupped his face in her hands. "I love you, Zach. I couldn't say it before. I couldn't even admit it to myself before because I didn't want to ever face that kind of loss again. But you're right. God is faithful through everything that comes. Even though the past year has been the hardest thing I've ever experienced, he took care of me and Alex. He gave us everything we needed."

His blue eyes widened, and a glow started in their depths. "I've wanted to tell you how I felt for days now, but I thought you'd pack up and leave."

He pulled her closer, and his lips came down on hers. His lips were firm yet exquisitely gentle. She wrapped her arms around his neck and sank into the passion and promise of his kiss. Time lost all meaning as she gave the last remnants of her heart to him.

When she finally broke the kiss, her breath was coming in small gasps. This was a man who would give his life for her and Alex.

He'd proven himself time and time again. She didn't have to be afraid.

"You realize now that it's safe I'll have to go home," she whispered. "You're way too tempting."

"That last part was my line." His white teeth gleamed in the moonlight. "I think a quick wedding is in order."

She gasped and put her hand to her throat. "Whoa, we're moving a little fast there, Cowboy."

"Not fast enough for me. I love you. We were friends first, which is the very best foundation for a good marriage, don't you agree?" He took her hands in his. "Marry me, Shauna. As quickly as we can get a license."

She searched his tender gaze. He seemed serious, and her heart thumped hard against her ribs. "This will be your first marriage. Don't you want a nice ceremony with a tux and everything?"

"That doesn't mean anything to me. We can invite the whole town for a barbecue afterward. People will be happy for us."

He was right. What did a fancy wedding mean anyway? "All right."

His lips descended on hers again, and she tasted how sweet life had become with Zach by her side.

EPILOGUE

One Month Later

The wedding had been small. Just a few close friends had gathered at the church. No one had given her away because she was giving herself to this wonderful man. Marilyn had Alex for the week, and tomorrow they would go on a honeymoon to a destination Zach refused to disclose, the rat.

"My feet hurt," Shauna moaned as Zach opened the truck door for her.

"I think I can remedy that." He swept her into his arms and carried her toward the front door of his house.

He staggered a little as he went up the stairs. "Um, you weigh all of a hundred pounds soaking wet, and I'm struggling here. I need to lift weights."

She clutched his neck as he practically fell against the doorjamb. "Maybe a hundred and five with all that apple cake Felicia forced me to eat. You can put me down."

"Not a chance." He rested against the jamb. "I should have gotten out my keys. See if you can fish them from my pocket."

She giggled and dug her hand into his left pocket. "Got 'em. Let me do the honors."

From this angle it was difficult to insert the key and twist it, but she managed, and he practically fell across the threshold with her. "I think you're faking all this, Cowboy."

"I'm not faking this, wife." He gathered her closer, and his lips devoured hers.

There were no restraints this time, no reason to pull away. She wrapped her arms around his neck and gave up every bit of love in her heart. "Care to carry me to the bedroom, or should I walk?" His smile held so much tenderness she couldn't look away.

He set her feet on the floor. "I want to give you a wedding present first."

"We agreed no presents! You promised." She had a cute little white number to wear to bed that she'd bought with him in mind. She wasn't about to tell him that now, though.

"This didn't cost anything." His blue eyes turned serious. "I started some digging to locate your brother and sister. I contacted CPS, and after much pleading and a few threats, I got the name of Connor's caseworker. I think we might be able to find him. We know who adopted him, but not where he is yet."

She gasped and would have fallen if he hadn't had hold of her. "Are you kidding me?"

"Nope. We'll know more in a few weeks."

She clutched his arm. "What do you know about him?"

"Just the names of his parents. Just be patient, Flygirl. We're getting close." He picked her up in his arms and started for the bedroom. "You can say thank you anytime."

She pressed her lips against his cheek. "I'd rather show you."

A NOTE FROM THE AUTHOR

Dear Reader,

I hope you enjoyed Shauna and Zach's story as we take off into a new series! It was fun for me to write this and settle into the beautiful state of Washington.☺

If you're like me, you often wonder why God lets bad things happen in our lives. I don't have all the answers, but I do know that with every single trial I've faced, I've come through the other side stronger and wiser. I can't always see at the time how God is using the trial in my life, but looking back, I often have more clarity.

I love hearing from readers! Drop me a note at colleen@colleencoble.com, or say hello over on Facebook. Can't wait to hear what you think!

Love,
Colleen Coble

DISCUSSION QUESTIONS

1. Was Shauna's hatred of Zach justified?
2. What is your first thought when bad things happen in your life?
3. Why do you think Shauna withdrew from friends and even church when Jack died? What would you do?
4. Valerie told Zach life goes on. Sometimes we don't want it to. Have you ever felt that way?
5. Felicia believed good and bad experiences work to shape us. Why do you feel that is true or untrue?
6. Is there any real justice in the world?
7. Have you ever been slammed with bad experiences and were waiting for the other shoe to drop? How did you get past it?
8. Have you ever done something to show you weren't afraid when you were actually shaking in your boots?
9. Have you ever realized years later how

God turned something bad into something good?

ACKNOWLEDGMENTS

I'm so blessed to belong to the terrific HarperCollins Christian Publishing dream team! I've been with my great fiction team for fifteen years in 2017, and they are like family to me. I learn something new with every book, which makes writing so much fun for me!

Our fiction publisher, Amanda Bostic, has been by my side through most of those fifteen years. She's my editor as well and really gets suspense. Fabulous cover guru Kristen Ingebretson works hard to create the perfect cover — and does. And, of course, I can't forget the other friends in my amazing fiction family: I've got a fabulous marketing and publicity team in Paul Fisher, Allison Carter, and Kristen Golden. Becky Monds, Karli Jackson, Jodi Hughes, Meghan Kraft, Kim Carlton, and Kayleigh Hines are always on hand to brainstorm titles and ideas. You are all such a big part of my life. I wish I could name all the great folks at HCCP who work on selling my books through different venues. I'm truly blessed!

Julee Schwarzburg is a dream editor to work with. She totally gets romantic suspense, and our partnership is pure joy. She brought some terrific ideas to the table with this book — as always!

My agent, Karen Solem, has helped shape my career in many ways, and that includes kicking an idea to the curb when necessary. We just celebrated seventeen years together! And my critique partner of nearly twenty years, Denise Hunter, is the best sounding board ever. Thanks, friends!

I'm so grateful for my husband, Dave, who carts me around from city to city, washes towels, and chases down dinner without complaint. My kids — Dave and Kara (and now Donna and Mark) — love and support me in every way possible, and my little granddaughter, Alexa, makes every day a joy. She's talking like a grown-up now, and having her spend the night is more fun than I can tell you. My new little grandson, Elijah, is seven months old, and I look forward to every moment with him. Exciting times!

Most important, I give my thanks to God,

who has opened such amazing doors for me
and makes the journey a golden one.

ABOUT THE AUTHOR

Colleen Coble is a *USA Today* bestselling author and RITA finalist best known for her romantic suspense novels, including *Tidewater Inn, Rosemary Cottage,* and the Mercy Falls, Lonestar, Rock Harbor, and Sunset Cove series.

Visit her website at www.colleencoble.com.
Twitter: @colleencoble
Facebook: colleencoblebooks